PRAISE FOR DANIEL JUDSON

"Daniel Judson is so much more than a crime-fiction novelist. He's a tattooed poet, a mad philosopher of the Apocalypse fascinated with exploring the darkest places in people's souls."

—Chicago Tribune on *The Water's Edge*

"Shamus winner Judson once again successfully mines Long Island's South Fork for glittering noir nuggets."

—Publishers Weekly on *The Violet Hour*

"A suspense masterpiece."

—Bookreporter.com on *The Violet Hour*

"Judson hits you with a 25,000-volt stun gun in chapter one and doesn't let up until the satisfying end."

—Alafair Burke, author of 212, on *Voyeur*

"Judson is a thoroughly accomplished writer."

—Kirkus Reviews on *Voyeur*

"A searing, brooding look at the bleak side of the Hamptons . . . an intense novel."

—South Florida Sun-Sentinel on *The Darkest Place*

"Action packed. Loss and redemption rule in Shamus Award–winning Daniel Judson's third novel, set in Southampton nights so cold that they could cool off a reader sizzling in this summer's heat. It's noir on ice."

—USA Today on *The Darkest Place*

"This taut thriller is far from predictable, and its dark and mysterious plot suits Judson's understated writing style."

—Publishers Weekly on *The Poisoned Rose*

THE
ROGUE
AGENT

OTHER TITLES BY DANIEL JUDSON

THE
ROGUE
AGENT

DANIEL JUDSON

THOMAS & MERCER

Text copyright © 2017 by Daniel Judson
All rights reserved.

Published by Thomas & Mercer, Seattle

www.apub.com

Amazon, the Amazon logo, and Thomas & Mercer are trademarks of Amazon.com, Inc., or its affiliates.

ISBN-13: 9781503940772
ISBN-10: 1503940772

Cover design by Rex Bonomelli

Printed in the United States of America

for my family,
those born to and those acquired

Prologue

Tom awakens to the sound of barking in the distance.

It takes all he has to keep from immediately sitting up, as any abrupt movement will disturb the sleeping woman beside him.

Not just asleep but deeply asleep, judging by the length and rhythm of her breathing.

Stella's state is the first thing Tom determines. The second thing he does is tune in to the far-off noise so he can assess its nature.

Is it the frantic, endless barking of a dog whose territory has been crossed by another animal? Or is it a more aggressive snapping, an indication of an intruder somewhere nearby? Maybe even more than one, possibly a team of men currently heading in their direction?

Men coming to kill them.

But Tom doesn't hear any of that.

The commotion coming from the farm two miles to the south is the lazy yelping of a hound bothered by the full moon.

The barking isn't anything to worry about.

And anyway, that isn't what had actually awakened him.

Tom checks the clock on his bedside table and sees that it is a few minutes past one a.m.

He has slept for three hours and will need to get up in less than three more.

That is, if he can fall back to sleep right away, which isn't always the case postdream.

Out of habit, he confirms that his .45-caliber pistol is where he left it, to the right of the clock, and that the old Marlin Camp carbine they had found upon moving in is still leaning in the corner.

Chambered in .45 as well, the Marlin has a sixteen-inch barrel that, while offering some accuracy at a range that the handgun can't, makes it particularly well suited for close-quarter combat.

For Tom, the real plus is that the carbine not only uses the same ammo as his pistol—a well-used 70-series Colt 1911—but also accepts the same magazine.

A significant convenience in the numerous scenarios for which he and Stella have prepared.

On the nightstand next to the pistol lie a half dozen fully loaded McCormick Power Mags, which Tom can easily gather together in an emergency. Next to them is a 600-lumen pocket flashlight.

He has long since come to terms with the fact that the need for such weaponry has extended into his civilian life. A peaceful wanderer once, he has now in Stella something he can never lose.

After a moment, Tom carefully rises from their bed and heads toward the bathroom to wash his face.

The nightmare always leaves him in a cold sweat.

Their apartment is above the small breakfast-and-lunch place that he and Stella run together—she waits on the eight booths and ten-seat counter; he buses tables, washes dishes, and handles repairs and what-ever else the business needs.

Open six days a week, serving from five a.m. to two p.m.

The staff is Stella, himself, and a gifted short-order cook named Krista, who came looking for work right when they feared they'd never find anyone. The timing of her appearance has always struck Tom as too good to be true, but such things do occur. And anyway, more than just qualified, she is, in Stella's words, capable, and that is what mattered, that is what they needed.

Stella would never have purchased the building had Tom not possessed the variety of skills necessary to bring the place up to code.

As a onetime US Navy Seabee, Tom could easily do whatever needed to be done, and yet a month's work—day and night, seven days a week—was what it had taken to get the dilapidated structure ready for both business and personal occupancy.

During that time Tom had also made a number of specific modifications to their bare-minimum living quarters, among them a makeshift safe room, which he'd rendered bulletproof by securing old phone books and encyclopedias to its door and walls, after which he'd covered the protective layer with ceramic tiles.

It had taken a week after completing that work for Tom and Stella to get the restaurant stocked and ready to open.

Their living area remains a work in progress, but these days they are more concerned with security—financial as well as tactical—than comfort. Stella had only a small amount of savings left over after closing on the property, and much of that was used up during the renovations.

The little she has left is all they will have to run on, should that time come.

In the bathroom, Tom opens the tap, knowing he'll need to wait a good half minute before the water begins its transition from frigid cold to hot. Looking into the cracked mirror over the sink, he is reminded of the nightmare by the sorrow evident in his eyes.

A nightmare he has been having with increasing frequency over the past year.

He had learned in the months following the murder of his mother and sister that four men had entered his childhood home that long-ago night.

And that is always how his dream opens—four men exiting their vehicle and walking toward the darkened and unguarded house, weapons concealed by long coats.

And then the men quietly enter the house.

Tom had been fifteen at the time, away at the military school his father had insisted he attend. And his father, an engineer, had been off on one of his many business trips.

This one had been a last-minute business trip. So, the two women who back then were Tom's world had been left alone, at the mercy of men who had none.

A home invasion gone wrong, according to the police.

Tom's dream, however, doesn't end with the men approaching and then breaching his childhood home.

He sees them enter and move as a pack through darkened rooms until they have found their prey.

And he sees his mother and kid sister—a woman and a teenage girl, identical in nearly every way—cornered by the men. The look on his mother's face is a mixture of anger and resolve.

His beloved kid sister is overtaken by fear.

Each time he wakes, Tom does everything he can to ensure the quick evaporation of the details his unconscious mind forces him to endure.

Details of events that are nothing shy of a horror show.

Based on what witnesses reported at the time, it is believed that the murders occurred soon after the men entered. But soon *is relative, and Tom knows full well how terror can turn minutes into hours.*

Often what's left in his mind is not just a memory of the unbearable but also the feeling that he had in fact been there and was a living witness to the sights and sounds and the raw emotions they stirred, helpless to do anything to stop what was unfolding before him.

Tonight's dream was no exception, and despite the film of cold sweat on his face, Tom decides not to wait for warmer water. Cupping his hands under the faucet, he lets his palms fill, then splashes his face, his head, the back of his neck with the icy flow. He does this several times before finally standing up straight and reaching for the towel hanging on its hook.

Only then does he realize that Stella is standing in the doorway.

————⏝————

She asks whether he's okay, and he nods, though unconvincingly.

Of course, she knows the reason he is up, but before she can say anything, he starts to tell her that it's okay, it's just a dream.

She quickly cuts him off. "We should have kept on moving, Tom. We should have looked for another property, something farther away." She pauses, then says, "We're too close here."

"It's not that."

"Then what is it?"

Tom has no answer.

He can tell by Stella's reaction that his inability to come up with a quick lie is comforting to her. A year and a half ago, when they began their wandering together, Stella said that what she wanted most was to know everything about Tom, which included a visit to the small town in Vermont where he'd grown up.

A town Tom hadn't seen since leaving it seventeen years before, when he was all of eighteen, one year of college behind him and no money to continue, nowhere to go but into the military.

They had eventually made it to his small town, and it was as they'd been driving away with every intention of resuming their wandering that they had spotted the building for sale.

Mere miles from where Tom had grown up and where his life had been forever altered, first by the murders of his mother and sister, and then by the death of his father two years later.

Tom's adult life, therefore, is a journey that began in violence.

A journey that carried him into and through yet more violence, both during and after his eight years of military service.

But it is also a journey that ultimately led him to Stella.

Step by step, decision by decision. Minute by minute, year by year.

What life isn't the bounding from bad to good, though, all seemingly senseless until the day it suddenly isn't?

He knows this much.

Tom has long since come to terms with what his life has brought, and with what he has had to do to stay alive.

What he and Stella have both done just to survive.

He'd do that and more again, should he need to.

In this regard, he considers himself a lucky man because his life has now but one purpose.

The recurring dream is a problem, yes. And though he knows that Stella would disagree, he considers it his problem.

Looking at her, Tom says, finally, "Here is where we're supposed to be, Stella. I believe that."

"You say that, I know. But you can't go on like this. The dreams used to be now and then. Then they were once a month. Now it's at least once a week that you wake up like this. You never had these dreams before we moved in here."

"I can deal with it."

"I know, you say that, too."

"It'll burn itself out eventually. The same thing happened when I came back from Afghanistan."

He had dreamed again and again of the grenade that had landed feet from him, of the force of the blast that had, seconds later, sent hot fragments tearing through his flesh, as well as the flesh of the man who at the last moment had lain down between the grenade and Tom.

The man who had almost died saving him.

It had taken five years of living as a drifter for Tom to stop dreaming of that night, and he is certain that in time he will stop dreaming of this, too.

"And if it doesn't burn itself out?" Stella says.

"We'll figure out what to do then. Okay?"

She says nothing. Tom can tell she is stopping herself from saying what is on her mind. He appreciates her restraint.

Finally, she touches his shoulder. "Jesus, your shirt is soaked. Get out of that and dry off, I'll get you a clean one."

Stella leaves. Tom pulls off the T-shirt and lays it over the edge of the tub.

The cold he feels as he heads back to the bedroom is something he has gotten used to. Insulating the upper floor is a project he plans on getting to before the summer heat.

If they are lucky and business continues to be as good as it is, they may actually be pulling out a profit by then.

Stella has retrieved a clean T-shirt from his makeshift dresser—a cardboard box. She turns and watches Tom as he walks to her. Her eyes immediately go to his scarred torso.

She tells him that his workouts are paying off, that he is looking even stronger than he was when they first met.

Tom understands that while her comment is intended as an earnest compliment, it is also an attempt to assure him that she no longer sees his scars when she looks at him—those made by the grenade fragments and those left by his many surgeons.

It is his evident fitness alone that draws her eyes.

He knows that this isn't the entire truth, but it is as close as they come to lying to each other, and for that he is grateful.

Stella, too, is stronger looking. In the past year alone, she has packed on close to ten pounds of muscle—an achievement made even more impressive by the fact that, at the age of forty-six, she is, in her words, no kid.

Hers is the kind of physique earned by working with one's own body weight—push-ups, pull-ups, burpees, dive bombers—and always after a daily five-mile run.

Physical conditioning is simply another of their many rituals performed in the name of security.

Should one day their enemies—or what worries Tom most, enemies posing as friends—find them, they may need to run.

And if they can't run, then stand and fight.

Either way, they long ago resolved that they would prepare themselves for whatever may come.

Heart and body and soul.

And not hesitate for a moment to leave behind everything for which they have worked so hard.

———— ⁀ ————

Back in bed, Tom holds Stella close until her breathing tells him that sleep has again found her.

It will be a while, he knows, before it reclaims him as well. So he lies there in the moonlit room, hoping not only for a dreamless sleep, but also for another day without any sign of those he has no desire to see again.

It has been a year and a half since he last heard from them.

From James Carrington and Sam Raveis and the man Tom knows only as "the Colonel."

It has been a year and a half since he killed for them—had been given no choice but to kill, and to do so more than once.

In the deepest part of himself, Tom hopes that he will never hear from them, and that every day that passes without contact means it is that much more likely they never will come looking for him.

That in their time of desperate need, they will wisely seek out others for help.

An odd thing, Tom muses, for a man to hope that he has been forgotten by all who have ever known him.

But this is precisely the thing for which he prays as he patiently waits for just a few more hours of precious rest.

PART ONE

PART ONE

One

In a Chelsea apartment overlooking the Hudson River, a spent prostitute passed out beside him, Gateno stared at his syringe.

It was an antique made of steel and thick glass that he had found in a flea market in Paris's seventh arrondissement decades ago.

He remembered that day well, the steady smile he had worn as he'd wandered the city, the satisfaction that had run through him like a current of electricity.

The night before, at the age of twenty-six, he'd made his first professional kill.

A flawless effort—he recalled every detail of that, too, thought of it often, in fact, much in the way another man might remember his first woman.

Fondly, proudly, nostalgically, even wistfully.

An act of self-discovery, and something he had wanted for a long time.

Generally, women were of little interest to Gateno, no more than a pleasant distraction in which he indulged once or twice a month. This prolonged period of time between sexual encounters was a carryover from his stint in the French Foreign Legion, when women had been few and far between and always enjoyed in exchange for cash.

Most of the habits that defined him had been acquired during those formative years—fighting as a mercenary in wars in which he'd had no political stake, doing so alongside men with whom he'd sweated and bled but ultimately knew little about.

A time of monklike isolation, physical and psychological demands, and skills acquired and sharpened. Most important, it had been a time of sanctioned violence.

Gateno had attempted to replicate as much of that as he could in his postservice life, though of course he had ultimately replaced certain hardships with comforts, some of which bordered on luxury. The loft apartment—the top floor of a renovated building across from the Chelsea Piers—was one such comfort.

Arched windows, polished plank floors, exposed brick. A sweatshop a century ago, but all traces of that had been erased.

A far cry from the desert conditions he had endured as a young legionnaire, or the years spent in a student-district hovel in Paris as he worked to make a name for himself.

It wasn't until he had branched out to America and performed well there as a freelancer that his standing in the industry of death had been secured. He'd earned a reputation for never confronting a physical boundary that he could not cross.

As well as for having no moral center to hold him back.

There was no one he would not kill—man, woman, child.

An orphan by the age of seven, for a long time he had wished that he'd been killed along with his parents. He would have preferred that over the life of poverty and degradation into which he'd been thrust.

How could one who had learned to devalue his life ever come to value the lives of others?

This ingrained amorality, combined with his ability to breach any perimeter, helped Gateno quickly rise to the top of his profession.

Once he had the means, his existence gradually shifted from the mere act of surviving to the ceaseless collecting of pleasures. And as each pleasure he sought was ultimately spent, he found himself consumed with the pursuit of another.

The naked prostitute beside him now was an indulgence in both pleasure and luxury—buffed and polished and sweetly scented, she was as eager to please as she was beautiful.

Dark-haired, like his long-lost mother, with a delicate face and soft skin and swimmer's build.

The service he used sent only the best.

His greatest indulgence, however, wasn't women for hire but rather the cocktail of illicit drugs he self-injected every afternoon.

A mixture of morphine, cocaine, and codeine that brought him to a state of exquisite indifference.

A godlike indifference.

Sitting on the edge of his bed, he stared at his waiting syringe.

Beside the antique was its carrying case—roughly the size of a paperback book, fashioned from worn black leather, its cover embossed with a gothic eagle, its broad wings spread wide and head turned to the left.

The *Hoheitszeichen*—the national symbol of the Third Reich.

It was a relic from a time long before he was born, but a cherished one, more for its rareness than its politics, though he did admire the cold savagery of the men who had followed that symbol, pledging to live and die by it.

So it served as a reminder of both the expectations of those who employed him and what was made necessary by his taste for certain luxuries.

Gateno had waited until four thirty before he began the ritual of preparing his syringe.

He took his time, enjoying the process before finally injecting himself and settling back, and was well into his state of heightened indifference when one of his several cell phones rang.

He took the call and stepped away from his platform bed. The drugged woman stretched across it in a tangle of sheets was sleeping, but there was no point in taking the risk of speaking in her presence.

Even an unconscious mind gathered and retained information that could later be retrieved under hypnosis.

Naked, Gateno walked to the large floor-to-ceiling window at the front of his apartment, not realizing till he was a few steps from it that the overcast April day he'd spent screwing a prostitute had given way to a rainy evening.

Heavy drops broke against the thick panes of glass.

He stood at the window and looked down at the rush hour traffic on Eleventh Avenue.

A river of blurred car lights flowed eight stories below.

Only one man had the number to this particular phone, so there was no need to bother with pleasantries.

"Go ahead," Gateno said.

"I need you to meet me."

"Where?"

"There isn't a lot of time. Come down to the piers. Start walking, I will find you."

Gateno was dressed and out his door in less than five minutes. His tailored raincoat and gentleman's umbrella protected him from the falling rain, but there was a chilled mist churning in the air that coated his dark face as he crossed Eleventh.

He was approaching Pier 39 when he saw the man he expected to see.

Not the man who had called him, but that man's personal driver and bodyguard.

Gateno knew him as Karl, and whether that was the man's real name didn't matter.

What did matter was that Karl was a brute—average in height but bull shouldered, with a torso like a keg and thick legs to support it.

14   *Daniel Judson*

Short but strong arms, hands like a butcher.

Contradicting the man's physical build was a pair of intelligent eyes.

Eyes that burned, eyes that were sharp.

Gateno did what he always did when he came face-to-face with Karl. He visualized the ways in which he would kill him if that ever became necessary.

A single shot to the forehead; a stiletto repeatedly plunged into his solar plexus; the edge of his hand landing with force just above his Adam's apple.

Gateno never met a man without imagining how he would kill him.

Killing an enemy was easy—an innate hatred of the "other" carried one to the required mind-set.

Enraged, one could tear a man to pieces.

But to kill on demand, without provocation or violent emotion, required a different frame of mind, and seeing in his mind's eye the killing of those he encountered was the first step toward that.

The two men stared at each other for a moment. Finally, Karl nodded and turned, prompting Gateno to follow.

The man Gateno had come to meet was known to him only as the Benefactor.

It was the Benefactor who had first brought Gateno to America, not as the solitary assassin he would later become but as part of a hit team sent to kill a deep-cover intelligence officer in his own home.

An audition, as such, and one that Gateno had easily passed, even though the job hadn't gone exactly to plan.

But while facing mission failure that long-ago night, Gateno had adapted, taking charge of the situation and in doing so setting into motion a chain of events that would eventually lead to his new employer's desired result—a fact the Benefactor had been quick to recognize.

You've got a bright future ahead of you, the man had said to Gateno afterward.

It had been nothing short of a turning point in Gateno's life.

Now he followed Karl to meet once more with the man to whom he owed so much. After a brief walk, Gateno spotted the Benefactor standing midway down a pier, holding an umbrella and facing the river.

As Gateno approached, he turned.

The Benefactor was always a well-dressed man. Beneath his dark raincoat was a Tom Ford suit—his trademark. He usually wore shoes handmade from Italian leather, but tonight, against the rain, he had on a pair of black mountain boots, no doubt handmade as well.

He was tall, in his early sixties, his dark hair graying at the temples.

This was the only man Gateno feared—not because Gateno couldn't easily kill him, which he had as a matter of habit envisioned countless times, but because the power this man wielded was the kind that would not cease with his death.

It was common knowledge that, in the event of this man's untimely demise, his killer would be hunted.

Hunted by men like Gateno, dozens of them dispatched on capture-or-kill missions.

Without question, it would be better for whoever did one day kill the Benefactor that he allowed himself to be killed instead of captured.

But Gateno had no intention of being that man, so he cleared his mind of these thoughts.

He needed to focus now.

Greeted with the usual nod, Gateno nodded back.

Karl was a few feet behind him. This, too, was typical, though Gateno wondered whether it was really necessary since the steady hiss of the heavy rain would likely prevent the brute from hearing his employer speak.

The Benefactor laid out what it was he needed Gateno to do tonight, then asked whether the instructions were clear.

Gateno told him that they were.

"I dislike having to ask this of you," the Benefactor said. "It's akin to using a Ferrari to haul garbage. But it is necessary if we are going to begin tying up these loose ends once and for all. Once my enemy is weakened, and once his witness is dead, then we can make our move against his people."

Gateno nodded. "I understand."

"You have crews standing by?"

"Always."

"You needn't waste your best men on the first attack. The second, however, cannot fail. I'll leave the details up to you, but I would prefer that you lead the second assault yourself. There is no room for error here."

"Of course."

"How soon can you have your teams in place?"

"I'll need two hours to assemble the right men for each job."

"You have it, but no more than that."

Gateno sensed that there was more to come, so he waited.

He didn't have to wait long.

"I will need to ask one more thing of you," the Benefactor said.

"Name it."

"You will need to leave when this is done. Immediately. Not just the city, but the country as well. As a matter of history, wars begin with a single shot, and it's a war we're starting. As a result, you will likely find that you've become a most-wanted man. There will be those who'll make it their mission to know what you know. For my sake as well as yours, this cannot happen. So I'd advise you to choose a location where you are known to no one. I'm afraid a less-civilized corner of the world would be the best option. Few would think to look for a man like you—a man with your tastes—in some South American slum or African hellhole."

Nothing like this had ever been requested of Gateno. Since he wasn't certain what to say, he said nothing.

"You will be compensated for your inability to work," the Benefactor said. "A generous monthly stipend by wire transfer. I cannot tell you for how long we will need you to remain unseen, but a message will be gotten to you via our usual means when the time is right for you to reemerge."

Gateno knew the system.

A fictitious obituary would appear in a Monday issue of *Le Monde*, both the print and online editions. The name, birthplace, and date of birth listed in the obit would serve as a code that would instruct him what to do next.

"I would not ask this of you if there were any other way," the Benefactor said. "We need your particular skills and unerring professionalism tonight. And then we need you not to exist."

If this man hadn't given him a chance two decades ago, recruited him and seen in him what no one else had, Gateno would likely still be in that student-district hovel, another Algerian refugee eking out a bare-minimum existence as a thug, forced to take greater risks for significantly less gain.

Or worse, having long since surrendered his reason to a twisted interpretation of religion, he would be in some desert terrorist camp, as willing to kill as he was to be killed.

Die for a cause, just to give his miserable life something that resembled meaning.

So what else could he do but accept the terms put before him?

Pay the homage due to the man who had always lived up to his name.

"I work for you," Gateno said. "I will do whatever you need me to do."

The Benefactor extended his gloved hand, and Gateno took it.

Later, Gateno prepared for the job.

He fieldstripped, lubricated, and reassembled his Walther PPK.

The weapon was chambered for the nine-millimeter Kurtz cartridge, and though that round was commonly believed to be near the low end of the lethality scale, Gateno had countless kills with it to justify his continued use.

Though it wasn't a pistol one would bring to a firefight, he was an assassin, and the PPK had been the assassin's weapon of choice throughout its ninety-year history.

In keeping with his fondness for specific artifacts, Gateno had chosen a Walther that had been manufactured in Germany in the late thirties and bore on its Bakelite grips a symbol identical to the one on his syringe case.

His obsession with antiques, however, did not extend to his preferred ammunition.

The Walther was loaded with state-of-the-art hollow points, plus-P rated for increased feet-per-second out of the muzzle.

The rifle he would use tonight in his role as team leader was a Barrett Model 82A1, chambered in .50 BMG and equipped with a SIG Sauer infrared scope.

The epitome of the modern-day sniper rifle.

Another current tech he had come to embrace affected the precaution he'd taken since his first professional kill. He'd made a record of every job—the target, the where and how and when, as well as the identity, or as much of the identity as he knew, of the person who had ordered the kill.

The digital age had made securing those records easier.

And it would be just as easy for him to retrieve his records, should he need them at some point to barter with the authorities for his freedom.

Or, in another circumstance he did not like to imagine, for his very life.

Signing in to his encrypted online storage account via his personal smartphone, he opened an existing Word document and added tonight's details to it. Saving and closing the document, he signed out.

His last act before leaving was to load his syringe with a lethal dose of liquid valium and inject the woman lying motionless in his bed.

That drug, combined with the heroin already in her system, was more than enough to guarantee death.

She had seen his face, and her body contained countless samples of his DNA, so there was no choice in the matter.

Not that he had any misgivings about killing another prostitute.

As the fatherless son of one, he felt as if doing so were his duty.

He waited as her breathing grew labored—waited to watch her breathe her last—and then, understanding that he would not return to this place, gathered his essentials and exited.

Once he had driven out of Chelsea, he contacted his courier and instructed her to arrange for the removal and disposal of the body.

She had been recommended to him by a fellow former legionnaire— a man he trusted with his life. And she had worked for Gateno since his arrival in New York, providing him with the things he needed to enjoy his life, as well as the basics.

As was always the case wherever Gateno went, it was preferable that as few people as possible saw his face.

Anonymity was a must, so even simple things like trips to the market were out of the question.

Cashiers had memories, and the city was a net of security and surveillance cameras.

And then there was the mixture of drugs he required, as well as the women he occasionally needed.

Gateno made that call, and upon ending it, he experienced the same intense sensation he felt every time he had closed one chapter of his life but had yet to begin the next.

It was a limbo defined by acts of intense violence.

He was prepared to throw himself into this temporary void with the devotion of a zealot, as was his custom.

More than that, violence was at the core of his nature—the thing he daydreamed about and the tendency that colored every action he took.

It was also at the root of every desire he pursued.

The next few days, and what they would require and what that would unleash in him, were the very things for which he lived.

Two

Cahill was waiting for the call.

He'd been told to expect it, had gotten ready by five and had been sitting in the dark since then, his burner phone within quick reach on the table beside his chair. But it was just after nine now and still no word yet.

Standing by was the least favorite part of his job.

He preferred to be in motion, rushing to complete his mission, because there was a sense of purpose that came with that, and purpose tended to clear all other thoughts from his mind.

A recon marine once, he'd long ago learned the art of pushing himself to the point where everything else fell away.

Thought, emotion, pain—until all that remained was his will.

It was a skill he had maintained and honed in his civilian life.

He wasn't overly fond of downtime, either, but a sympathetic physician close to his family had provided him with the pills necessary to reach and hold on to unconsciousness whenever he had trouble sleeping.

He had come to rely on those too much, but that was a problem for another time.

Standby status—the lingering space between his two escapes—was something that he was required to endure.

It was during these hours—long hours, lately—that his disciplined mind would fail him, and he'd find himself thinking of her, remembering everything about her, every detail of her face and body, her voice, the feel of her.

These precious details, unfortunately, also included how she had died.

How *he* had gotten her killed.

Had he not loved her, had he never met Erica, she would still be alive.

A simple and painful truth he often couldn't comprehend.

Of course, Cahill had seen men and women die before—combatants and civilians in Iraq and Afghanistan, among other places.

He'd seen mutilated bodies—those torn by weapons of war as well as those upon which unspeakable acts of torture had been inflicted.

Dead men hanging from ceilings by meat hooks, their naked torsos bound with heavy chains, hacked-off limbs scattered on the blood-drenched floor below them.

Children and women, too.

He had managed to shake off all the effects of those images within moments of witnessing them, choosing instead to focus only on the resolve they stirred in him, the dogged determination to hunt those responsible.

Cahill knew that in war it was emotions—any and all emotions—that more often than not made casualties of men.

Though he had years ago hunted down and killed the men who'd murdered Erica, the memory of her death was like a parasite he could not expel. Or ignore.

So during these hours, as he waited for the call that would at last send him into motion, he did the only thing he could do. He spoke to her, sometimes aloud, other times by writing her a note.

It was for him the only way through.

Listening to the hard April rain, he felt the need tonight to put his words down on paper.

Pour out his regret and grief and anger in a way that was tangible. He was close enough to crazy these days that he didn't want to add talking to himself to the list of warning signs.

Tearing a page from a notepad, he placed it out of habit on a hard surface and began his nightly purge.

He checked his watch when he was done.

Twenty minutes had passed, and the rain had stopped without his having noticed.

He was surrounded by silence.

He read over what he had written—raw and rambling, but that was the point.

No one would ever read it or know he had even written it.

Just another in a long line of private correspondence with the cherished dead.

Correspondence in which he'd begged forgiveness from the only woman he had ever loved.

He didn't bother to reread the letter, simply signed his name and then folded it by thirds.

Neatly, precisely.

Rising from the table, he stepped into his small kitchen and, removing the Zippo lighter from his pocket, lit the note on fire.

At the sink, he held the paper with one hand, turning it so the flame always had something to consume.

He continued to hold it until the fire touched his fingertips, then dropped it into the drain.

Only when nothing but ash remained did he open the faucet and wash all traces away.

He stood there for a while afterward, wanting to scream, to burst, but that wasn't him.

All that he could do was endure this storm of emotion until the call came.

He was in the darkened kitchen, standing silent and motionless, the Zippo still in his hand, when it finally did.

———————

Cahill returned to the living room and answered the burner phone just as the fourth ring had begun. "Yeah."

The voice on the other end was the one he expected to hear.

"You're needed," Raveis said.

Cahill knew the procedure.

Specific details would be sent by text following this call.

Still, he wanted to know what awaited him tonight. "Medical?"

"Exfil, too."

Cahill had recently been cross-trained as a medic, could handle everything from a simple field dressing to minor surgery.

But secreting assets out of the city was still his specialty.

"The old tavern?" he said.

The code name for a safe house seventy-five miles northeast of the city.

With full med facilities and a staff doctor, someone whom Cahill had known most of his life and trusted as he trusted no other.

The very place, in fact, where Cahill had spent three months receiving his extensive medical training.

Raveis answered, "For now, yes."

"Copy that."

"Our overseas friend has the asset," Raveis added. "He'll provide any assistance you need. And just to be safe, I have two airlift crews on standby." He hesitated for a moment, then added, "It seems we may have a breach somewhere."

By saying that, Raveis had broken his own cardinal rule regarding cell phone communications, what could and couldn't be said, and Cahill wondered whether that meant the man was rattled.

All Cahill knew for certain was that emergency medical assistance, followed by an exfil to Connecticut, would be considered a worst-case scenario.

Something big was going down.

Big enough to possibly distress Sam Raveis—a man Cahill had never before seen distressed.

Cahill responded in the only manner protocol allowed. "Copy that," he said again.

The text came through thirty seconds after the call had been terminated. The secure app installed on the burner phone gave Cahill five seconds to read the information before the text would self-delete.

It wasn't an address but rather a single word: DUMBO. Down Under the Manhattan Bridge Overpass—an acronym for a neighborhood in Brooklyn.

Cahill knew exactly where he was headed.

With luck, he'd be across the river in a half hour.

That text disappeared, and a second immediately followed, this one containing the number of the burner cell currently being used by Hammerton, their "overseas friend."

There were few men that Cahill trusted implicitly, but John Hammerton was one.

Cahill wrote the number on the palm of his left hand, purposely jumbling the last four digits in case he was somehow intercepted along the way.

It seems we might have a breach somewhere, Raveis had said.

Now more than ever, Cahill needed to follow any and all protocols.

Powering down and pocketing his phone, he hurriedly gathered together his things.

A biometric safe hidden in a cabinet contained several clean burner phones as well as his firearm of choice and a half dozen loaded magazines.

A Kimber Ultra Raptor II—a compact .45-caliber 1911 with a three-inch barrel—went into a neoprene holster on the inside of his left ankle.

Two seven-round mags went into a similar holster on the inside of his right.

Secured on the outside of his right boot was a leather sheath housing a KA-BAR knife.

Seven-inch blade of sintered, 1095 carbon steel.

His Carhartt jeans had been modified to allow him fast access to his firearm.

The inner seams of the pant legs had been unstitched, starting at the bottom cuff and extending up to midcalf. Strips of noiseless Velcro had then been sewn into the thick denim and the seams reclosed.

All it took was for him to drop to his right knee and pull the Velcro apart with his left hand, and the grip of his Kimber was there for him to grasp with his right.

The same motion to his right pant leg would allow him access to both his spare magazines and the KA-BAR.

These were movements he had practiced daily till they had become second nature.

He still practiced them, devoting several minutes of every day until the mechanics were fluid.

Even though he had two spare mags on his left ankle, Cahill slid a third one into his left hip pocket so that he could quickly acquire it should the ones at his ankle for any reason be out of easy reach.

He'd learned the hard way the need to carry as many mags as possible.

Taking two burner phones from the safe, he swung the heavy door closed and locked it, then grabbed his fully stocked medic's rucksack and headed out the door.

His small apartment was one of four on the top floor of a building in Harlem, the ownership of which could never be traced to him.

Such precautions were essential.

The property was held in a land trust that was controlled by an attorney who had been hired by a businessman with no known ties to the Cahill family.

A wealthy and prominent family, the Cahills had real estate holdings in numerous parts of the world, a handful of which had been acquired for the sole purpose of providing a well-stocked place for their only son to lay low in when necessary.

Cahill had recently taken up residence in the five-story structure.

He was, in fact, the building's only occupant, which no doubt added to his feelings of grief and separateness.

But his isolation kept others safe, and so living disconnected from people was a burden he stoically bore.

We learn from our mistakes, he told himself often.

Because if we don't, people die.

He rode the freight elevator down to the enclosed loading dock where two vehicles waited—his twenty-plus-year-old Mustang GT and a GMC panel van, both parked with their noses facing the garage door.

Heading toward the vehicles, Cahill removed the phone he'd used to communicate with Raveis from his pocket and dropped it through a small opening cut into the lid of a 55-gallon steel oil drum.

The drum was filled with a mixture of paint stripper and methylene chloride.

By the time Cahill had reached the white panel van parked mere feet away, the device and all the information stored within it had been destroyed beyond recovery.

Climbing in behind the wheel, he turned the ignition and pressed the automatic garage door opener clipped to the sun visor.

He listened to the engine as the wide door rose.

The van was a decoy vehicle, a mock-up of a contractor's truck, but its V-6 engine was finely tuned, its tires and suspension the best that money could buy.

Blending in was important, but so was getting away, should the attempt at camouflage fail.

Steering out of the garage, Cahill pressed the opener again and watched in the rearview mirror as the overhead door lowered behind him.

Once it was down, he tucked the opener into his medic bag and headed east along 125th Street.

He had crossed Third Avenue and was approaching Second when the downpour resumed, the heavy drops drumming the roof of the van like flak.

Three

Hammerton guarded the locked door, listening as he stood beside it for any indication of activity in the hallway beyond.

He'd quickly rigged the fire exit at the end of the hall with a simple makeshift alarm—a glass bottle of sparkling water that he had balanced on the door's lever-style handle.

Pushing the lever downward to open the door would send the bottle crashing to the linoleum floor.

The long and narrow corridor, its walls made of heavy prewar plaster, would easily carry down to him the sound of glass shattering.

The elevator reaching this floor, its heavy doors parting automatically, he would certainly hear as well.

An industrial warehouse that had been converted during the real estate boom two decades ago into a mix of offices and artist studios and storage space, the building was likely empty at this hour, or close enough to it, and this made his job just a little easier.

The arrival of anyone on this floor would be something he would need to pay close attention to.

The simplicity of this was appealing.

But that simple act was made considerably more difficult by the sharp and persistent ringing that blared in his ears like an alarm.

The source of the steady, shrill pitch—gunshots that were like cupped hands repeatedly slapping his ears—had occurred an hour before.

The discharging of firearms, both small and large, was something he had encountered many times in his life, first during his stint in the British SAS and then in the decades of private-sector work that followed. But tonight's shots had been fired in a confined space—one right after the other—and that, combined with the lack of any ear protection, had proved to be the critical difference.

The damage caused to his inner ear—the drums as well as the sensitive cilia that vibrated with every sound wave—was likely irreversible.

The ringing itself would fade sooner or later, but the loss in his hearing, no matter how minor, was not something he could afford.

Closing in on sixty years old, Hammerton was all too aware of the fact that his abilities were waning. He still had the hardened body of the trooper he had once been, but he also woke each morning to aching joints that could not be attributed to strenuous activity.

His eyes, though still good at long distance, could no longer focus on anything within the distance of two feet. Add another foot or so to that handicap and the front sight of his SIG P226 would be nothing more than a blur.

And then where would he be?

He knew that he wasn't at that point yet—he remained capable and effective, and tonight had proved that.

The wounded man he was now guarding would certainly be dead had Hammerton not still possessed much of his vigor and skill.

But the armor was showing cracks, there was no ignoring that, and one day—sooner than he had assumed—he would need to find another way to earn his living.

Or maybe somehow land some major score so that he wouldn't have to work.

This wasn't the time for those concerns, though.

All that mattered now was whether or not someone entered the hallway.

That and keeping the man whose life was in his hands safe until Cahill arrived.

After that, all that would remain was for the three of them to make it out of the city alive.

———

"You don't happen to have a cigarette, do you?" the wounded man said.

Hammerton turned to look at him but remained by the door.

He was uncertain how far he could step away from it before any sounds coming from beyond it would be drowned out by the ringing.

The room was a storage area but large—larger by double than Hammerton's Lower East Side apartment.

Despite its size, it had just two windows, each one a foot tall by three feet wide and located high up on only one wall.

With the overhead fluorescent lights off, the only available illumination came from what spilled in through those two small windows.

Street light from eight stories below muted by a curtain of heavy rain.

Hammerton could see the outline of Ballentine, who was seated on the floor, his back flat against the wall.

With his right hand, Ballentine held a blood-soaked rag to his left shoulder. His left arm hung limp, his left hand resting in his lap.

Despite the ringing in his ears, Hammerton could hear the man's excited breathing.

Young, maybe twenty-five, tops. A good-looking kid. Fit, so the fast breathing was likely from lingering panic rather than the exertion of getting him to this safe location.

Hammerton had all but dragged the kid along.

"I asked if you had a smoke," Ballentine said.

Hammerton hesitated before finally approaching the kid, removing his waxed canvas shoulder bag as he knelt beside him. He reached into one of the bag's outer pockets and produced a pack of Marlboros.

Digging out one of the remaining cigarettes, he placed the filtered tip between Ballentine's lips and lit the end with a Zippo lighter. "I'm told these things will kill you."

Ballentine took a breath, held it, and let out a plume of blue smoke. "No kidding. As good as aspirin, if you ask me."

"Cahill will be here soon."

Ballentine nodded. "You don't happen to have another bottle of water in that bag of yours, do you?"

Hammerton shook his head. "Sorry, mate. You'll be all right, though. The bullet missed the bone. Meat heals fast, trust me."

"It still fucking hurts."

"Always does."

"You've been shot?"

Hammerton didn't answer.

Ballentine drew on the cigarette several times before speaking again. "They came out of fucking nowhere."

"Yeah, they tend to do that."

Seated in his watch car, Hammerton had seen their vehicle—a late-model Ford sedan, likely stolen, with plates that had been stolen from yet another vehicle—pull to a stop and double-park outside the brownstone in which Ballentine lived.

Just as Ballentine had been climbing the steep stoop.

It was a borrowed apartment, one that Ballentine had claimed was a well-kept secret and was certain would remain so.

Hammerton's first impression when he had met the kid was that he was, at best, overly confident.

And anyway, Raveis didn't believe in well-kept secrets, thus Hammerton's presence.

The Ford hadn't screeched to a halt, nor had its four doors been flung open suddenly, its occupants rushing out.

It had pulled up slowly, almost silently, cruising to a gentle stop, as if the driver had been intent on looking like someone innocently searching for a specific address.

But the vehicle had appeared just as Ballentine arrived, and this had triggered a reaction in Hammerton's gut, one he knew not to ignore.

He had quickly memorized everything he could about the vehicle's physical appearance and was writing the marker numbers down in the notebook he always kept open and ready when the doors finally opened.

Three of them, not four.

One man emerging from each opened door, leaving the driver behind the wheel.

A small squad, relatively speaking, but small squads were better suited to getting in and out quickly.

Whoever had sent them was unaware that Ballentine had been assigned protection. Not that more men would have been sent, necessarily, but it was likely those that had been would have acted differently as they emerged.

Would have been more aware of their surroundings and less focused on the target ahead of them.

By the way these men moved from their vehicle—the quickness with which they strode toward the stoop stairs in a tight formation—there hadn't been any doubt in Hammerton's mind of their intentions.

This was an ambush.

Abduction or assassination, but that didn't matter at this point.

What mattered to Hammerton was the level of professionalism these men did or didn't possess.

How well trained and well armed they were, and which of the many possible mistakes that could be made they'd make first.

There was of course only one way to find that out.

In the end, as was often the case, it was sheer luck that had allowed Hammerton to get the drop on them.

It was his job to do so—to blindside those who sought to blindside the person he'd been assigned to protect.

Exiting the watch car, Hammerton had gone to work.

Four

An arguing couple a half block down the sidewalk had caught the driver's attention, allowing Hammerton to approach the Ford undetected.

The steady rain helped with that, too, covering the sound of his boots on the pavement as he closed the distance.

Within a few fast seconds he was just three feet away from his first target.

A suppressor attached to his SIG, Hammerton put a single round through the man's left ear.

Moving around the front of the Ford, he kept his eyes fixed on the three-man hit team.

The first man had reached the stoop, climbed its five steps, and was entering the street door of Ballentine's building.

As a ploy to lower Ballentine's guard and throw off anyone who might be watching, he was holding a grocery bag to his chest with one arm and moving as if in a rush to catch the interior foyer door with his free hand before it swung closed.

None of the men had turned back, which told Hammerton that the metallic clack of the pistol's slide racking had been absorbed by the rain and hadn't alerted them to his presence.

Still, he wasn't in position yet, and at any moment, one of them could simply glance back over his shoulder, eliminating the crucial element of surprise.

Reaching the stoop, Hammerton watched as the other two men entered the street door. Ballentine turned back to hold the foyer door open for the man with the grocery bag.

As if that man belonged there, he thanked Ballentine, then turned and placed his back against the door to hold it for his two friends.

Ballentine continued on his way, starting up the stairs.

He'd gone only a few steps up when the lead man placed his bag on the floor and reached into his raincoat, producing a short-barreled carbine suspended from his neck by a sling. Pulling the stock tight against his shoulder, the man began to raise the muzzle upward.

The other two men removed pistols from their waistbands.

One blocked the doorway, facing forward, while the other began to turn to cover the street door.

Hammerton was inside the foyer and just feet from the turning man.

His SIG was raised, the man already in his sights.

Without hesitation, he put a round through the man's neck, severing his spine.

The man dropped to the floor.

Hammerton stepped over the body and quickly closed the distance to the next man, who had heard the commotion behind him and was turning.

Hammerton immediately shifted to close-quarter tactics.

Instead of his arm outstretched in a two-hand grip, he lowered his weapon to his side, bracing his forearm horizontally along the natural notch of his hip bone, and used his free hand to grab the man's weapon by its barrel.

Hammerton didn't struggle for control of the weapon, simply redirected it long enough to square his body with his target's and unleash a double-tap into his center mass.

The second man fell, giving Hammerton a clear view of the final man—the man armed with the short-barreled carbine.

Ballentine had bolted at some point, was halfway up the stairs as the final man took aim.

Hammerton was out of time, so he simply shifted his weight to his left leg and twisted his torso to the right as he brought his SIG to his solar plexus, gripping it again with both hands.

He squeezed off another single shot, but not before the man pulled the trigger.

The carbine had been set on full auto. Bright orange lit the stairwell, and in the enclosed space, the painfully loud burst of multiple rounds carried shockwaves that were palpable.

Hammerton's single round—a clean shot through the spine—dropped the man, but his finger did not immediately release its grip on the trigger and the weapon continued to fire.

Hammerton counted a total of seven shots in that burst.

It wasn't until the man was motionless on the floor, the rifle clutched in his dead hand finally silent, that Hammerton moved to stand over him.

He recognized the weapon as a KRISS Vector SBR—a modern-day equivalent to the Thompson submachine gun.

He kicked the weapon clear of the man's hand and as a precaution put a second round into the back of his head, then looked up at Ballentine, who was lying on his side halfway up the stairs, grasping his left shoulder with his right hand.

A pistol lay a few steps down from his feet.

"Fuck," Hammerton whispered.

He climbed the stairs two steps at a time, reached Ballentine, and knelt beside him, examining the wound.

They were lucky; only one round had actually struck, leaving a flesh wound that was far from fatal.

Hammerton's concern switched instantly from tending to the wounded man to extracting him from the scene.

No doubt others—many others, both inside this building and out—had heard the unusual sound of automatic gunfire.

"Get up," Hammerton said.

"I think I've been shot."

"Get up. I need you to walk."

"Jesus. How bad is it?"

"Get up, come on. We need to get out of here."

Ballentine looked at his bloodied hand. "Oh shit, I'm bleeding."

Hammerton lost his patience, grabbed the kid by his belt, and yanked him to his feet. He maintained his firm hold as he half pulled, half guided the kid down the stairs, letting go only long enough to retrieve the dropped pistol and tuck it securely into his waistband.

At the bottom of the stairs, the kid stumbled and began to fall, but Hammerton yanked him to his feet and kept him moving.

Facing the foyer door, which was propped open by the body of the second man, Hammerton let go of the kid and, resuming his Weaver stance, scanned what he could see of the street.

"Stay right behind me," he ordered, then stepped over the fallen men and moved through the narrow foyer to the street door.

There he paused, his SIG still raised, and scanned the area—the vehicles parked along the curbs, the dozen stoops to his right and left, then those across the street.

He saw no overt threats, but he also saw a number of places in which covert ones could find easy cover.

But there was no staying where they were; stationary targets quickly drew fire.

Lowering his hands, he concealed his firearm inside his open jacket and led Ballentine down the stairs and past the Ford with the dead man slumped behind the wheel.

Less than a minute after the ambush had begun, Hammerton was speeding away in his watch car, Ballentine stretched out on the back-seat, bleeding.

Hammerton was back at his post by the locked office door.

His ears were still ringing.

Ballentine had smoked the cigarette down and was working on his second. After a moment, he spoke. "Who were they?"

"You tell me."

"I mean, how did they find me? I did everything I was told."

"Everything isn't always enough."

Ballentine was quiet for a moment more. "Thanks," he said finally. "For doing what you did back there."

"It's my job."

"How'd you get so good at it?"

"It's interesting that you think I'm good at it, considering you got shot."

"It could have been a lot worse. It *would* have been a lot worse." Ballentine shook his head. "I let them in, like an idiot. Then I just froze."

Hammerton thought about letting the kid off the hook, telling him that everyone panics the first time they come under fire, that no amount of training can prepare a man to face down a muzzle aimed right at him.

But it suited Hammerton to have the kid scared and humbled, so he said nothing.

Luck was on his side tonight, because before the kid could ask him anything else, Hammerton's cell phone vibrated.

He looked at the display. "He's here."

"Who?"

"Your own personal Jesus Christ."

Hammerton stepped to the kid and bent to help him up.

"What the fuck does that mean?" the kid said.

Hammerton ignored the question. "C'mon, get up. We need to move."

Five

Hammerton sat in the van's driver seat while Cahill examined Ballentine in the back.

The renovated warehouse had a loading dock, but the bay was an open one, no overhead door, so Hammerton was keeping a close watch on the activity on the street outside.

The rain kept pedestrians off the sidewalk, and this part of DUMBO was relatively quiet at night, so vehicle traffic was minimal.

His SIG, reloaded, lay within quick reach on the passenger seat beside him.

The back of the van was crowded with the kind of gear one would expect of a general contractor: power tools secured to one wall, a row of toolboxes for hand tools placed beneath them, and a two-foot-tall wooden chest fitted with a latch and padlock running along the other wall.

The chest hid a state-of-the-art stretcher, but that wasn't needed because Ballentine was able to sit up.

He'd insisted on it, in fact.

He was facing Cahill, who was seated on an overturned milk crate.

The drawers of the metal toolboxes contained everything Cahill would need to patch a person up, or, in more desperate situations, keep him or her alive during the two-hour journey to Connecticut.

Cahill had decided to clean and close Ballentine's wound before proceeding with the exfil.

For that, the van needed to be stationary, and though this was a risk, it was a calculated one. If there had been a breach and someone knew of the location of this safe house, then certainly that someone would have arrived by now.

Cahill prided himself on his newfound set of skills, worked them with great care. And despite the fact that all gunshot wounds initially reminded him of Erica, focusing on this task eased his troubled mind—for a while, anyway.

Each person he aided felt a little like redemption.

Cahill injected Ballentine first with four hundred milligrams Ciprofloxacin to prevent infection, then followed that with a shot of Novocain, after which he threaded a surgical needle with a 2-0 nylon suture and began to stitch the wound closed.

He spoke to Ballentine during the procedure, informing him of each step he was about to take prior to taking it.

It wasn't until Cahill was a few stitches from finishing that the kid spoke. "You're Cahill, aren't you? Charlie Cahill. Right?"

Cahill continued stitching. "It doesn't matter who I am."

"It does to me."

"Why?"

"You knew my brother. In Afghanistan. Frank Ballentine. He was one of your recon marines."

Cahill disliked coincidences. Years ago, when he had learned that Frank Ballentine had been finally discharged, Cahill had recommended him to his handler, Sam Raveis, for contract work.

And Raveis had sent James Carrington to recruit him.

But here was Ballentine's kid brother, also brought into the fold, and done so without Cahill's knowledge—not that informing Cahill was required, though he would have expected to be consulted.

Certain precautions were taken when bringing in family members.

More than all that, though, here was Ballentine's kid brother, shot by assailants who somehow knew what shouldn't be known—the address of an operative's apartment.

But Cahill's days as a special operator were behind him. He was support staff now—nothing more, nothing less. Exfils from New York City when required, field medicine when necessary.

To ensure he never caused the loss of another life, Cahill followed orders and stuck to protocols as if they were commandments.

The younger Ballentine had broken one of the more sacred of protocols by asking Cahill's name, but there wasn't anything Cahill could do about that other than to shut the kid down.

"I need you to stop talking," he said. "You're going to sit back here, and I'm going to get you out. Are we clear?"

"Where are we going?"

"Out of the city. That's all you need to know for now."

"For how long?"

"I don't know. But they're going to want to debrief you, and someone's going to keep an eye on your wound to make sure it's healing right. Expect to be there for a few days, at the least."

"No."

"No what?"

"I'm not leaving."

"It's not your choice."

"The fuck it isn't. And anyway, it's not about choice. I can't leave. Not without them."

"Who?"

"Ula, my partner. If my cover is blown, hers could be, too. I leave, they're in danger."

"They?"

"She has a fifteen-year-old daughter."

Cahill leaned back, paused a moment, then looked toward Hammerton.

Seated behind the wheel, Hammerton was watching them via the rearview mirror.

He said nothing, and neither did Cahill.

It was obvious to both men that the nature of the mission had now changed from simple exfil to rescue.

Finally, Cahill let out a breath and faced Ballentine again. "Where are they?"

"A motel. We needed a place for them to wait for me if something happened, and we needed to scramble. A safe place."

It took Cahill a moment to reply.

He'd once thought the same thing—that a motel was the safest place for the woman he was determined to protect.

The woman he loved.

Erica.

It had, of course, proved to be anything but safe.

He didn't need to check the rearview mirror to know that Hammerton was still watching for his reaction.

Though Cahill did his best to keep his face void of expression, he had no doubt that the effort itself was visible to the man behind the wheel.

The sight of a man about to come face-to-face with his past wasn't easily mistaken. Or easily hidden.

There wasn't any time to waste.

"What motel are they at?" he said.

Six

Brooklyn to the Bronx via the BQE was the fastest route, but it was also a zigzag—first north, then east, then west, then north again.

Hammerton drove, pushing the speed limit as much as he dared.

Ballentine was on the chest in the back, Cahill still seated across from him.

In Ballentine's hand was a smartphone. He had used it to text his partner a predetermined code, one that told her that he was on his way to get her and her daughter.

Having such protocols in place was standard op procedure.

Thirty minutes had passed since Ballentine had sent the coded message, however, and he had yet to receive a reply indicating receipt and compliance.

Ballentine stared at the phone. Finally, the kid looked at Cahill. "Should I try again? It's possible it didn't go through, right? I mean, that happens."

"What's your name?" Cahill said. "Your first name."

"Dante."

"Seriously?"

"Yeah."

"What's your background?"

"What do you mean?"

"What were you before this? Before signing on with Raveis?"

Ballentine hesitated. "I was in school."

"School?"

"Grad school."

"But before that?"

"I'm not following."

"You served at some point, right?"

"In the military? No."

Cahill shook his head. "Jesus." To the best of his knowledge, only former military were recruited by Raveis to work as private contractors, and those recruits had almost exclusively been members of special forces units, those of either the United States or one of its allies.

Cahill had been thinking up to this point that the kid was the exception to that rule—that rare recruit whose raw talent outweighed his having been a simple soldier or marine or seaman. But the kid's apparent nervousness had told him that this wasn't the case, and Cahill couldn't help wondering what the hell a former grad student was doing in the field.

Not just a grad student, but the younger brother of one of Cahill's former recon marines.

"You had your training, though, right?" Cahill said. "At one of Raveis's compounds?"

"Not exactly."

"What do you mean?"

"Raveis trained me privately. Off the grid."

"Why?"

"It's a long story."

Cahill was about to ask him to elaborate on that but thought better of it. "You remember your training, though, right?"

Ballentine nodded.

"Then answer your own question," Cahill said. "Should you send another message?"

"No."

Cahill paused. "Listen, I'll make it easier for you. Just do what I say from now on, okay? Everything I say, exactly as I say it. No questions, no hesitation, just immediate compliance and swift action. Understand?"

Another nod. "Yeah."

"Good." Cahill let out of breath. "So how is your brother anyway?"

"You haven't heard?"

"Heard what?"

"He's dead."

Before Cahill could ask how, the smartphone in Ballentine's hand buzzed. The kid immediately looked down at the display. "She's ready and waiting."

There was sorrow on Ballentine's face, so Cahill decided not to pursue the subject of his older brother.

More than that, he wanted to offer the kid something in the way of kindness.

"See, you worried for nothing," he said. "Now put the phone in your pocket and look at me."

Ballentine did as instructed.

Cahill gave the kid his speech, how this was what he did for a living, and he wouldn't get paid what he got paid if he wasn't good at what he did.

The part about this being his living wasn't true, but that didn't matter.

The second half of his speech was true, and did matter.

He told the kid that he'd led men into danger before—younger men, men who were even more scared and distracted.

Men who were far from home, facing incursions into landscapes that were nothing shy of hell on earth.

He knew all about leading men, knew that his own confidence would instill the same—or at least some degree of it—in the kid.

Cahill could portray confidence, had always done so, even in the worst situations, and he was doing so now, despite his own lingering distraction and fear.

Despite the unbearable grief and remorse that burned still fresh in his mind.

The memory of the one death he couldn't shake.

Hammerton announced that they were five minutes away.

Cahill offered Ballentine the weapon he had drawn but dropped on the stairway—a subcompact Beretta Storm, nine-mil.

Ballentine took it and checked the indicator located behind the ejector port to confirm that a round was still chambered, then removed the double-stack mag to determine that it was full.

He reinserted the mag and leaned forward, sliding the pistol into his small-of-the-back holster.

Cahill was comforted by the fact that the kid could at least perform a simple weapon check expertly.

A small comfort, yes, but at this point he'd take all that he could get.

"Just do what I tell you," he told Ballentine. "We'll get your people and get you out. All right? Everything's going to be okay."

Seven

The Baychester Motel was closed for renovations, though one look at the property told Cahill that any work that may have been begun had stalled, and had likely done so a while ago.

He watched through the windshield as the van approached the construction site, saw three two-story brick structures set in a U shape around a parking lot that was closed off by a cyclone fence, its gate not only standing open a few feet but also leaning inward at a forty-five-degree angle.

Each wing of the motel had twenty rooms—ten on the ground floor, ten on the floor above—and more than half of them had their windows and doors boarded over with weather-beaten sheets of plywood.

The parking lot's pavement had long cracks through which tall, dead weeds had sprung.

Cahill's first thought was to question how this place, in a desolate corner of the Bronx, could be considered a safe location for a woman and her teenage daughter to wait for evac.

If anything, the enclosed and deserted property struck him as the perfect scene for any number of crimes.

But as the van pulled up alongside the gate and Cahill saw farther into the empty parking lot, he recognized, in those rooms that had not been sealed up, a dozen positions that would offer someone both perfect cover and an unobstructed view of the gate.

Having many vantage points to choose from—and others to move to should one need to displace—was a significant advantage when choosing an Alamo.

Also, the fact that the property was seemingly abandoned meant there would likely be no one to witness the arrival and departure of two women.

What was more important to Cahill, however, was that this derelict place was different in every imaginable way from the New Haven motel where his beloved Erica had been shot and killed.

He was determined not to ever endure again—tonight or any other time—what he had barely survived two years ago.

Therefore, his mind clung to all the detectable differences between that motel and this one as if his very sanity depended on them.

But while Cahill opted to keep his impressions of this location to himself, Hammerton did not. "What the fuck is this? You sent them here?"

Ballentine moved forward and leaned over the back of the empty front seat, looking out the passenger window. "Raveis told me that this was my extraction point. I told Ula about it, in case I needed her to meet me here."

Cahill wasn't surprised by this, knew that Raveis had a network of safe houses throughout the Greater New York area.

The locations were on a need-to-know basis, and Cahill had been apprised of only a few—the storage unit in Brooklyn and the "old tavern" in Connecticut among them.

But in the vastness of the five boroughs, not to mention the far reaches of the tristate area, the options for such places were countless.

Cahill stood and, bent at the waist, moved forward as the other two men studied the motel.

"So where is she?" Hammerton said.

"Looking at us," Ballentine answered.

"From where?"

Ballentine moved between the two front seats and sat by the passenger door. He pointed to the northern wing. "Up there—the room in the dead center of the wing facing us. Room 205. And my guess is right now she has you in her sights."

Cahill leaned between the two seats for a clearer view. Room 205 was one of the rooms without its windows boarded over, and the only room with its shade almost fully drawn. "Is she coming out?"

"No. I'm supposed to come in and get her."

Cahill understood the reason for that, nodded, and said to Hammerton, "We'll be right back."

Leaning across Ballentine, he opened the passenger door.

Ballentine climbed out, and Cahill followed. They crossed the sidewalk to the broken gate, moved through it, and faced the open parking lot.

Half a football field wide.

Cahill's training told him to make use of available cover by walking along the wing to his right, but he knew the woman watching them would prefer that he remain in her direct line of sight as much as possible, so he had no choice but to lead Ballentine into what would be the perfect kill box.

A wing straight ahead, one to their left and another to their right, and no easy escape behind them.

Too many windows to keep track of as they moved.

Despite this exposure, Cahill maintained an easy pace, keeping his arms hanging at his sides, his hands open.

It took a minute for them to cross the distance and climb the single flight of cement stairs to the second-floor landing.

Here the occupant of 205 could no longer see them and no doubt had abandoned her position at the window for one deeper inside the room.

Cahill and Ballentine reached the door, but neither stood in front of it. Cahill crossed to the left of it, Ballentine remained to the right. Ballentine knocked lightly once, then twice, then three times.

From inside a woman said, "Enter."

Just one word was enough for Cahill to detect an accent, one he believed to be Middle Eastern.

Ballentine opened the door and moved inside, doing so with his hands held out and up slightly.

Cahill took a last scan of what was behind him—the empty lot and the two wings that flanked it, the cyclone fence, and the van waiting just beyond it.

He didn't like the idea of having to move through that again as they departed, but there was nothing he could do about that now.

Finally, his hands held out and open, he, too, entered the darkened motel room.

Eight

He could not see at first.

The streets immediately surrounding the Baychester Motel weren't exactly abandoned, but they weren't high-traffic areas, either. The distance between the street lamps—those that worked—reflected this. So while the light outside had been little more than ambient city light, it was still enough that Cahill's eyes had to adjust to the darkened room.

Such a transition would offer a significant advantage to those waiting inside.

The first thing Cahill determined was that the room was unfurnished—he sensed openness, and the few footsteps he took had echoed more than he would have expected.

The room wasn't completely void, however.

To his left, in front of the only window, was a pile of what appeared to be sandbags stacked to form a barrier.

Cahill recognized a fixed and reinforced position behind which a shooter could find cover and take careful aim.

As his eyes adjusted, he realized that the contents of the stack weren't sandbags but rather sixty-pound bags of cement mix laid end to end, three stacks long and four tall.

Ballentine had stepped to the center of the room and was facing the back wall. Cahill turned his attention there and saw a woman standing in front of the closed bathroom door as if guarding it.

He made quick work of sizing her up.

She was in her late thirties at the most. Her thick, dark hair was pulled back into a ponytail, and she was dressed in tactical boots, dark jeans, a black field jacket, and a scarf.

In her gloved hands was a Kel-Tec Sub-16 carbine, its folding stock extended and shouldered, its suppressed muzzle aimed at Cahill's center mass.

The weapon was attached by a short bungee sling to a harness she wore under her open jacket.

Cahill froze, didn't even breathe. His only movement was in his eyes, which shifted from the suppressor to the woman's right hand.

Her fully extended index finger was resting outside the trigger guard, so he knew she was well trained.

From there he looked at her face and saw something that alarmed him.

There was a wildness in her eyes.

Dark-gray eyes, he noted.

They weren't, he believed, wild from fear or panic, but rather from something else, something . . . deeper.

Cahill scanned the room for a second occupant—a teenage girl— but he and Ballentine and the woman ready to fire were all he could see. The girl was probably hiding in the bathroom.

He realized then that the wildness in the woman's eyes was the look of a mother determined to protect her child at all costs.

Ballentine put himself between the woman and Cahill. A simple adjustment of her aim put Cahill back into her sights.

"It's okay, Ula," Ballentine said. "He's with me."

But she didn't budge, nor did her demeanor alter. She said in a deep voice, "The word, please. Say the word."

Cahill understood the protocol in play here.

Should Ballentine ever arrive here with another person, he was to speak one of two preselected words, and the woman's actions—shoot the stranger beside him or not—depended on which word he spoke.

But Ballentine was obviously drawing a blank. "Shit," he muttered.

"Tell her the word." Cahill kept his voice as calm and even as he could.

Ballentine glanced over his shoulder. "Give me a second," he snapped. "I'm not used to all these guns being pointed at me—"

"Say the fucking word," Cahill urged.

Ballentine's mouth opened as he searched for the word, but nothing came out. He shook his head once, then again, and finally blurted out, "Darayya." He let out a breath and repeated, "Darayya. It's Darayya."

Cahill recognized that as the name of a suburb of Damascus, Syria.

The woman named Ula lowered her carbine, though she kept the stock pressed against her shoulder. Her eyes remained fixed on Cahill. "Who is he?"

Cahill spoke before Ballentine could answer. "It doesn't matter. I'm here to get you out; that's all you need to know."

Ula ignored him. "What happened, Dante?"

Again, Cahill cut Ballentine off. "You two can catch up later. Right now I need you and your daughter to come with us."

Ballentine took a less forceful approach. "Tell Valena it's okay to come out," he said softly. "They'll take us somewhere safe."

Ula glanced at Ballentine's shoulder. Blood had seeped through his dressing. "You're injured."

"Don't worry about it." He nodded toward the bathroom door behind her. "Tell Valena to come out. We need to get going, now."

She took a breath, held it for a few seconds, then let it out and announced, "Clear."

Cahill and Ballentine watched the bathroom door, expecting it to open, but it didn't.

Then Cahill sensed motion to his left, someone suddenly standing there.

He turned and saw the girl.

She'd been hiding beside the stacked bags of cement, wedged in between the stack's far edge and the cinder-block wall, and had risen to her feet without Cahill detecting her.

She was holding in a two-handed grip a pistol he immediately identified as a Czech-made CZ-75 nine-mil.

The girl, like her mother, held the weapon expertly.

And like her mother, she had dark hair that she wore pulled back into a ponytail and was dressed for urban combat.

Unlike her mother, however, the wildness in her dark-gray eyes *was* fear.

Cahill would have been surprised to see anything less than that.

He said to Ula, "Have you seen any activity since you got here? Vehicles up and down the street a few times? Unusual pedestrians walking by? Anything?"

"Nothing."

"Are you sure?"

It was obvious that the follow-up question irked her. "Yes."

Cahill ignored her reaction. "You and your daughter follow me. Ballentine here will be right behind you. Are we clear?"

Ula waved for her daughter to join her.

The girl did, handing the pistol to her mother, who slid it into her carbon-fiber belt holster without taking her eyes off Cahill. She then folded the carbine's shoulder stock, effectively cutting the length of the weapon by more than a third, which would allow her to conceal it, more or less, inside her field jacket.

As Ula did this, her daughter reached behind her and removed something from the small of her mother's back—a six-inch-long tactical flashlight.

The girl had done this without missing a beat. It struck Cahill that they worked together as a well-drilled team.

"Actually," Ula said, "it will be better if you two follow us. Only a fool or someone with a death wish would walk through that kill box out there."

She stepped back and, still facing Cahill, opened the bathroom door.

The small room was lit, though dimly. Cahill saw something he did not expect.

A hole had been cut into the tile floor, and sticking out of it were the top few rungs of an aluminum ladder.

Someone had taken the time necessary not only to fortify this room with bags of cement mix but also to create a second means of entrance and egress, and then had cleaned up afterward.

A quick look at Ballentine told Cahill that the kid was just as surprised by this revelation.

"My daughter and I are going out the way we came in," Ula said. "I'd suggest you follow us."

She led the girl through the bathroom door. Taking the flashlight back, she switched it on. The flashlight in her left and the carbine's grip in her right, Ula aimed both items down through the opening.

She made a visual search of the room below, shifting her position around the edge of the makeshift escape hatch till she had covered a full 360 degrees.

Handing the light back to her daughter, who kept it aimed down the hole, Ula said to the men, "I'm going to need you two to keep up."

She swung her carbine to her left side and let it hang there from its sling, then began to climb down the ladder.

Nine

Cahill was the last one down, and the moment he stepped off the ladder, he dropped to one knee and drew his Kimber from its ankle holster.

Rising, he followed Ballentine, who was behind the pair of women.

Standing close together, Valena aiming the light and Ula holding the carbine, they headed toward an opening in the wall separating this room from the one next to it.

A half dozen or so cinder blocks had been knocked out, likely by jackhammer, leaving an opening that was large enough for a person to move through.

It was necessary to duck, and to be mindful of debris littering the floor, but that barely slowed the women as they moved into the next room, then through a similar gap into the room next to that.

They passed through four walls before reaching the final room of that wing.

Here there was no evidence of any further demolition, and to Cahill's eye, no way out other than the door.

Ula strode to it and stood to the right of it, opening it slightly.

This room's window wasn't boarded over, so Cahill hurried to it and stood to its left, leaning forward enough to peer out.

Nothing had changed from the last time he had looked.

He saw the same empty parking lot and fence, and the van was still twenty feet beyond the broken gate.

The distance they needed to cross to reach the waiting vehicle, however, seemed somehow greater than it had been when he'd first assessed it just moments ago.

Maybe his judgment was tinged by the fact that retreat generally took longer than forward motion, and unlike his and Ballentine's two-man advance, it was a group of four that would be retreating now.

Ula barely paused at the door. She announced, "We're moving," then swung the door open.

After one more visual sweep, she led her daughter outside.

Ballentine followed, his Beretta drawn.

Cahill would have preferred a longer pause, but there was nothing he could do about that. Ula had taken point, and the race for their transport out had begun.

Stepping to the door, he made his own quick survey before proceeding into the open.

Ula led them along the front of the western wing, using the shadow of the second-floor landing directly overhead as cover.

Though this was smarter than all of them rushing across the open parking lot, they were still in clear view of a number of rooms in the eastern wing, as well as those in the wing they had just vacated.

The potential of interconnecting fields of fire had been reduced but not eliminated, so Cahill whispered, "Watch the windows. You cover the ground floor. I've got the second."

Ballentine did as ordered, only looking away every few steps to confirm that the women just ahead of him were still in motion.

They had passed the halfway point in fifteen seconds, made the far end of the building in another fifteen.

Ula stopped them at the corner, but again for only a brief pause as she studied the street.

She breathed evenly, her eyes scanning from left to right.

Steady but quickly.

Cahill noticed that the woman's daughter kept her eyes almost always on her mother, watching for the cues that would tell her what to do next and precisely when to do it.

They were in sync at a level reached only by those who had trained and fought together for long periods. But it was more than that, too.

It was, to him, something akin to a predator and its cub.

Everything the mother did, the daughter observed and absorbed.

Every skill the daughter displayed had no doubt come from the mother, a woman as skilled as any man Cahill had fought beside.

Or against.

Within seconds of pausing at the corner, Ula and her daughter were hustling in double time again, moving along the fence toward its broken gate. Doing so brought them into the open, and Ula made a point of concealing her carbine inside her open jacket.

This was, after all, New York City, and even though this neighborhood was far from densely populated, there was no point in taking the risk of drawing attention.

Ballentine had clearly noticed Ula's attempt at discretion, because as he broke from cover to follow, he made a point of concealing his subcompact Beretta by drawing his arms in tight and placing his right hand over his stomach with his left covering the pistol.

A "safe carry" posture employed by some law enforcement.

As a result, the way he moved was awkward looking at best, but Cahill didn't bother to correct the kid.

As for himself, Cahill simply lowered his right hand so it was hanging beside his thigh and walked as naturally as he could.

Ula and her daughter reached and cleared the broken gate. Ballentine followed and caught up with them on the sidewalk, was alongside them as they approached the van's back panel door.

Grasping the handle, Ballentine slid the door back, letting the two women enter first, then followed and pulled the door closed.

Cahill was climbing into the passenger seat and closing his door when Hammerton pressed down on the accelerator, swinging the wheel with both hands and steering the van into an aggressive U-turn.

The wide, curving arc turned into a slight fishtail, but Hammerton compensated, straightening the vehicle out before proceeding to backtrack toward the BQE.

Cahill had yet to fasten his seat belt, and the three passengers in the back had barely managed to sit down, when the first gunshot came.

For the former recon marine there was no mistaking the report of a .50-caliber rifle.

And the devastation that massive round caused.

A .50-cal BMG bullet traveled at roughly four times the speed of sound, so Cahill should have only heard that familiar *thump* seconds after the powerful round had already torn its way through the van's radiator and penetrated deep into the V-6 engine.

But in combat the human mind can play all kinds of tricks, and to his senses the sound of the shot being fired arrived virtually at the same instant as the deep ping of the armor-piercing round's impact.

Even in the immediate shock and confusion, Cahill was able to glean a crucial fact: the shooter had fired from extremely close range.

The bullet wrought its unmistakable catastrophic damage to the engine block, causing the motor to instantly seize and the vehicle to slow dramatically.

A fast follow-up shot to the same location brought the van from a crawl to a dead stop.

Unlike the first round, however, the second was a tracer—an incendiary round that glowed red-hot as it flew toward the target, allowing the shooter to track the projectile's arc and make quick-aiming corrections without needing to observe its impact.

In this case, though, the pyrotechnic served no other purpose than to set the disabled engine ablaze.

But Cahill was able to use its fast, perfectly straight line of flight to determine the point of origin, and his eyes went to a black SUV parked at the curb two hundred yards straight ahead.

The shooter was standing inside the vehicle and using its open sunroof as a fixed firing position.

Cahill saw the silhouette of a head and a pair of shoulders, but only for a fraction of a second, because the shooter quickly ducked back inside, pulling the long rifle with him.

And almost immediately, another vehicle pulled out from its position of concealment behind the SUV.

Its headlights off, the second SUV barreled toward them.

Flames emerged around the edges of the van's hood, the fast-rising black smoke forming a swirling cloud that obscured Cahill's view through the windshield.

But he didn't need to see the vehicle approaching.

He could hear its gunning engine as it closed the distance.

Loud and getting louder.

Ten

Cahill turned in his seat and grabbed Hammerton, pulling the man with him as he rushed into the van's back compartment.

A burst of automatic gunfire shattered the driver's door window the instant Hammerton was clear.

Cahill dove for the storage container that doubled as a med bed and flung it open. As he did, Hammerton lunged for Ballentine and Valena, who were standing frozen, stunned by the sudden violence.

Hammerton placed his hands on the top of their heads and half guided, half shoved them to the floor.

He pressed them down till they were flat on their stomachs, but he remained on his knees, his eyes on the double doors at the van's rear.

He drew his SIG and leveled it at the entrance, ready to fire should the doors be opened from the outside.

The only person still upright was Ula. She had removed the Kel-Tec from inside her field jacket and swung the folding stock to the open position. It locked with a solid click, and she shouldered the weapon as she strode, bent forward at the waist, toward the back door.

As she closed the short distance, the automatic gunfire resumed, these rounds puncturing the van's right-side panel and passing through the interior before exiting through the left side.

The shooter's aim, however, was high, so he either hadn't antici-pated that his targets had dropped down low as they retreated, which meant he was inexperienced, or his intent wasn't to kill but rather to lay down suppressing fire.

Cahill decided it was the latter since that was consistent with the sniper in the SUV disabling the engine instead of taking out the men behind the windshield, which he could have accomplished just as easily.

Which Cahill would have done had he been sent here to kill.

So an abduction, he thought. *But who is the target?*

That didn't really matter, though. If even just one of them was meant to be taken alive, their assailants would have to attack with restraint.

Cahill and those with him, of course, had no such restrictions.

It was kill or be killed, as simple as that, and there was freedom in this.

He tucked his Kimber into the waistband of his jeans, then reached into the storage bench and grabbed his Heckler & Koch MR556A1—an AR-15-type carbine.

A magazine was preinserted, and the bolt had been locked back in the open position, so he slapped the catch lever with his palm, sending the carrier forward and chambering the 62-grain, steel-core, 5.56 NATO round.

Grabbing two more mags, he quickly shoved them into his jacket pocket as he rose to a crouch, then slipped on the attached single-point bungee sling and readied his weapon.

Ula was standing to the right of the double doors, watching him and waiting for her cue to move. Cahill had no doubt that she had made the same assessment he'd made—that the only advantage they had right now was to go on the offensive.

Come out shooting and prevent the ambush from turning into a siege, one they couldn't possibly hold.

Everything he'd seen that woman do—everything about her—told him that she had been a soldier, likely a leader of soldiers and a good one at that.

Cahill glanced at Hammerton. His SIG was still aimed at the rear doors, and though his being armed with a nine-mil pistol meant he was outgunned, he indicated with a single nod that he was ready for what needed to be done.

The second SUV skidded to a stop, aligning itself nose-to-nose with the van.

Its headlights came on, flooding the interior with a stark mix of bright light and severe shadows.

In this starkness, Cahill could see Ula's face clearly.

Her eyes went to her daughter, her focus drifting, but only for a second.

Car doors opened. Boots hit pavement.

She looked at Cahill again, her eyes as sharp as before.

A mother determined to protect her child, no matter what it took.

Cahill rose from his crouch and, bent at the waist, walked toward her.

She waited till he was next to her—till they were face-to-face, looking each other in the eye—and then she turned, unlatched the door, and kicked it open.

Shifting her finger inside the trigger guard of her Kel-Tec, she came out shooting, Cahill right behind her.

Eleven

The bleeding wouldn't stop, no matter what he did.

The backseat of the SUV was slick with blood, and Cahill was covered in it, too—not just his hands and forearms as he worked to keep her alive, but his torso and face and jeans.

Not all of it was her blood.

They'd had no time to retrieve any of Cahill's medical gear from the van prior to hijacking their attackers' only remaining vehicle—not that it would have mattered, because Ula was losing blood fast from multiple entrance and exit wounds, as well as the torn organs and severed arteries that had been struck as the three fast-moving rounds had cut through her, and nothing Cahill could carry in a kit would be enough against that.

Hammerton had been shot up as well, though not nearly as badly.

In the far backseat, the former SAS trooper was doing his best to sit upright.

Ballentine and Valena were the only ones intact, at least physically. Ballentine drove as the girl sat in the passenger seat, looking back and watching Cahill as he worked frantically on her mother.

If he could even just slow the bleeding . . .

Several times Ballentine told Valena to look at him, speaking to her calmly and assuredly.

This told Cahill they'd had significant interactions prior to tonight.

She wasn't just the daughter of Ballentine's assigned partner.

She knew and trusted Ballentine.

Cahill wondered, though, exactly what Ballentine's relationship was to the woman who'd fought so expertly and bravely.

Were they partners in another sense?

Despite the obvious closeness between Ballentine and the girl, she didn't listen to him, couldn't stop herself from staring at the horrific scene playing out one seat behind her.

She showed all the signs of someone slipping deeper and deeper into shock.

Cahill glanced over at her several times, wishing she'd do as Ballentine was telling her to do, but that was the least of his problems.

Here was another woman dying.

Another woman gushing blood, this time from multiple gunshot wounds.

He thought of his last moments with Erica, with her slumped in the passenger seat of his Jeep, a single nine-mil round lodged in her chest, the jagged edges of its blossom-shaped hollow point severing vital tissue as she struggled to breathe.

Conscious till the moment she died.

And it had been anything but a fast death.

Cahill felt a deep sorrow rising within, one that threatened to spill over into tears, but he fought against it, had to tell himself that this woman wasn't Erica, that he wasn't back there again, helpless, watching the woman he loved die.

There wasn't a day—or a night—when he didn't relive that terror.

But he needed to focus now, needed his mind clear and sharp and decisive.

He repeated four words like a mantra whenever the shit was coming down around him.

You're a fucking marine.

You're a fucking marine.

You're a fucking marine . . .

He let logistics occupy his mind.

The safe house in Connecticut, complete with a skilled physician and operating facilities, was still an hour away, but the chances that Ula would survive that long were slim.

Added to that was the fact that the vehicle they had commandeered was likely equipped with a GPS tracking system, so even if he could keep her alive, they would need another way of reaching their destination. Otherwise a fresh team of gunmen would follow them there, and the firefight they had just barely survived would simply resume.

And do so in a place Cahill was determined to keep secret.

He didn't see any other choice, so he said to Hammerton, "Get the phone out of my jacket pocket."

Hammerton had been in the back of the van when he'd been hit by bullet fragments—one piece lodging in his right thigh, the other cutting clear through his left palm, both pieces of jagged lead coming from rounds that had traveled through sheet metal and broken apart before reaching him.

A great deal of their kinetic energy had been lost, but the fragments caused damage nonetheless—his leg was all but useless, and he now had just one good hand.

Still, he managed to push through the pain and lean forward. He removed the cell phone from Cahill's pocket.

Cahill was digging into Ula's open leg wound with his index and middle fingers, searching for the damaged artery.

The femoral artery—nicked at best, completely severed at worst.

But even the best-case scenario wasn't good.

Cahill said to Hammerton, "We're going to need an airlift. Now."

Hammerton nodded and used Cahill's phone to make the call.

It took ninety seconds for their current location to be pinned down and the best landing zone to be determined. During that time, Cahill located the artery and assessed that it had been severed—the worst possible scenario.

The only good news was that the artery hadn't retracted up into her pelvis. If that had been the case, and he couldn't reach it and pinch it closed, she'd be dead in minutes.

He worked quickly, his heart pounding, and held one end of the artery closed with his index and middle finger, preventing her heart from pumping out what blood remained inside her.

He'd bought her just a little more time.

It was a matter now of making it to I-684—still a good fifteen minutes from their current location.

A long time, particularly since the ninety seconds he'd just endured had felt like an eternity.

Even though I-684 wasn't a heavily traveled highway at this time of night, it would still be far from empty. But its six lanes, separated into three northbound and three southbound by a wide, grassy median, was the nearest place a civilian helicopter could land safely.

And do so, if they were lucky, without drawing too much attention.

But the stealthy exfil of an asset was no longer the mission here.

That objective had not survived first contact with the enemy.

In combat, plans seldom endured beyond the firing of the first shot.

⁓

The SUV reached the makeshift landing zone, between the first and second exits on I-684, just as the helicopter appeared over the western tree line.

The copter—a Bell 429—hovered for a moment as the pilot searched the median below for level ground, then finally touched down.

Ballentine pulled the SUV to the shoulder, shifted into park, and killed the motor.

A two-man crew dressed in black fatigues exited the copter. One carried a collapsible stretcher, and both wore medic bags slung over their shoulders.

They hurried to the SUV and began the process of transferring the wounded.

Hammerton was first, Ballentine and Valena wedged in beside him like crutches and helping him across the grass.

Cahill maintained his hold on Ula's femoral artery as the two men placed her on the stretcher, then ran along with them as they rushed toward the copter, passing the slow-moving Hammerton.

He couldn't move through the rear door with her, and there was no way he would be heard over the sound of the spinning rotors, so he indicated to one of the medics that he was holding an artery and couldn't let go.

That medic propped his end of the stretcher on the floor and got in beside Cahill. He removed a clamp from his kit and expertly applied it.

A part of Cahill still didn't want to let go, but he did, stepping aside as the second medic pushed the stretcher in.

As Hammerton was being helped onboard, Cahill looked back at the SUV.

Two details remained: All evidence connecting him and the others to that vehicle—blood, fingerprints, hair—had to be eliminated. And he needed to gather any and all intelligence that he could.

Running back across the grass to the SUV, he quickly located the vehicle identification number at the bottom of the driver's side windshield and snapped a pic of it with his phone.

He then hurried around to the back and did the same with the license plate.

There wasn't time for anything more than that.

Dropping down to the ground, Cahill scrambled beneath the vehicle's rear bumper, removed the KA-BAR knife hidden in his right boot, and thrust the thick blade into the bottom of the fuel tank, piercing the sheet metal.

Withdrawing the blade from the puncture released a steady stream of gasoline onto the pavement.

Back on his feet, Cahill dug into his jeans pocket with his bloodied hand for his Zippo lighter.

He waited till the fuel had surrounded both rear tires before stepping away and thumbing the flint wheel, engaging a flame.

As he strode toward the copter, he flung the lighter onto the shimmering puddle spreading fast behind him.

Even over the sound of the rotors he could hear the sudden *whoosh* of the fuel igniting.

And despite the rotor wash, he felt a gust of heat rush his back.

By the time he was aboard the copter, the SUV was engulfed in flames.

He didn't bother to look back, just sat in a jump seat and watched as the medics worked on Ula.

Steadily, efficiently, professionally.

No hint of the inner turmoil Cahill had fought to control as he'd struggled to keep her alive.

As the copter lifted off, he felt the familiar sensation of gravity tugging at his insides.

Banking sharply and heading toward the northeast, the Bell flew at top cruising speed just above the tree line.

⁓

She died midflight, ten miles from their destination.

It wasn't a quiet death, and there was no escape from the horror of it for anyone in the crowded cabin.

The only consolation—a small one—was that she had lost consciousness well before the level of blood loss triggered a seizure.

Her body shuddered violently, her lungs expelling a whining, pitiful moan.

An agony for those witnessing it, one that carried on unbearably for minutes.

Cahill did the only thing he could do: close his eyes and wait for the inevitable.

Once the seizures were done—once there was nothing to hear but the powerful engine above the cabin and the rotors cutting air—he opened his eyes and studied his fellow survivors.

For the girl, Valena, shock had given way to raw anguish. Tears smeared her young face.

Based on the closeness between mother and daughter—and the fact that Ula had brought her daughter into harm's way—there was likely no father in the picture.

He'd never before witnessed the very moment at which a child had become an orphan.

He watched her till he felt compelled to offer her some semblance of privacy and turned away, looking next at Hammerton, who had already cast his gaze downward and was whispering to himself a quiet prayer.

Finally, Cahill turned to Ballentine and saw on the kid's face something he had seen many times before.

The expression of dismay that comes with the realization that one is in over one's head.

That not only had one failed magnificently, but one had done so at a time when failure was not an option.

There were men who never came back from such a traumatizing event, yet at this moment there was no way for Cahill to know which kind of man the kid was.

And anyway, what did that matter now?

Ballentine eventually met Cahill's eyes, though he held them only briefly.

He, too, bowed his head, but his lips were motionless.

Turning away, Cahill looked out the window and down at the dark terrain below. It wasn't long before he glimpsed a cluster of brick buildings surrounded by playing fields.

This was Taft School—the prep school he had attended, and a visual landmark he had anticipated.

One that meant the old tavern was just fifteen seconds away.

Only at this moment did Cahill become aware of his own injuries—flesh wounds, from what he could surmise, some to his forehead and face, one to his left arm, another to his neck.

He had no idea how close that last wound had come to his carotid artery, but whether it missed by an inch or just a fraction of one, there was no mistaking that he was alive because of dumb luck, and he disliked owing his life to chance.

He'd spent the last fifteen years in the pursuit of skills meant to keep him—and others—alive.

That insatiable acquisition of capabilities defined his adult life and was a quest he had begun in the very buildings now below him.

A reckless and troubled teenage boy in need of direction, finding it the day he put on a pair of boxing gloves.

Tonight's narrow escape was simply a reminder that all preparation was in fact an illusion.

Yes, fortune favored the prepared, but at any given moment, even the elite were vulnerable to bad luck.

But he pushed this thought from his mind, along with everything else that would interfere with his ability to reason.

Pain, rage, fear, sorrow, and confusion.

There were just too many questions that needed to be answered for him to be wasting time and energy on anything other than what was critical. And what was critical was the little he currently knew, and everything he didn't know and was determined, whatever the cost, to find out.

Exactly fifteen seconds after passing beyond the bare trees that bordered the northeastern edge of the campus, the old tavern finally came into view.

A hilltop farmhouse now, but originally a roadside inn during the American Revolution.

A safe house—Cahill's own safe house, self-funded, so known only to a few, and complete with surgery facilities and a state-of-the-art survivalist bunker that doubled as a secure command-and-control center.

It was also the home of Sandy Montrose—one of the few people Cahill could implicitly trust.

A lifelong friend and, along with her veterinarian husband, Cahill's instructor in all things medical.

The Bell began its controlled rotational turn, maneuvering for the small clearing behind the three-story barn that served as a makeshift landing pad. As the copter lowered, Cahill spotted two people standing on the edge of the driveway.

Sandy and her husband, Kevin, both waiting to render expert aid.

She would patch Cahill up, just as she had done on that night Erica had been gunned down.

The night Cahill had both survived and died.

The copter dipped behind the barn, cutting off Cahill's view of the driveway.

He returned his attention to those seated around him in the blood-drenched cabin.

The waiting wounded, and the one fallen.

Then he looked at the dead woman's daughter.

Her legs drawn to her chest, she was hugging her knees with trembling arms.

No longer crying, she was now in shock.

The copter touched down, but Cahill didn't take his eyes off the girl's vacant face.

———

Kevin Montrose tended to Cahill's wounds, not Sandy.

In one of the farmhouse's upstairs room, the veterinarian stitched closed the gash on Cahill's neck before addressing the abrasions that cluttered his face like constellations.

Both men remained silent throughout the procedure, and when it was completed and Kevin was gathering his gear, Cahill simply nodded his thanks, then asked whether Kevin would send Sandy up when she was ready.

"Of course," Kevin said. "Need anything else?"

Cahill shook his head.

Twenty minutes passed before Sandy entered the room.

Cahill asked about Hammerton's condition.

"He's good," Sandy said. "It helps that he acts like he's indestructible. How are you?"

Cahill ignored the question. "They're coming here. The Colonel and Raveis. Are you okay with that?"

"Of course. I'm guessing that means you're going operational again."

Cahill nodded. "Yeah."

"You got out for a reason."

"That doesn't really matter now, does it? There's a dead woman in your barn anyway."

"From what Hammerton says, it doesn't sound like that was your fault."

Again, Cahill ignored what she'd said. Sandy was about to speak again when he cut her off.

"Frank Ballentine's dead," he said.

As Cahill's closest friend, Sandy understood the significance of that. She watched him for a moment. "How?"

"I don't know. But I need to find out."

"How can I help?"

"Stay out of harm's way. And watch your backs. Something's not right."

"What do you mean?"

"They rushed Ballentine's kid brother into the field. Raveis trained him, but it's obvious he wasn't ready."

"Why would they do that?"

"Can't think of a reason that doesn't bother me."

"Kevin and I will stay strapped," Sandy said.

Staying strapped meant carrying a sidearm at all times, with a carbine or rifle either slung or nearby.

"You see something you don't like, anything, head straight for the bunker."

"We know what to do."

While she had taught him field medicine and emergency war surgery, he had trained her and Kevin in close-quarters battle.

How to clear a house, room by room, when to barricade and defend, when to escape and evade.

"Don't worry about us," she added.

"Easily said."

"When will Raveis and the Colonel be here?"

"An hour or so."

Sandy nodded, watched him for a moment more, then said, "Charlie, you seem a little . . . spooked. What's wrong?"

"I saw a man tonight . . ."

Twelve

Gateno was on the run, one of only two survivors of the second assault team.

The other survivor was the driver of his SUV, but once they had arrived at their destination—a small warehouse on the eastern edge of Williamsburg, into which the driver steered the shot-up vehicle—Gateno waited until the man had gotten out and pulled the garage door closed before discreetly drawing his Walther and shooting him in the back of his head.

The man hadn't even heard the shot that killed him.

Dragging the body to the center of the room and leaving it there, Gateno quickly grabbed a nylon duffel bag from a cupboard. It held a change of clothing—jeans and polo shirt, leather peacoat, work boots, and a billed cap.

It was critical that the man leaving the warehouse in no way resemble the man who had fired shots from a Barrett rifle outside the Baychester Motel less than an hour ago.

He had accomplished his objective as the Benefactor had laid it out, though he would not call the attack his most proficient.

But that didn't matter.

What did was that it was time to disappear, which appealed to him now.

It would mean a break from this—from the risks, but also from the prisoner-like existence that had been his stay in Chelsea.

All of New York City just eight floors down, and no ability to enjoy it.

The idea of living somewhere he wasn't known—and the freedom to build a daily routine that included exploring new sites—felt right.

Would he kill if he didn't need to?

How long would it take before he felt the urge to seek out a prostitute, use her up for hours on end, and then erase any and all traces left of himself by eliminating her?

Where the Benefactor said he needed to go—one of the more dangerous parts of the world—would provide opportunities for both aspects of his nature.

But there was housekeeping to do before he could get to that life.

Firing up the furnace, Gateno incinerated the clothing he had worn during the attack, then disassembled the Barrett and laid its pieces beside the dead body.

Next, he removed the laptop he kept locked in a heavy safe, placed it on a workbench, and powered it up, then signed in to his online storage account.

Opening the only document contained there, he added key details of the two attacks.

He listed the names of the men he had employed. In most cases he only had a last name, but he didn't need anything more than that.

Then he typed a large *D* beside each name, an indication that every man listed—every man who had seen his face—was deceased.

All killed in action, with the exception of the two he had killed.

Scrolling through the document, he found an entry he had made one year ago.

Here was the name Ula Nakash.

Next to it he keyed in three letters: *WPD*—wounded, presumed deceased.

The last he'd seen, she was flat on her back, in the process of bleeding out onto the pavement.

He knew enough about wounds to know she wouldn't have lasted much longer.

Scrolling back to the end of the document, he entered the physical description of the man who had been with her.

The man who had seen him as the SUV passed, who'd caught at best a fleeting glimpse. But even a brief look at his face was not something he could ignore.

Whatever the identity of that man, he was a skilled shooter.

No, he was more than that.

He was a gunfighter.

But Gateno had killed men like that before.

Once his notes were updated, he saved the document, then transferred a copy to an encrypted flash drive and signed out.

If he was going to run, he wanted this information on his person.

Pocketing the flash drive, he stepped to the microwave oven at the other end of the workbench. Placing the running computer inside, Gateno closed the oven door and set the timer for two minutes before pressing the "Start" button.

He heard the cracking and snapping of circuits being fried as he stepped away.

The final act was to open the drums of kerosene and diesel fuel scattered around the warehouse.

The cement floor was a shallow lake in less than a minute, the dead man lying at the center of it, propellant soaking his clothing and skin and hair.

Gateno didn't need to drop a match on his way out the door; he had rigged a small incendiary device, the timer to which he could activate by a panel above the light switch.

He took one last look before flipping the switch and leaving.

Outside, he walked to the prearranged rendezvous point a few blocks east, where his courier would be waiting.

He arrived only to find no sign of her vehicle.

This part of Brooklyn had been staked out—no traffic cameras, no private business security cameras, a true blind spot in a city that had precious few left, so nothing to record him as he made his way out.

He waited for a moment, felt briefly trapped.

It was a feeling he disliked greatly.

Moving on foot one block in any direction would expose him to traffic cameras.

He began to scout windows, looking for shooters.

As much as he trusted the Benefactor, there would come the day when the man would want him dead.

Gateno trusted his gut, believed that he would know that day when it was upon him, but now he wondered whether he had missed the signs.

More than that, could it have been the Benefactor's intention that he not survive that second attack?

Before his concerns could overtake him, Gateno spotted his courier's car.

As it got nearer, he recognized her behind the wheel.

Still, his hand was in his jacket pocket, gripping the Walther, just in case.

The vehicle slowed and stopped exactly where it was supposed to, and he closed the remaining distance.

He glanced quickly into the backseat to confirm that it was indeed empty before climbing into the passenger seat.

As he did, his cell phone vibrated. Gateno took the call, but before he could make his report, the Benefactor spoke.

"Our inside man confirms Nakash is dead, but the situation is changing rapidly now. We may need another hit, one that requires a full assault team. I have one assembling at a staging area right now.

Its leader is someone who has my full confidence. I need you there immediately."

Gateno replied, "Of course."

He was given the address.

The call was ended. Gateno pocketed the phone.

He thought about what he had just been told, and what it could really mean.

If the Benefactor wanted to eliminate his assassin in the name of tying up loose ends, then sending him to meet his own death squad would be one way to do it.

Gateno thought, too, about the promise that had been made during their meeting at the Chelsea Piers.

The promise of a well-funded life away from all this with the assurance that someday he would be brought back in.

It had struck him as odd then, and it struck him as odd now.

Gateno gave the courier the address and asked how long it would take them to get there.

"Two hours."

He nodded.

She was young, maybe in her midtwenties, had dark hair, dark skin, was slim but strong.

In some ways she reminded him of the women he'd paid for back in Algiers.

He knew her only by a first name, and whether or not it was a fake didn't matter to him.

"Rene," he said, "I need you to do something for me."

He removed the flash drive from his pocket and held it for her to see. "If something happens to me, you are to take this to a lawyer in New York City named Selad Ouellette. Say that name again."

Rene repeated the name.

"He will, upon delivery, pay you ten thousand dollars for this. Do you understand?"

She nodded, then asked, "What do you think might happen to you?"

His reply was blunt. "Forced retirement."

"I don't understand."

Gateno ignored that, nodded toward the item in his hand. "It is important that you do not lose this, or that anyone take it from you. So at the first rest area we come to, I would like you to pull over, go to the ladies' room, and secure this inside your body. Do you understand?"

Rene nodded again.

Gateno knew she would.

She was a courier by profession, accustomed to smuggling contraband in a variety of ways.

He removed a wad of hundreds from his jacket pocket, peeled off ten, and handed them to her, along with the flash drive. "For your troubles," he said.

She took the money, then steered through city streets until they reached the highway.

A small compass was mounted on the dashboard.

Gateno watched the thing, knew by it that they were heading north.

The first rest area came into view twenty minutes later.

⌣

The staging area was a private hangar at the far end of a small regional airport.

Rene parked outside the hangar, then followed Gateno to the entrance to the right of the main door.

He paused to grip the Walther in his coat pocket before entering.

A group of men were milling about inside.

Gateno counted twelve.

The hangar also housed three vehicles, two SUVs and a panel van.

Most of the men were dressed in black tactical clothing.

The few who weren't stood apart from the rest of the group.

Gateno easily recognized the type of men they were.

They came from different parts of the world, but each one no doubt had been forged in a crucible similar to the one that had forged him.

Poverty, desperation, military service, then a career as mercs, killers for hire.

The only difference was that Gateno had preferred to work alone.

He would form and lead a wet team when necessary, but he never wanted to be part of one.

A man stepped out of the crowd and approached Gateno and Rene. He was in his forties, tall and powerfully built, walked with the swagger of someone who knew exactly what he was capable of.

Knew the power he wielded—had wielded in the past and would wield again.

The man told Rene that she was free to go.

She left, and as she did, he nodded to the other two men dressed in civilian clothing.

Gateno sensed what was coming and knew what that would mean to his plan regarding the flash drive hidden inside his courier.

The two men followed her out, and Gateno waited for the sound of a pistol fitted with a suppressor being fired.

Two such sounds were heard a moment later, after which the men returned inside.

Their leader sent four of the men dressed in black out to tend to the dead body.

Gateno doubted these men would do more than a quick search of the dead woman's clothing, so his fail-safe remained viable, to a degree.

His entire life was a series of calculated risks.

And while he had no attachment to the girl he knew as Rene, he nonetheless found himself staring at the man who had ordered her death and imagining the ways in which he would kill him, should it come to that.

The leader looked at Gateno and said, "We're on standby. If the order comes, though, my men and I are tasked with getting you in. Then you do what you're supposed to. Up to that point, and after you make the kill, I'm in charge. Understand?"

"I don't have a problem with that."

"So do you have a name, or do I call you what he calls you? The Algerian?"

"The Algerian is what I prefer."

The team leader nodded. "Okay."

Gateno said, "And how shall I address you?"

"The same way my men do. Call me Gunny."

So, a marine.

A call came to Gunny's cell phone.

Stepping away, he answered it, listened more than he spoke, then ended the call and turned back to Gateno. "There's another target, one the Benefactor referred to as 'the child.' I was told you'd know what that means."

Gateno nodded. The child was no longer a child but an asset the Benefactor's enemy had kept hidden for a long time. "I do."

"So what does it mean?"

"It means we may get to kill someone the Benefactor has feared for more than two decades."

PART TWO

PART TWO

Thirteen

In a small rented house a half mile from the Taft School, James Carrington was awake.

He had heard the low-flying helicopter just after midnight, had continued to listen as the copter touched down less than a mile to the north.

Fifteen minutes later, the copter had taken off again, reversing its course, the dull thumping of the rotors finally fading away.

It was dawn now, and quiet, though he doubted this stillness would last for very long.

In fact, he was counting on it coming to an end, and his current existence with it.

Exiled from his private security firm for his excessive drinking, among other things, he'd endured a year and a half of teaching history to the children of the wealthy—a nightmare more tedious than horrific, but one from which he was nonetheless desperate to be released.

The late-night arrival of a copter just up the hill carried with it the possibility of exactly that.

A retired navy captain, he had been making a handsome living for five years as a recruiter, specializing in selecting and screening ex-military personnel for private security work, with a handful of the men and women he employed being "encouraged" to pursue work as government contractors.

An even more select few were recruited for private-sector special operations.

It was an "up-sell" few ever turned down.

The money alone was reason enough, though there were, even among ex-military, those who did not trust government and therefore didn't have the heart for that kind of work.

Carrington's drinking had brought that success to an end, and this posting as a teacher at a small prep school was an opportunity for him to redeem himself.

He would do this mainly by remaining sober, though staying put was just as important, for the simple reason that he'd be easily found should the day come when he was needed.

When the one and only card he held would be required by those who had once employed him, and his banishment would end, either once and for all or only briefly.

But even a day away from his humiliation would bring relief.

Of all the possible scenarios that Carrington could imagine that required the transfer via helicopter of a person or persons to the farm-turned-veterinarian-hospital atop Litchfield Road, none were good.

One scenario in particular could even be bad for him.

But in the end, his desire for escape overrode his apprehension.

All that mattered to him was getting out of this life and back into his old one.

Or maybe even one better than that.

So he was up before his alarm, waiting. Sitting on the edge of his bed and looking toward the only window of his back bedroom, he watched the dawn give way to a gray spring morning and wondered when and how they would approach him.

And what exactly would play out after that?

The walk from his house on the corner of Main Street and Hawley Lane to the campus took six minutes if he cut through Evergreen Cemetery—a shortcut he avoided only on winter mornings when the snow was too deep.

Leaving at a quarter to eight, he followed Hawley to its end, crossed North Street, and entered the hillside cemetery through its main gate.

Walking to the top of the main road, he stepped off the pavement and crossed a few rows of graves before making his way through a border of hedges and onto the far edge of the campus.

From there he saw the playing fields below and the cluster of brick buildings beyond them.

He'd expected the caravan of SUVs that Raveis always traveled in to come rushing upon him as he made his habitual walk, but there was no sign of them.

And no such activity ahead as he continued down to the empty playing fields and approached the residence halls.

Any point he had passed so far would have been more than suitable for the kind of private meeting that Raveis preferred.

The man was shadow that moved in shadows.

Carrington began questioning whether or not the escape he craved would arrive today after all. Passing the residence halls and following the curving walkway around to the front parking lot, he noted only the usual vehicles.

But when he was only a few dozen steps from Taft Hall, where his office was located, he at last spotted what he'd been expecting since last night.

Three black SUVs traveling in a tight formation.

The caravan was coming from the direction of the farm. Had Raveis's men just now driven up from New York City, their vehicles would have approached not from the north but rather from the south.

Carrington felt the urge to panic, but he fought it.

Aware of the SIG P230 in his leather satchel—a violation of campus rules and grounds for immediate termination and possible arrest should it be discovered—he watched as the two SUVs turned into the circular driveway and accelerated toward him.

The expertly driven caravan came to an abrupt stop a few yards away.

The location that had been chosen for the ambush, as well as the manner in which the vehicles had approached, like police cars overcoming a criminal, was intended to maximize Carrington's discomfort—a specialty of Sam Raveis, though Carrington thought "obsession" might be the more accurate description.

He realized then that it had been foolish of him to expect anything resembling stealth.

The three vehicles parked nose to bumper, but only the doors of the middle vehicle opened.

Carrington expected to see several of Raveis's men pour out, but to his surprise, only one individual exited, and he wasn't one of the many armed private contractors that were almost always with Raveis.

Stoic-faced men dressed in black suits.

These men, though, were visible seated inside the vehicle, watching him, open hands resting within easy reach of holstered firearms.

The man who emerged from the vehicle was Raveis himself, dressed, as always, in an expensive and well-fitting suit, his dark hair cropped and combed, his face freshly shaven.

Carrington had always thought of Raveis as a finely crafted piece of military-grade weaponry—polished to the point of gleaming but nonetheless menacing as hell.

Raveis looked at Carrington, both men remaining expressionless.

Despite the fact that Carrington had imagined this moment countless times—obsessed about it, even—he was uncertain now how to react.

After all, how does a person in exile greet the very man who exiled him?

The man who had pushed for a punishment more severe.

Knowing Raveis as he did, Carrington decided to be the first to break the standoff. "Good morning, Sam."

Raveis's expression didn't lighten. He shifted his attention to the building behind Carrington—stately, ivy-covered, narrow windows made up of small leaded panes.

Outwardly, Carrington's life looked idyllic.

For some men it would be, but not Carrington.

And Raveis knew this. "You and I are going to take a little ride, Jim."

So, down to business. "Where to?"

"Where do you think?"

Carrington glanced toward the north. "How about you tell me what's going on first?"

"There's only one reason I'd be here like this, Jim. I'm sure you heard the activity last night—unless you slept through it. All your urine tests have come back clean, from what I've been told. But maybe last night was the night you suddenly fell off the wagon. Maybe last night you got blackout drunk."

Raveis paused, but Carrington didn't take the bait.

"Or is there something I don't know about?" Raveis said. "Some other reason, maybe, for me to be paying you a surprise visit like this first thing in the morning?"

"Nothing that I can think of," Carrington said.

"Because we sent you here to keep you out of trouble, Jim. I'd hate to think you were getting into some on your own. I know they don't pay you a lot here. Believe me, I feel terrible about that."

"I'm sure you do."

"As far I'm concerned, you got off easy. If it had been up to me, you'd be in federal prison right now."

"Convicted of what crime, exactly?"

"Whatever crime I wanted you convicted of."

Carrington ignored that, too. "You need me to bring in Tom," he said. "That's why you're here."

Raveis nodded. "It's your lucky day. We need him. And we need him fast."

"Yeah, well, fast is going to be a problem."

"Why?"

"I only have one means of contacting him to set up a meeting. He insisted on it being that way. If I break protocol and contact him in any other way, he'll take it to mean I'm compromised. He'll disappear and go even deeper than he is now."

Raveis didn't hide his irritation. "You and your fucking codes."

"This one's all him, Sam. I didn't come up with it."

"You taught him what he knows."

"You give me too much credit. He's smarter than the two of us combined. You know that."

"What kind of delay are we talking about?"

"The device I'm to contact him on is only monitored between four and five in the afternoon."

"Why that hour only?"

"He didn't say, and I didn't ask."

"You know where he is, though."

"You're telling me you don't?"

"I'm under orders never to look."

"Thank God the Colonel's in charge. Of course, what are orders to you, right?"

Raveis ignored that. "You didn't answer my question. Do you know where he is?"

Carrington hesitated. "Yes. But I can't tell you. That was part of the deal."

"Can you at least confirm that he's in the country?"

"He is."

Raveis glanced at his watch, looked again at Carrington, and said, "We're going to need you to come in for the next few days."

"What has happened?"

"I'm taking you to the old tavern for safekeeping. You'll be briefed there. As you're our only means to Tom, I'm required to keep you alive. That was the Colonel's deal with him."

Carrington knew about that—or enough about it.

If there is anything I can do for you, I will do it, Tom had said to the Colonel before disappearing. *But the only person I want to contact me is James Carrington.*

And what if something were to happen to him? the Colonel had asked.

You'll have to make sure nothing does.

It was Tom's deal with the Colonel that had saved Carrington from a fate far worse than this one.

He was grateful for that, despite his many misgivings about his current posting. But that deal had also made clear that Tom refused to be squandered, so whatever had happened last night had to be bad enough to set in motion the delicate process of bringing him in.

As much as Carrington wanted out of his dull daily grind, he did not wish to achieve this at the expense of the man who had sacrificed so much for him.

"I have to cancel my classes," Carrington said. "I'll go inside and make the call."

Raveis shook his head. "You have a cell, Jim. You can make the call as we drive. You're not leaving my sight. And there's even less time to waste now."

Fourteen

Tom stood in the doorway as Stella completed putting on the first layer of her workout clothes—a sports bra and boy shorts.

She looked over her shoulder at him. "You just missed it," she teased. "I was naked."

Tom smiled. "Damn it." He entered the room and crossed to its only window, looking down at the empty parking lot.

Then he scanned what he could see of their property's perimeter.

Once a Seabee, always a Seabee.

"So, we might skip the CrossFit tonight," Stella said. "We'll see how we feel after our run."

Rarely did Stella and her short-order cook, Krista, miss their eight-mile run. Taking just over an hour, it ended at the neighboring farm where Krista rented a room. There, in the makeshift gym she had set up in the barn, they pushed through another forty-five minutes of grueling CrossFit training.

"Long day," Tom said. The diner was closed on most days by two thirty, but there had been a later-than-usual lunch rush today, ending with a party of six walking in just minutes before closing, so the place hadn't been cleaned and restocked for the next day till three thirty.

It was a quarter to four now.

Normally Tom was done with his own workout by this time, not about to begin it.

Done and showered and dressed, ready to monitor the smartphone he only powered up for one hour a day, every day.

He glanced at his watch.

Stella saw that. "I'll be out of here in a minute."

"It's okay."

She stepped into her sweatpants and pulled them up. "Shoot."

"What?"

"I left our dinners in the walk-in downstairs."

At the end of every shift, Krista made three plates of food—two for Tom and Stella, one for herself. Lots of protein and vegetables, and one cup of brown rice, though sometimes she'd treat them all with a plain baked potato.

"I'll get it after my workout."

"Thanks."

"Of course."

"I'll text you when we're done with our run, let you know whether I'm staying for CrossFit or not."

"Sounds good."

A figure appeared below, emerging from the line of pine trees that surrounded the property. It moved at a light sprint across the gravel parking lot, then came to a stop.

"She's here," Tom said.

Krista was twenty-six—nine years younger than Tom and twenty years younger than Stella.

She had always struck Tom as an odd young woman—edgy and intense, yet shy to the point of being unable to look Tom in the eye.

When talking about her in private with Stella, he jokingly referred to her as "their feral." Stella insisted she was merely a stray.

Upon hiring the girl, she had almost immediately taken her under her wing.

They'd begun their nightly workouts within a week.

Tom did notice that Krista seemed more at ease with Stella, and that, among other things, she was able to look Stella in the eye whenever they spoke.

Stella suggested the reason for this was Tom's generally rough appearance and somewhat stoic demeanor, yet softening his manner around Krista hadn't changed her reticence.

But he had a business to run and a building to maintain, so he didn't think too much about it.

One thing he did think about was that for the year and a half Krista had worked for them, she had never once mentioned anything about a significant other—neither to him nor to Stella.

As far as either of them could glean, she had no wish to find someone, nor any concern that she didn't have one.

She doesn't even like to talk about it, Stella had said.

Though she wasn't Tom's type—heavily tattooed, with visible piercings—she was by no means unattractive.

Tremendously fit, with a pleasing if plain face and an obvious intelligence, there was no reason, beyond the acute shyness, for her to be spending her life working and training with little else to occupy herself.

Still, despite her quirks, she was an ideal employee—she'd never once called in sick or requested time off or arrived late.

More than that, she worked six days a week and did so with the same devotion to their business that Tom and Stella had.

What more could any fledgling business owner want?

Tom watched as Krista stood in the parking lot, her chest rising and falling evenly. The nearly three-mile sprint from her place to the diner had barely winded her.

And then she did the same thing she did every time she made this run: she checked her wristwatch, as if timing how long it had taken her to cross the distance between her home and place of work.

As much as Tom tried, he couldn't gauge her reaction to today's time—was she pleased that she had topped herself, or dissatisfied that she had fallen short of yesterday's sprint?

It was an odd thing, spending so much time with someone he could not read, not even slightly.

Someone who was as enigmatic as a cat.

Tom didn't realize that Stella was behind him until she spoke.

"I'm going."

He faced her. Her second layer of workout clothes was the sweatpants and a sweatshirt, both baggy. Though loose fitting, they did little to hide her athletic physique.

Rounded delts, strong back and legs.

Even when she was exhausted by a day's hard work, she stood with a cadet's posture.

"Be careful," he said.

She smiled, securing her long curls into a ponytail. "Always. Don't forget our dinners." She kissed him, then nodded toward his watch. "Good luck."

This was their daily ritual—Stella's acknowledgment of the hour of waiting ahead of Tom, and Tom's insistence that it was all merely a formality.

A result of the bargain he'd made for their freedom to make their own way.

Stella stepped to her side of the bed and retrieved the fanny pack she wore when running. She placed her Smith & Wesson .357 inside it.

Putting the pack on, she returned to Tom and kissed him once more. "I love you. I'll see you in a little bit."

"I love you, too."

He watched from the bedroom window as Stella joined Krista in the parking lot.

The two spoke as Stella stretched.

Then they ran off together, shoulder-to-shoulder, their initial pace steady.

After they were gone from his sight, Tom went down to the diner. Leaving the lights off, he moved behind the counter and into the kitchen.

Whenever he wasn't on the floor helping Stella by busing tables and running food, he was in the kitchen, either washing dishes or assisting behind the line during rushes.

A newbie to the business, he was becoming a jack-of-all-trades.

One of the curses of ownership was a compulsion to check and recheck things, and Tom did just that as he made his way to the walk-in.

He checked that the burners were off and that all the pilots were lit. Then he made sure the small refrigerators were closed all the way and that the walk-in unit was shut and bolted.

Finally, he confirmed that the Craftsman tool chest containing Krista's collection of precision cutlery was padlocked.

She'd been lugging the cutlery back and forth in a toolbox till Tom had found the five-drawer chest at a tag sale.

Even as he had handed her the only key, and even as she had thanked him, Krista had strained to meet his eyes.

Retrieving the two plates from the walk-in, Tom locked up again and returned upstairs, placing the plates in the small college-boy refrigerator in their rudimentary kitchen.

It was five minutes to four when he began his own workout.

Pull-ups from a door frame, followed by squat thrusts, then those followed by diamond pushup—hard reps, fast up and slow down, all with a knapsack containing a forty-pound bag of rice on his back.

He finished his first set by four o'clock, then walked into the bedroom and removed from under his side of the mattress the burner smartphone his former CO had given him.

Powering the phone up, he laid it facedown on a table and returned to his workout, doing another hard set—fifteen pull-ups, fifty squats, thirty push-ups.

After a brief rest, he completed a third set.

He'd just begun to sweat and breathe hard and was getting ready for his least favorite part of the routine—the three-minute continuous run up and down the stairs with the knapsack held to his chest—when he heard a sound he hadn't heard in the year and a half he'd been listening for it.

The one sound he didn't want to hear.

The deep buzzing of his muted smartphone, vibrating on the wooden tabletop.

He hadn't bothered assigning a specific pattern to help him immediately differentiate between an incoming call and incoming text.

There was really no point since only one person had this number, and that person would only text.

Tom's protocols had been very specific.

And while there was a remote chance that this was a call from someone who had misdialed, or even from some telemarketer or scammer working from a list of computer-generated numbers, Tom knew in his gut he wasn't that lucky.

The rapid buzzing, as insistent as an alarm—and arriving a few minutes past four—could only be one thing.

Walking to the table, Tom waited a moment before picking up the device, then turned it over and read what was on the display.

Fifteen

A text containing three digits.

9-9-9

The predetermined code telling Tom that his former commanding officer was requesting a meeting.

It was from the correct number—the only one to which Tom would respond.

Of course, a part of him wanted to return the device to the table and walk away, pretend he simply hadn't heard the buzzing.

But immediately the phrase that had been drilled into him by the sender of the text pushed those thoughts from his mind.

The only way out is through.

And yet Tom froze, unwilling to move in any direction at all, much less forward.

The idea of never seeing Stella again—of risking his life in any way, and of possibly leaving her with all they had taken on—stirred in him deep sorrow.

He'd been fortunate enough to go off to war with no one waiting for him at home—no loved one or lover, not one person for whom he needed to stay alive, so no reason for him to hold back.

For the eight years he'd been a member of the ten-man Seabee Reconnaissance Team that James Carrington had commanded, Tom had followed orders without hesitation, no matter the danger involved.

He had learned early on that only those with no one to hurt could experience true fearlessness.

That obviously was no longer the case.

He had done his part for his country, first in Afghanistan and then during the five years after his discharge, when a message not unlike this one had turned his life upside down.

And he had more than enough scars to show for both his foreign and domestic battles.

But Stella was his cause now. They'd done their share of surviving—the war and the recession and the long, slow recovery from both. It was their turn to thrive.

And they seemed now poised to do just that.

As distressing as the idea of being separated from her was, even for the hour it would take him to meet with Carrington, it was Tom's firsthand knowledge of the men Carrington would likely bring along that deepened any hesitation he had.

Out there in the world were men and women for whom duty to country and personal enrichment were two sides of the same coin.

There was no reason to think that Tom would be spared encountering such men and women this time around.

He had, though, discerned whom among them to trust and whom to always view with skepticism.

Those who had his back, and those to whom he should never show it.

In truth, only a few had proven themselves trustworthy.

Three men, in fact.

And one of them was now calling for Tom to come in from hiding.

Thumbing an icon on the phone's display, Tom opened his Amazon Photo account, into which he had uploaded two dozen or so photographs he had taken shortly after his and Stella's arrival.

All of them were of local landmarks and Vermont scenery, and there was nothing specific or particularly telling about any of them.

He scrolled through those pics, choosing three, and composed a reply text that contained just three numbers.

3 8 11

The third, eighth, and eleventh photos in the queue.

As a matter of security, the phone that Carrington had used to send the coded request for an immediate meeting was not linked to Tom's photo account.

But a separate tablet that Carrington always kept in his satchel was, so using that device he would log in to Tom's account and use those numbers to identify the pics Tom wanted him to view.

One was of a maple tree in autumn, its branches holding leaves that were the color of fire.

Another showed a historic church, taken from its front steps and angled steeply upward to capture its tall steeple.

The final pic was of a small-town Main Street and showed a long row of shops and restaurants.

Tom had, in fact, taken several shots from that same angle, some during the day and others at night.

The one he had chosen happened to be a nighttime shot, but that wasn't what mattered.

What did matter was what was in the background—a clock tower located in the center of a wide village green at the far end of the street.

Though that clock wasn't prominent in the photo—cell phone pics weren't the best choice for distance shots—it was focused well enough for Carrington to note the position of its two hands and determine the time that Tom would meet him.

Five o'clock.

Carrington would only request a meeting using the *999* code if he was nearby. And Tom wanted this over with as quickly as possible.

The other two pics revealed the location of the meeting, which was to be one of a handful of places that Tom had scouted and determined were tactically beneficial to him.

It had been a hectic few days, back when they'd first bought the property, with Tom taking the time to do the necessary photoreconnaissance as well as establish multiple points of egress from all possible meeting places.

He was an expert in identifying the strengths and vulnerabilities inherent in any terrain.

Once he'd completed his reconnaissance and had everything he needed, he'd met with Carrington in person at a neutral location to convey the protocols he required.

He had laid them out, one by one.

Any deviation, Tom had warned, would set Stella and him in motion.

It didn't matter—couldn't matter—if the deviation was due to a simple error.

Whatever the cause, they would grab what they needed and bolt.

If Tom knew anything, it was how to keep moving.

I'm sorry it has to be that way, he had said. *But Stella comes first.*

Carrington had nodded and replied that he understood.

After that meeting, Tom and Carrington had parted ways.

And every afternoon since, Tom had powered up his spare smartphone at four o'clock, only to power it down again at five and return it to its place in his nightstand drawer.

The meeting would take place at the corner of Maple and Church Streets on the far edge of a town called Smithton.

It wasn't just any town, though.

It was a town just a few miles east of the town in which Tom had been born and raised—a location he therefore knew like the back of his hand.

The tactical advantages that Tom gained by his familiarity with this area far outweighed the bad dreams his being back here had stirred.

Dreams of the family he'd lost, and of how he had lost them.

But Tom was determined to be in charge this time around and to never again be used like a pawn.

And he would endure whatever was necessary to hang on to the edge that control offered.

He waited for Carrington's reply text.

At any point in their communication, if Carrington were under duress, he could warn Tom off by skipping a step.

Tom trusted that the man would do that.

So every stage in communication that was achieved left Tom waiting for the next stage—or its absence.

It took longer than Tom thought it should for that message to come through, but finally it did—another three-digit code, this one conveying the identities of those who would be meeting with him, just as Tom had instructed Carrington to do.

1 2 3

Of all the possible variations, this was the one Tom had hoped he wouldn't receive, because it meant that the top players would be in attendance.

So whatever was going down, it was serious enough to bring them to the middle of nowhere.

Further communications weren't required, so Tom quickly powered down the phone.

He paused again, but not for long.

The sooner he got this over with—the sooner he heard them out—the better.

Grabbing a small military map bag from the bottom drawer of his nightstand, he shoved the burner phone into its front pocket, where his SureFire pocket flashlight was stored.

The main pocket of the bag was divided into two separate compartments, and into one went his spare magazines, leaving the other for his Colt 1911, which he kept in its leather, inside-the-waistband holster.

He didn't bother to shower, just changed into clean jeans, a T-shirt, and his worn-out work boots. Against the evening chill, and to conceal his pistol, he pulled on a zip-up, hooded sweatshirt.

The location Tom had chosen was thirty-five minutes away, and he wanted to get there early, so that meant he had to leave now.

If Carrington and his party arrived at five, and if the meeting didn't take too long, maybe fifteen minutes tops, chances were good that Tom would make it back home before Stella returned from her postrun workout—that is, if she didn't skip it tonight.

He made this his goal, setting that time frame as the schedule he would keep.

Informing Stella now of this new development would only cause her to worry. If it turned out that he wasn't going to be home when she got there—either because she decided to skip her CrossFit workout or because his meeting ran long—he'd let her know then.

He recognized, though, the hope that he wouldn't have to tell her anything at all.

His promise to the Colonel the last time he'd seen the man was that he would help if he could, and right now he simply couldn't, as there was no way he was leaving Stella with an all-consuming business to run as well as no one to defend her.

Not that she couldn't take care of herself—her long-deceased father had been a state trooper commander, and the Smith & Wesson .357 she carried with her had been handed down to her by him, along with all the necessary knowledge to handle it both safely and effectively.

She could take care of herself, yes, and had done just that two years ago, when men with the hearts of animals had come to kidnap her with the intention of using her to control Tom.

Of doing the worst to her, if that's what it took to achieve their goal.

But despite Stella's skills—despite her heroic heart—Tom had no desire for her to be put in harm's way again.

He found himself, even as he prepared to leave for the meeting, coming to a difficult conclusion.

He would—had to—say no to the Colonel.

Taking the Marlin Camp carbine from its corner by his side of the bed, Tom carried it to the makeshift safe room down the hall and hid the weapon beneath a loose floorboard—a precaution he always took when leaving the premises.

He paused to look at what else the secret compartment contained: a fireproof money box, which he eventually removed and opened.

Inside was a mix of personal documents, his and Stella's—both their original documents and those they had recently acquired.

Documents that had made it possible for them to safely settle down and start over.

The box also contained a small card made of copper that was stamped with Tom's full name and the name and signature of the current attorney general of the United States.

Also stamped into the metal was a phone number for Tom to call, should he find himself in trouble with law enforcement.

That number is monitored twenty-four-seven, the Colonel had said when handing the card to Tom. *Of course, this doesn't mean you shouldn't avoid trouble, Tomas. But something tells me you don't need to be reminded of that.*

Tom pocketed the courtesy card, then hurried downstairs, locked up behind himself, and made his way across the gravel parking lot to his pickup. The vehicle was parked just beyond a pair of industrial-size dumpsters at the far edge of the lot, where a cluster of pine trees created a pocket of shade in the summer and kept some of the snow off the plastic lids in the winter.

Getting in behind the wheel, he laid the map bag on the passenger seat, cranked the ignition, and checked his watch.

It was 4:15.

Maybe a half hour of daylight remained.

Smithton was a valley town, surrounded almost entirely by steep hills, and night always seemed to come fast there, or at least that was how Tom remembered it.

Shifting into gear, he steered onto the two-lane road and headed east, the falling sun at his back and the cradle of his current nightmares ahead.

Sixteen

Tom did his best against the onslaught of long-forgotten memories that the familiar landmarks beyond his windshield triggered.

He saw the roadside meadow he had wandered in as a child; the general store where he'd spent his allowance on treats as a boy; the second-run movie theater in which he had spent rainy Saturdays as a teenager and then later in high school took dates to.

But for every fond memory that was evoked, there was an equal number of unwanted reminders of the lives cut short.

He passed the funeral home in which his mother and sister, and then his father two years later, had lain in repose; then the Episcopalian church in which the memorial services had been held; and finally, the cemetery in which their remains, along with generations of Tom's ancestors, had been buried.

He felt, though, very little connection to the life he had lived prior to joining the navy.

Despite the reminders springing up all around him, that life remained strangely vague to him, as though it weren't his at all but instead belonged to some distant relative who had come and gone long before him and whose actions were something Tom had merely heard about from someone who had heard them from someone who had heard them from someone else.

A string of events that felt more like narration than personal recollection.

What Tom did feel as the landmarks rolled past was a sharpening of his conviction to preserve everything he now had.

Preserve the life he had built with Stella, this chance they had taken together in hopes of achieving some semblance of financial security, as well as that quiet existence, free from any and all violence, that they both deeply craved.

Not a lot to ask, to want to be left alone.

Though he had the habit of carefully but quickly studying each individual who entered their restaurant, or whom he passed while out running errands, Tom had never once glimpsed the kind of man for whom he was always on the lookout.

There were two very specific yet opposite types, actually: Those who dressed in suits and were well groomed with neatly cropped hair. These were the kind of men who accompanied Sam Raveis everywhere he went, surrounding him like multiple silent shadows. The other type had bearded faces and stoic scowls and wore their hair long. These were former military elite who worked now as private-sector special operators and often dressed with at least one, though often more, military affectations—tactical cargo pants, combat boots, a long-billed cap, Oakley sunglasses, an earth-toned safari shirt. These contractors were always easy for Tom to spot simply by the efforts they made to look like mere drifters.

Every moment of every day, Tom had kept an eye out for those two variations, doing so as if the sight of them—even one of them, walking into the restaurant one morning—carried with it the potential for immediate violence, or at the very least, the abrupt and irrevocable end of the world as he and Stella knew it.

Though Tom's protocols required that no security personnel be present at any meeting he was called to, he had no doubt that such men would be waiting somewhere beyond his sight, armed and at the ready.

He and Raveis had one thing in common: a belief in secure perimeters.

It wasn't long before Maple and Church Streets were just a few blocks away, so Tom removed the holstered Colt from the map bag and laid the weapon within quick reach on the seat.

Then he drove a grid of the surrounding blocks, looking for any vehicles that didn't fit in this quaint Vermont town—a watch vehicle disguised as a laborer's van; nondescript sedans with out-of-state plates; a random black SUV, or even a caravan of them.

He saw nothing that stood out, but after parking his pickup in a lot behind a bank and exiting his vehicle in full view of the bank's external security cameras, he nonetheless followed a circuitous route as he made his way on foot to his destination.

The holstered Colt was tucked into his waistband at the four o'clock position, concealed by his open sweatshirt, and the map bag with the two spare mags and tactical flashlight was slung diagonally over his shoulder.

Stopping in front of a hardware store, Tom waited in the darkness that was growing around him for the arrival of the man who was the closest thing to a father he had.

The man who'd had, more than anyone else, the greatest hand in shaping Tom into what he was today.

He remembered the first time he'd met Carrington.

Tom had been qualifying on the M16A3 at the Naval Construction Battalion Center in Gulfport, Mississippi.

Carrington had shown up at the range and talked for a moment with Tom's then-commanding officer before the two men had approached Tom.

After introductions, it had been explained to Tom that Carrington was looking for the right man to fill an open slot in his Seabee Engineer Reconnaissance Team.

A SERT was composed of three elements: liaison, security, and reconnaissance.

Carrington was the officer in charge of the security element.

You've got everything the captain here is looking for, and then some, so I recommended you.

Dropping all military posturing, Carrington had stepped in close to Tom and extended his hand.

As they shook, Carrington had smiled warmly. *Pack your gear, son. You're with me now.*

Tom had served eight years under James Carrington, ultimately being awarded both the Purple Heart and Silver Star by the man.

Carrington had retired from the navy shortly before Tom's eight years were up, and a month after Tom's discharge he had met with Tom in New York City and offered him a job as a private-sector security contractor.

A lucrative job, Carrington had assured him. *And one with a real future for someone like you.*

But Tom had never seen himself as the type of man the private paramilitary industry produced, so he'd turned Carrington down.

More than that, though, Tom had wanted to find his own way, to make his own decisions after spending most of his adult life following orders. He had spent the following five years as a wanderer, drifting around the Northeast, going from odd job to odd job, spending his nights reading, never really straying too far from this Vermont town, and doing so without realizing it.

Every step he'd taken during those five years had brought him closer to his chance meeting with Stella.

And it was that chance meeting with Stella that had set him on the course leading him to this street corner right now.

Tom pondered the significance of his meeting Carrington here tonight—the father figure he'd encountered shortly after his father's death, coming to the same town in which his father was buried.

Some kind of full circle?

But then he pushed all that from his mind; this wasn't the time for such thoughts, nor was it time for memories, pleasant and unpleasant.

Now was the time to stay sharp, focus on what mattered, and not be distracted by what didn't.

What Tom could control and what he couldn't.

With his hands hanging ready at his sides, he proceeded to scan his surroundings.

This part of town was quiet, which was one of the reasons why he had chosen it as a meeting place.

Right now, there were maybe ten pedestrians on the sidewalks and half a dozen vehicles parked along both sides of the street.

Secluded enough that no one would get in the way, and yet not so secluded that a man waiting on a corner would stand out.

Everything Tom did was done to avoid drawing attention to himself.

It wasn't long—two minutes, tops, of Tom standing there in the open, and that felt long enough—before James Carrington finally came into sight.

Tom watched the man approach. He was only fifteen years older than Tom and had never seemed to age during the eight years Tom had served under his command, but that wasn't the case any longer.

There was gray in his hair, some lines around his eyes, and dark half circles below them.

Tom knew that the man had quit drinking, and he would have thought the soft life of a prep-school instructor would have him looking better than when Tom had last seen him, when the time since the man's final drink had been only weeks, not years.

But Carrington had always been tireless—as a commander, then as a recruiter for the CIA and private-sector employers like Raveis.

Tireless men often didn't slow down well. Tom remembered having seen the same thing in his father in the two years following the murders of Tom's mother and sister.

A career as a civil engineer lost to a two-year quest for vengeance.

Carrington extended his hand. "It's good to see you, Tom."

Tom took his hand and they shook. "It's good to see you, too, sir."

Carrington smiled. "You don't have to lie. And I'm sorry about this. I really am."

"What's going on?"

"They'll debrief you. I'll take you there, but that's the extent of my involvement."

"I'd rather you were present when I talk to them."

Carrington shook his head. "I don't have clearance anymore."

Tom said nothing.

"I wasn't about to bring you in without knowing what it was they wanted, so I pushed them a bit and got them to give me the general idea. You should hear them out, Tom. Okay?"

Tom nodded. "Understood."

Carrington paused. "How is Stella?"

"She's good."

"And the business?"

"Busy. We appreciate you helping us get things started the way you did. Neither of us would have thought of that on our own."

"It was the least I could do. Wish we could have more time, but they're waiting, right where you said they should be waiting."

Tom nodded.

Carrington extended his hand again, and Tom took it.

As they shook, Carrington turned their hands so his was above Tom's.

Tom saw on the back of Carrington's hand a sequence of numbers, written in black ink.

He recognized them immediately as coordinates.

Latitude and longitude.

"How's that remarkable memory of yours doing?" Carrington said. "Still able to look at long numbers and instantly memorize them?"

Tom met Carrington's eyes.

"If you need anything, Tom, just shoot me a text. One of three words, it doesn't matter which one."

"What three words?"

"Marcus Aurelius wrote that there are three contingent disciplines necessary to overcoming any obstacle. What are they?"

It only took Tom a moment to answer. "Perception, action, and will."

Carrington smiled proudly. He'd always considered himself as much a teacher to his men as a commander. And he'd had no better student than Tom.

"If you need me," Carrington said, "I'll be there for you. Remember that. Okay?"

"Yes."

They released hands.

Carrington paused one last time. "We both know what kind of man Raveis is. And I know you trust Cahill and the Colonel. But the stakes are high, and even good men can do fucked-up things when their backs are against the wall. So be careful, Tom. Watch your back, and remember who you are. Never forget who you are. Understand?"

Tom nodded. "Yes, sir."

Carrington turned and retraced his steps across the street. Tom watched till the man was gone from sight, then started for the corner.

He had only taken a few steps when the smartphone in his pocket vibrated.

The pattern of the buzzing—a quick pair, followed by another, then a third—told him that this was a text from Stella.

Removing the phone and glancing at its display, he saw the phrase for which he'd been hoping.

Staying for CrossFit.

This text was followed immediately by another.

I love you!

Tom composed and sent a brief reply, which was characteristic of him since, as far as Stella knew, he was working out as well.

Getting himself ready, as he did every night, to stand and fight, should they need to.

Or if it came to it, grab her and run, just as they had done once before.

As he approached the corner, he checked his watch.

5:16.

He still had every intention of getting back home before Stella did.

Seventeen

The black Chevy SUVs hadn't been parked along Bank Street when Tom had run his grid moments ago, but as he rounded the corner he saw them lined up along the curb.

Gleaming, aggressive-looking hulks.

Raveis traveled in a caravan of three, but there were four here tonight, and even a variation as slight as this one was enough to get Tom's attention.

His gut told him that something more than added security was in that fourth SUV.

But he didn't break his stride as he walked toward the two center vehicles, one of which he was certain would be occupied by the three men who had traveled so far to see him.

The rear driver's-side door of the second vehicle opened as Tom got closer. A suited figure exited, and to Tom's surprise it wasn't the clean-cut yet hard-edged male he was expecting but rather a female.

Late twenties, five ten, athletic, her fine blonde hair pulled back into a ponytail that swung as she moved.

As a Seabee, Tom had been around enough marines, male and female, to recognize a former jarhead when he saw one.

The rear passenger-side door opened as well, and another suited figure exited, this one not only a man but also the exact sort of man Tom had been expecting.

Hurrying around to the other side of the SUV, the man stood just a few feet behind the woman.

Tom knew the security procedures and stopped when he was within arm's reach of the woman. He held his hands out to the side as she frisked his torso.

She found the Colt almost immediately and removed the weapon from its holster, passing it back to the man behind her, who released the mag and cleared the chamber of its round before placing the items into the pockets of his jacket.

The woman then moved down, patting Tom's hips. She removed his smartphone and keys, slipping them both into the right pocket of her slacks before completing her search by crouching down and brushing Tom's legs and ankles, inside and out.

Standing again, she said to Tom, "I'll take the bag, too."

Tom recognized a Southern accent.

Pulling the strap over his head, he handed the map bag to her. The woman shouldered it and gestured toward the third SUV. "You can go ahead now, sir."

Carrington had said there would be three men at this meeting, but as Tom stepped to the vehicle's open door, he saw only one man seated inside.

Of the three he was expecting, here was the one man he didn't want to see.

"Get in, Tom," Raveis said.

But Tom didn't move, instead asked where the others were.

"They're waiting for you in a secure location," Raveis answered. "C'mon, we're wasting time. Get in, I'll take you to them."

Tom hesitated, then climbed inside.

The SUV's two rows of backseats were positioned so they faced each other. Tom opted to sit diagonally across from Raveis—the furthest possible point from the man in that confined space.

The suited bodyguard closed the door, and Tom watched through the window as the blonde woman handed him a set of keys.

Tom's keys.

The bodyguard turned and walked away, moving quickly as he headed in the direction of the bank where Tom's pickup was parked.

Obviously, Tom wasn't the only one to run a full recon of the area.

Tom assumed that the man was to follow them to the meeting place. The idea pleased him, because it meant with his truck there, he would be in a position to control his exit.

All he needed to do was endure the ride to the meeting and the meeting itself, and his life would be his own again.

The blonde hurried around to the other side of the SUV, got in, and sat beside Tom.

The instant she closed the door, the caravan was in motion, its bumper-to-bumper formation as tight as a train.

Raveis said to Tom, "This is Grunn."

Tom didn't recall Raveis ever having introduced a member of his security detail before, but he couldn't care about that now.

He glanced at the woman briefly before looking back at Raveis. "So what's going on?"

"You'll find out soon enough. But it's bad. Worst-case-scenario bad. Right now, though, I have questions of my own. We only have a few minutes, so keep your answers short and to the point. The first thing I want to know is why you chose to settle down just outside your home town."

"I didn't choose to, it just worked out that way."

"How, exactly?"

Tom explained that Stella had wanted to see where he'd grown up, and on their way out of town, intending to keep on moving, they'd driven past a property for sale.

A ghost of a business, standing alone on an empty stretch of road.

Stella had seen in that place the possibility of starting over, maybe even achieving some financial security, which had always mattered to her.

All Tom had been concerned with was the state of the structure—what it would take to bring it up to code—and the layout of the surrounding property, how defendable the building and its perimeter were.

That was all that mattered to him.

Once a Seabee, always a Seabee.

Raveis said, "We had staked you both fairly well, I thought. The idea was for you to remain in motion while things played out on our end."

"That payout was generous, but it wasn't going to last forever. Living in hiding is costly. And as far as things playing out on your end, how many men would you need to have killed before Stella and I were safe? I mean truly safe."

"We are none of us truly safe these days," Raveis said. He studied Tom for a moment, then said, "The issue of you being too close to your home town aside, I suppose it makes sense that you would choose Vermont. Being a constitutional carry state, residents aren't required to obtain a permit to purchase and carry a firearm. I know it's important to you that you don't break any laws. I know that's your thing, and I think I understand why. It took me a while, but I get it. It seems to me, though, that using falsified documents to get a Vermont state driver's license under an alias isn't exactly law-abiding behavior. Neither is using the lax motor vehicle salvage laws they have up here to sell your pickup to your new self. That was smart. No paper trail for anyone to follow. Tom Sexton junked his truck, and some stranger up in Vermont purchased it." Raveis paused. "I'm curious, whose idea was all that?"

"It doesn't matter."

"I employ a lot of people, Tom. Type A, ambitious people, all of whom possess a deadly set of skills. I learned early on that it's a good idea for me to determine which are the smart ones. So, I strongly disagree. It does matter whose idea it was."

"It was mine," Tom said.

Raveis nodded. "But Carrington provided you with the necessary fake documents, correct?"

Tom didn't answer.

"And Stella's obtaining the license for the business in the name of her deceased mother, was that your idea, too, Tom? I only just learned that the deed to the property is in her mother's name as well. And so are Stella's bank account and the accounts she has with your vendors. From what I understand, theft of a dead parent's identity by a surviving child isn't an uncommon thing. Still, kudos to you for coming up with that. And that's what you're telling me, right? That all this fraud you and Stella have committed was your idea. Carrington simply assisted, providing you with whatever you needed when you needed it."

"Yes."

"So I guess that makes you the smart one."

Tom remained silent.

"I'm sure the IRS wouldn't be happy to hear that you and Stella haven't reported any income in the past two years," Raveis said. "Of course, how could either of you file a return? Technically, you have no earnings to report. You're not even you, and the means by which you earn your living is owned by a woman who has been dead for decades. As far as we're concerned, Tom, you absolutely did the right thing. If you can't keep moving, then dig in deep and fortify. I doubt, though, that it would matter to the IRS that you had no other choice. I don't really see them taking into consideration the fact that you did what you did to prevent your enemies from finding you. Finding and killing you and Stella. That's if she was lucky, of course. We both know what the men who want you dead are capable of. We both know what Stella would be forced to endure before she was finally killed. How could anyone blame a man for doing what he needed to do to spare the woman he loves from that?"

Raveis paused, then said, "The Colonel has clout, and he'd do anything he could for you, but it's the fucking IRS we're talking about here. The only truly unstoppable force in our government. Of course, what they don't know won't hurt them, right? And someone would have to go out of his way to tip them off. All it would take is a phone call. But I don't see anyone doing that to you. Right?"

Tom glanced at Grunn, then looked back at Raveis. "What is it you want?"

"Obviously, the Colonel has a soft spot in his heart for you. Who knows, maybe someday you'll know why. And Cahill believes you saved his life, not once but twice. He says he'd fight beside you any day. These things matter, Tom. These are the reasons why you've been indulged the way you have been. I certainly wouldn't have let you walk away from us like you did. And I would not have let you disappear from our sight. And no way in hell would I have allowed you to make that drunk our only means of contacting you. Lucky for you, though, the Colonel runs the show. He considers you one of his most valuable assets. And I agree with him on that. But right now we're in unknown territory, and what the Colonel is about to ask of you, well, frankly, you can't say no to. He'd never say that to you, and neither would Cahill, which means I have to."

Raveis paused again. "So between you and me, Tom, as of this moment you're back on the clock. In exchange for your cooperation, I'll see to it that the cover you've built here holds. I'll even reinforce it with everything you'll need to make who you and Stella are now even more real. I can do a lot more than Carrington did. I can create pasts that no one will have any reason to doubt. But before I start this process, I need assurance from you that you won't refuse the Colonel."

It took Tom a moment to answer. "I told him two years ago that if I could help, I would."

"That's the B answer. Want to try for the A answer?"

Anything shy of total compliance was unacceptable to Raveis, but the last thing Tom wanted was to appear compliant. "Your deal sounds fair to me," he said finally.

The more one gives to a man like Raveis, the more he will want.

Raveis shook his head. It was obvious he was frustrated with Tom's minor defiance, but he'd made his point.

"If you need to text home, do it now," Raveis said. "We're almost at our destination. We'll be going dark soon."

Raveis nodded toward Grunn, who had already removed Tom's smartphone from her pocket and was now holding it out for him to take.

Tom did, and began composing a text.

Three numbers was all it would take for him to inform Stella of what was happening.

They had three-digit codes for every possible contingency.

Tom tried not to imagine Stella's reaction to the information he was about to convey, knew it'd be a mix of powerful emotions that would no doubt include fear and worry.

He had done everything he could to keep her free of such states of mind, but this was the moment they'd prepared for, the one she had been dreading.

They'll only ever want to talk to me, he had said back when they'd first worked out the codes. *And always remember that I'll never be away for more than an hour without contacting you.*

It was difficult to believe that a few words he'd spoken so long ago would provide her with much comfort now, but he had no choice except to hope for that.

Hope that she knew him and trusted him—knew what he was capable of and trusted that he would always make his way to her, wherever she was and no matter who stood in his way.

Friend or foe, or those dangerous few who had it within them to shift from the former to the latter.

"We're approaching the blackout threshold," Grunn announced.

Tom handed his phone back to her and watched as she powered it down and pocketed it.

Being cut off from Stella like this, even temporarily, gave Tom an uneasy feeling, but he wasn't surprised that it was necessary.

While there were men who wanted him dead—Chechen thugs who'd lost a fortune on a series of weapons caches hidden in major US cities that Tom had helped expose—it was the man he was heading to meet who had made a career out of acquiring powerful enemies.

The fact that the Colonel had ventured so far from where his security could be guaranteed was more of an indication of the seriousness of the matter at hand than anything Raveis had said.

The threshold Grunn had referred to was the honeycomb of cell towers that could easily be used by anyone with Tom's number to track and pinpoint his location, either live or after the fact.

And along with Tom's location, the location of anyone with whom he was meeting.

He had given his number to just two people—Stella and Carrington—but in today's world, that didn't necessarily mean they were the only ones to possess it.

Clean phones didn't remain so for long these days.

Grunn announced that they had passed into the blackout zone and were now ten minutes from their destination.

Tom said to Raveis, "You have one hour, starting now."

Without waiting for the man's reply, Tom turned his head and looked out the window at the last remaining moments of daylight.

Every now and then he saw in the passing roadside scenery yet another landmark that carried with it a remembrance of the life to which he felt no connection.

The life that had been stripped from him so long ago.

Along with the people who had once been his entire world.

He was thinking now the same thing he had thought every day since finding Stella, repeating it as if it were a prayer.

Never again.

Never again.

Never again . . .

Eighteen

A fingernail moon was rising above the dark tree line to the east when the caravan turned off the main road and began winding its way around the wooded edge of a secluded lake.

Several minutes passed before the four vehicles finally slowed, eventually turning into a small parking area close to the shore.

Tom identified the area—little more than a patch of dirt—as a boat launch.

When the SUVs came to a stop, Grunn exited and made her way around to Tom's door. Opening it, she held it for him.

There were no other vehicles in the lot, or for that matter anywhere in sight.

Tom didn't move.

Raveis said, "They'll meet you once I'm gone. Grunn here is staying with you. She's one of my best close-protection agents. She'll make sure you get back home, and she'll be outside your place twenty-four-seven for the next few days."

Tom didn't like the fact that the one thing he had control over—his leaving here, alone—had been taken away.

Nor did he like the fact that the only real information Raveis had shared with him so far was that whatever it was they needed him to do would likely take a few days.

The idea of being pulled from his life for a few hours was bad enough.

But being torn from it for days—days during which he would certainly be in danger and Stella would be out of his sight—was unfathomable.

He decided to focus on the more pressing problem first. "Where's my truck?"

"It's on its way. All this added security is for a reason, Tom. You'll understand when you talk to them." Raveis looked at him for a moment, then said, "Keep up your end of the bargain, and I'll keep up mine."

Tom stepped out into the chilly evening air. The air lakeside was significantly cooler than it had been in town. His hooded sweatshirt was barely enough.

Grunn swung the door closed, and the SUV made a U-turn and headed toward the road.

Two of the remaining three SUVs moved to take formation, one ahead of Raveis's vehicle, the other tailing it. This train, now only three cars long, pulled onto the road and sped away, leaving the fourth SUV behind in the dirt lot.

Its motor was turned off, and its headlights and running lights went dark.

All there was to hear now was the quickly fading sound of the caravan moving away.

Tom wondered whether maybe they'd brought him here to kill him.

It seemed as good an explanation as any.

Facing Grunn, he met her eyes but kept the center of her torso within his peripheral vision. He knew that any movement she might make would generate from there.

"It should only be a few minutes more," she said.

Tom nodded, studied her for a moment longer, then said, "Do you love someone?"

The question caught her off guard. "I'm sorry."

"Do you love someone? Is someone waiting for you to come home?"

She hesitated, opening her mouth as if to speak, but ultimately she didn't answer.

"Someone's waiting for me," Tom said.

Again, Grunn didn't seem to know how to respond. And Tom didn't see the need to elaborate.

Turning his head, he watched the road, but he needed to wait only a few seconds before a pair of headlights came into view.

Behind that vehicle were a number of other vehicles.

It didn't take long for Tom to determine that the lead vehicle was his pickup, and that among this collection of vehicles was a black Mercedes sedan with New York State markers and heavily tinted glass.

Unlike Raveis, the Colonel was a man who generally preferred a lighter touch, in every way possible.

This included his traveling with a much smaller security detail.

Smaller, but better armed.

What was rolling up now, though, was nothing short of a show of force.

It was also a display of wealth; the support vehicles were Range Rovers, not Chevys.

The sight of this surging tonnage, as well as the sound it made as it headed toward the boat launch, allowed Tom to dismiss any thoughts of assassination.

And yet his overall state of concern was in no way diminished.

What was it Raveis had said?

It's bad. Worst-case-scenario bad.

And you can't say no.

Tom and Grunn stepped to the edge of the lot as the vehicles flowed in—Tom's pickup, followed by the Mercedes, then a trio of Range Rovers, all parking in a line, placing themselves like a barricade between Tom and the road. A cloud of dirt had been kicked up and was still swirling in the air when the vehicles went silent and dark.

Then all four doors of the rear Range Rover opened, and men poured out.

Men in suits, men just like Raveis's men, though these were armed with carbines that hung from single-point slings fitted beneath their open jackets.

These four men split quickly into two pairs, the first pair heading for the SUV that had remained behind, the second rushing toward the Mercedes.

Everything about them—the way they moved, the manner in which they held their weapons—indicated that they were former special operators.

The elite of the elite.

The driver and front passenger of the Mercedes, similarly armed, had also exited and were standing by both rear doors.

As the door facing Tom was opened, he saw two men seated shoulder-to-shoulder inside.

Closest to the open door was Charlie Cahill, and beyond him was the man Tom knew only as the Colonel.

Cahill exited the Mercedes and approached Tom. As he did, Grunn stepped off to the side.

She walked far enough away to be just out of earshot yet remained close enough to keep a watch on Tom.

What Tom couldn't determine was whether she was his protector or his keeper.

He desired neither.

Reaching Tom, Cahill extended his hand, and Tom took it.

As they shook, Tom saw a number of cuts on Cahill's face—cuts that were clearly recent because they had only just begun to heal.

Then Tom noted on the right side of Cahill's neck a fresh bandage roughly the size of a postcard.

"It's good to see you again, Tom," Cahill said.

Tom replied that it was good to see him, too.

He looked over Cahill's shoulder. The Colonel had exited the sedan, his armed man shadowing him as he moved.

Tom glanced once more at the vehicle from Raveis's detail, then at the two men standing with their backs to it and facing the road like sentries.

Guarding the SUV—or rather, guarding who or what it contained.

"What's with the war footing, Charlie? What the hell is going on?"

Cahill said, "We have a traitor among us. The list of people we can trust right now has suddenly grown very short."

The Colonel had rounded the rear of the Mercedes and was crossing the dirt lot.

Cahill glanced over his shoulder at him, then looked back at Tom. "He wants to talk to the both of us. Then you and I will talk alone. There's a lot you need to be brought up to speed on, but we'll do our best to get you back home before Stella's done with her workout."

Tom wondered how Cahill knew about that, but he said nothing.

It was time for him to listen.

More than that, Tom's list of those he could implicitly trust—with his life and Stella's—was always short.

If any of those men had decided to betray Tom, well, there wasn't much he could do to stop them.

The only thing within his power was what he would do after that.

The Colonel reached them, and he and Tom shook hands.

Pull-ups from a door frame, not to mention months of carpentry and plumbing, made for strong hands. Yet despite Tom's recent increases in strength, the Colonel's grip was still among the most powerful he had ever felt.

Tom had never made an effort to learn the identity of the man or to determine the details of his background—in which branch of service he had risen to the rank of colonel, or which of the half dozen government intelligence agencies his organization was allied with now.

But Tom had the overall impression that the Colonel had been a combat officer before retiring.

Barrel chested, bull shouldered, six feet tall, and with salt-and-pepper hair buzzed close to the scalp, he was a man who was vital in every way possible, even now that he was well into his sixties.

Releasing Tom's hand, the Colonel smiled.

There was a look of fondness in his eyes, just as there had been the first and only other time Tom had stood face-to-face with him.

At the Cahill family compound on New York's Shelter Island.

It had been just hours after that meeting that Tom and Stella had slipped away and disappeared.

Over the past two years, Tom had wondered at times about the way the man had looked at him that night, as if they were somehow old friends.

Maybe it was just the appreciation that a onetime commander had for all men who have fought, and almost died, for their country.

That same look of fondness was in his eyes tonight.

"Sorry about coming at you like this, son," the Colonel said. "I hope Raveis wasn't too much of an asshole."

"No, he was fine," Tom replied.

The Colonel smiled again. "Let's not have your first words to me in two years be an outright lie. That's no way to start things off."

Tom nodded. "What can I do for you, sir?"

The Colonel glanced at Grunn before gesturing toward the shore. "Let's take a walk together down there."

Tom, the Colonel, and Cahill made their way to the water's edge and faced each other.

Beside that secluded lake, with the stillness of a Vermont night surrounding them, the Colonel began to speak.

Nineteen

"There was an attack last night," he said. "An orchestrated attack resulting in one death. We don't know yet who the target of the attack was, because a few hours prior there was an attack that failed, and we can't rule out the possibility that the first attack was merely a diversion intended to draw out the true target. We also don't know for certain, but we suspect that the second attack was an attempted abduction."

Tom said, "What makes you suspect the first attempt wasn't the mission?"

Cahill answered. "Hammerton was acting as security for one of our operatives. The four men sent in that first attack didn't strike him as being anywhere near tier one. As you know, probably better than anyone, Hammerton's instincts are impeccable."

Knowing what Tom knew about the Brit—having fought beside him, but more importantly having *thought* beside him—he saw no reason to doubt the man on anything. "Hammerton was involved in the first attack."

"Yes."

"Is he okay?"

"He made it through the first attack fine," Cahill said. "But he was wounded during the second attack."

"How bad?"

"Minor injuries."

Tom glanced again at the bandage on Cahill's neck, wondered whether that qualified as a minor injury. "Where is Hammerton now?"

The Colonel answered. "He's back in New York. He's fine, Tom. I promise."

Tom thought about that, then looked back at Cahill. "I take it the second attack was tier one."

Cahill nodded. Tom got the sense that the former recon marine was bothered by something about that event, but before he could ask a follow-up question, the Colonel spoke again.

"The operative Hammerton was assigned to watch is named Dante Ballentine." He paused to give Tom a moment to place the name.

Tom of course recognized it immediately.

Carrington's Seabee Reconnaissance Team had served as support to marines stationed at the forward-operating base, Nolay, in Sangin, Afghanistan.

Among the marines operating from that base had been the Force Reconnaissance unit for which Cahill had served as a squad leader.

It was there that heavily armed insurgents had ambushed Cahill's squad while it was making its way back from a three-day patrol. Tom had led a late-night rescue squad composed of a ragtag mix of Seabees and marines, and had done so against the direct orders of a superior officer.

He had saved all of Cahill's men while losing none of his own, actions that had, once the issue of a court-martial had been dropped, resulted in his being awarded a Silver Star.

During the fighting retreat, however, with Tom and Cahill providing rear security, a Russian-made grenade had landed in the sand just feet from Tom.

Instantly, Cahill had dropped to the ground and laid his body between the grenade and Tom.

Tom had spent the next two months recovering from the fragments that had come to a rest inside his torso after first moving through Cahill.

Though he barely remembered that night anymore—rarely relived it in his sleep, that is—Tom of course remembered the men Cahill had led.

And the marine who had pulled Cahill and Tom, their bodies torn, to safety.

A marine sergeant named Frank Ballentine.

Tom looked at Cahill. "He's related to Frank."

Cahill nodded. "His kid brother." He paused. "Frank went missing six months ago. He was on assignment when he disappeared."

The Colonel said, "Dante approached Raveis, saying he wanted to help find his older brother, or at least learn what had happened to him and bring his family some closure. We recruited him, Raveis trained him, and he was put into the field six weeks ago."

"He approached Raveis, so that means he knew what his brother was involved in. Isn't that against protocol?"

"It is," the Colonel conceded. "Frank left a recorded message for his brother to find."

"Left a message how?"

Cahill answered, "He had an app on his phone. If the device was inactive for more than eight hours, a prerecorded voice memo was automatically forwarded to his brother's phone."

"The voice mail directed Dante to an online storage site," the Colonel said. "Frank had uploaded to it everything he had. His contacts, as well as all the intel he had collected so far. Frank's partner had received a similar message from him with instructions to go into hiding and wait for his kid brother to make contact."

"Why send his partner into hiding to wait for his brother?"

"Apparently, just prior to his sudden disappearance, Frank had come to suspect that our organization had been breached at some level. Since Dante came to Raveis directly, as Frank had instructed him to do, the list of people who knew about Dante was limited to myself, Raveis, and Frank's partner. Obviously, we took Frank's concerns seriously and kept Dante sequestered from all aspects of our operation while he was trained."

"What about the people who trained him?"

"Raveis trained him, just the two of them, twenty-four-seven, for six months. The result was an operator that was entirely clean. He was a ghost, even to our own people, but what really made him special was the fact that his motivation was pure. He and Frank were close. He wanted this as much as we did—more than we did, even. That was his edge as far as we were concerned. That would make up for whatever shortcomings he came to us with."

"What shortcomings?"

"His youth, plus his complete lack of experience prior to training with Raveis."

Tom considered the advantages inherent in controlling a ghost as it sought unseen to avenge the loss of a loved one.

He understood the temptation that would cause a man as careful and deliberate as the Colonel to take such a gamble.

"You said Frank had a partner. Where is he now?"

"She," Cahill corrected. "Unfortunately, she was killed in last night's attack."

Tom waited a moment, then said, "So who was she?"

"One of our best recruits, it turns out," the Colonel said. "Her name is Ula Nakash. Carrington brought her to us three years ago. She had served in the Syrian military for several years before spending four more years in the Military Intelligence Directorate. She emigrated to the United States with her daughter after her husband, an officer in Israeli intelligence, was murdered. She was skilled and smart, but more importantly, we shared a common enemy."

"What do you mean?"

"Her husband was assassinated. The man suspected of ordering it and the man we believe carried out that order have been at the top of our most-wanted list for a long time."

"Who are they?"

"The man we believe ordered the hit is a power broker who calls himself the Benefactor. He is allied with no government, though we know his services have been hired by several, mostly dictatorial regimes in the Middle East and Africa. He has no political affiliation or agenda, is in every sense of the word a true mercenary. The more chaotic the world, the better business is for him, so if he isn't being paid to destabilize a region by some strongman or multinational corporation, he is quietly taking steps to destabilize it himself, for his own gain. He has arranged the assassination of both political and business leaders, has sold weapons to freedom fighters and terrorist groups, often arming both sides of a single conflict, and is even suspected of having brought down a commercial airliner as a means of taking out just one target. The man suspected of carrying out the hit on Ula's husband, along with countless others, is a professional killer known only as the Algerian. He has been an assassin-for-hire for twenty-five years, but the intelligence community believes he has been working exclusively for the Benefactor for close to twenty. He's the ghost of all ghosts. Little is known about his background. He seemingly came out of nowhere. There are no photographs of the man, no fingerprints, nothing. No one can ID him because no one has ever survived one of his hits. And there have been no eyewitnesses, with one exception."

Tom said, "Frank's dead partner."

The Colonel nodded. "Correct. Ula's death sets us back significantly."

"You had a composite sketch of him drawn up, no?"

"Yes, but a sketch can't positively identify him. A sketch can't be fed into facial recognition software. More to the point, a sketch isn't enough for me to authorize a kill order. When Carrington found Ula and brought her to our attention, she had already done more than anyone to track the Algerian. And she'd done it on her own, with little money. Bringing her onboard represented the only significant progress we'd had in two decades."

"Frank and Ula were looking for the Algerian when he disappeared."

"Yes. They had picked up a trail that indicated the man was in New York."

"What kind of trail? You said he was a ghost."

Cahill answered this. "One of the few pieces of information Ula had brought us regarding the Algerian was that he has a fondness for two things: dark-haired prostitutes and a very specific combination of drugs. Frank went undercover as a drug runner. He served as the middleman between the out-of-state source of that product and those who sold it on the street. It took some time, but he gained a number of regular customers."

The Colonel took over. "We believe one of these dealers was the Algerian's seller. Surveillance indicates that this seller sold the product to a street-level career criminal who then delivered it to a young woman. This woman, we believe, is the Algerian's New York City courier. She's what allows him to remain in the shadows. And she's our only link to him. We've run the photographs of her through facial recognition, but no hits. It's fitting that a ghost would employ another ghost. Whoever she is, though, she's good at disappearing. Every tail we put on her, she loses. When Frank disappeared, we immediately feared that he'd been killed. Maybe he did something that blew his own cover. Maybe he slipped up somewhere. But we also had to acknowledge the possibility that someone on the inside had blown his cover, that someone within the ranks of our organization was actively betraying us. That possibility was elevated to certainty by last night's attack."

"How?"

"We were hit coming out of a safe house," Cahill explained. "A safe house even I didn't know about."

Tom again sensed something in Cahill's voice.

A regret, or maybe some kind of self-recrimination.

Tom realized that before him now was not the man he had last seen two years ago.

Not the type A, onetime elite marine who, without a hint of recklessness or bravado, had exuded confidence.

That mix of high intelligence and physical prowess—a prowess bordering on quiet menace—that was the foundation of every good special operator.

And was to some degree missing now.

While hardly crippled by this absence, Cahill nonetheless seemed less self-assured than he had once been.

He had been driven by vengeance the last time Tom had worked with him, hunting down the man who had ordered the death of the woman he loved.

On that man's order, a bullet had been put into her chest.

Cahill, with Tom beside him, had done the same to that man.

Tom had little doubt that Cahill could live with that action, though it was possible he'd found it difficult to deal with what had led to it.

His failure to protect the woman he loved.

And here now was another dead woman, killed in some firefight in which Cahill had been involved.

Tom had questions, naturally, but he focused on what was at hand: what these men wanted from him, and for how long he would be required to be away from the woman he loved. "How is it you think I can help?"

The Colonel said, "There's someone we need protected. We're asking you to take that person in, Tom."

Tom glanced at the SUV from Raveis's detail that had remained behind.

Looking back at the Colonel, he said, "You and Raveis have safe houses everywhere. All over the world, from what I understand. And you each have your own private army, exempt from a number of state and federal laws. So why me? Why here?"

"Our list of people we can fully trust has suddenly been cut very short. Out of an abundance of caution, we need to assume that all our safe houses have been compromised. When you left us, I gave orders that no one was to look for you. We understood that Carrington knew where you were, and that he could reach you when the time came, and that was good enough for me. As far as I was concerned, considering what you did for us, and for your country, you more than earned the right to slip quietly away. It turns out, though, that the steps you've taken to make sure no one could find you—your friends and enemies alike—is what makes you even more of an asset to us than you already were. It makes you—it makes the life you've built here—exactly what we need right now."

"I can't put Stella at risk. Not again."

"You're not bait this time, Tom. And you'll have a security detail watching your perimeter. My best-trained and most reliable personnel. The only people who'll know about your guest—who'll know *who* she is and that you've taken her in—are the three of us plus Raveis, Carrington, and Hammerton. My organization is highly compartmentalized, designed with a number of fail-safe measures that enable it to become even more so in a state of emergency, which is what we're in tonight."

"Who would I be protecting?"

"Frank's partner had a daughter. Her name is Valena. She lost her mother last night. Unfortunately, that's a particular type of grief that you know something about."

"I'm not a counselor," Tom said.

"We understand your reluctance. Ballentine wants to get back out there. Ula's death wasn't entirely in vain. He's even more motivated now than he was before. Raveis believes we should give him that second chance. He thinks we don't have any other choice, and I agree. But we need Ballentine focused. His recent failures aren't lost on us, so Cahill here is returning to the field and will serve as his handler. With our organization compromised, though, you're our only way of guaranteeing the girl's safety until we can make other arrangements, which will take time. Apparently, Dante had formed an emotional attachment to Ula, one that extends to her daughter. Without giving away your location, we informed him who would be watching her. It seems Frank had told him what you did back in Afghanistan. And he knows what Frank did for you and Cahill. So the idea of you being the one to take the girl in and watch over her eased his mind considerably."

"I can't just spring this on Stella," Tom said. "I can't just show up with a refugee for us to take in."

More to the point, of all the scenarios he had anticipated facing, this wasn't included among them.

He couldn't have predicted this one if his life had depended on it.

So he had no three-digit code to text to her that would cover this.

"We understand your situation," the Colonel said. "But we are pressed for time. Grunn will drive you back in your pickup. Once you're clear of the blackout zone, you can use your phone to contact Stella."

Tom looked at Cahill, then back to the Colonel.

It took a moment, but he finally nodded.

As Raveis had said, there was no way Tom could say no.

"How is Stella, by the way?" the Colonel said. "She's a lovely woman. And she suits you; that much is obvious to everyone. It's not always easy for men like us to return to the world, so it pleases me to see that you've taken the steps you've taken. It took time for you to find your place, but that's the nature of the beast. It took time for me, too. In one way or another, it takes time for all of us."

After his discharge—after eight years of following orders—Tom had chosen to live as a wanderer, sometimes working, sometimes not; sometimes sleeping in cheap motels, sometimes living out of his pickup.

Alone every night for five years, he'd read to pass the time.

He'd met Stella by chance when he stopped for an early lunch in an old railcar diner in a small town he had intended on just passing through in northeastern Connecticut.

His fondness for all things historic had required that he do that.

They had barely said more than a few words to each other when Tom had decided that he would end his wandering there, in that town.

But because of him—because he loved her—Stella had faced death once already.

Faced men who'd been sent to harm her and kill her.

Men who hurt and murdered for no other reason than to earn their money, though Tom knew it was also likely these men sought to fill darker needs.

And now here was Tom, about to report to Stella that while he wasn't returning to the world in which men such as those dwelled, he was skirting the edge of it.

His only hope was to take the Colonel at his word when the man had said Tom's service would last only for as long as it would take them to make other arrangements.

"Stella's fine," Tom answered. He felt no compulsion to say more than that. "But if you don't mind, I'd prefer Cahill drive me back home."

The Colonel smiled, looked at Cahill, then back at Tom, and nodded. "Of course. You two can catch up. Grunn and her partner will follow you. They'll be in charge of your security detail. But they work for you, Tom. You make all the decisions. It's their job to make whatever you decide work. If you want them to remain out of sight—if you want to try to keep their presence from Stella—that's their burden, not yours."

Tom didn't consider for a second keeping Stella in the dark, even though a part of him wished he could, for his sake as well as hers.

"Any further communication from me will come to you through them," the Colonel said. "And should you need to reach me, for any reason, any time of the day or night, they will put you in touch with me right away. Understand?"

"Yes, sir." Tom glanced at Grunn standing just beyond earshot. The idea of allowing strangers into the secret life he had built—even strangers assigned by the Colonel—made him uneasy.

It was an emotion that must have showed on his face, because the Colonel was quick to add, "They're among the best we have, Tom. Fully vetted, impeccable credentials. You can trust them with your life, because I trust them with mine."

Tom looked at the Colonel and nodded. "Very good, sir."

"Regretfully, here's where you and I say goodbye. For now, at least." The Colonel extended his hand again, and Tom took it.

They locked eyes as they shook hands.

Releasing his powerful grip, the Colonel said, "When all this is over—when our objective has been attained and we can all stand down—you and Stella will spend some time at my home, meet my wife and my family, share a meal with us, talk about the things we will do now that we no longer do this. I hope that's as appealing to you as it is to me."

Tom told him that it was.

"Stay safe, son."

"You, too, sir."

The Colonel turned and approached Grunn, speaking to her for a moment before making his way toward the waiting Mercedes.

His armed men scanned the surroundings as he moved. Once he was back inside the sedan with the doors closed, they hurried to their respective vehicles.

Twenty

Within a matter of seconds, the Colonel's contingent had pulled out of the boat launch and was speeding away down the dark lakeside road.

All that remained now were Tom, Cahill, Grunn, and her partner.

The only vehicles were Tom's pickup, the fourth SUV from Raveis's caravan, and one of the Colonel's trio of Range Rovers.

This would be Cahill's ride out once Tom had been dropped off.

The doors of the Range Rover opened and its driver and passenger stepped out, quickly taking sentry positions.

Like those they replaced, these men were well armed. Tom knew by the length of the barrels that these men carried M4s.

Select-fire military-grade weapons, not semiautomatic AR-15-type carbines.

Tom looked at Grunn and her partner, who were waiting in the parking lot. He and Cahill approached them. Grunn handed Tom his smartphone and makeshift ammo bag as her partner gave to Cahill Tom's keys and a gallon-size Ziploc bag containing Tom's Colt.

Cahill kept the keys but passed the Ziploc bag on to Tom.

The weapon had been unloaded, its slide locked back in the open position.

Also in the Ziploc were the single ejected round and the fully loaded magazine that had been removed from the pistol.

Together, Tom and Cahill crossed the parking lot to Tom's pickup.

Climbing into the passenger seat, Tom realized that he had never sat there before.

It was, he knew, a minor detail, but it was also symbolic of the powerlessness that he was required to endure for now.

His only comfort was that it was Cahill behind the wheel of his truck.

If Tom had to be subordinate to anyone, even for the duration of a car ride home, he was glad it was this man.

Cahill inserted the key into the ignition and started the engine.

Tom confirmed that they had ten minutes or so before they would be clear of the blackout zone.

He had no idea what he was going to say to Stella, but there was something else he would need to do with these few moments before coming up with the right words to say to her.

Cahill steered the pickup out of the boat launch and onto the narrow road, checking the rearview mirror as he drove to make sure that the Range Rover and SUV were behind him.

Tom watched him for a moment. "I need you to do something for me," he said finally.

Cahill nodded. "Okay."

"I need you to tell me what's going on."

"What the Colonel told you is pretty much all I know, too. He's serious about compartmentalizing. There were a few things he couldn't even share with me."

"No, I meant I need you to tell me what's going on with you."

Cahill didn't respond, but as if to validate Tom's concerns, the expression he'd seen twice already returned.

Tom had seen haunted men before, men plagued by memories that would never fully leave them, memories that were prompted for immediate and vivid recall by everyday sights and sounds.

He had been one of those men, and for that time he had avoided catching his own reflection anywhere—bathroom mirrors, storefront windows as he walked down streets, even the rearview mirror of his pickup as he drove from one place to the next.

He was one of the lucky ones, though, because his memories—and the effect their sudden return had on his limbic system—had dissipated over time.

Every mile he'd driven during his five years of wandering, every book he'd read on his Kindle, every day that had passed without violence or the threat of it—all this had put the price of war farther and farther behind him.

But now here was Charlie Cahill with the same dark expression—a mix of distraction and pain and remorse.

As well as that all-too-familiar stare, simultaneously cast inward and far away.

Tom had never thought he'd see that telltale mask being worn by his friend, because he'd never met—never fought beside—a man as composed and as capable as the onetime recon marine.

And yet the source of Cahill's current pain evidently wasn't the events of his multiple tours of duties in the corps.

That injury had come while he was in the employ of Raveis and the Colonel, when he had failed to save the woman he loved from the men sent to kill her.

There was no doubt in Tom's mind that he would be just as torn up as the man beside him if he had to face that same failure.

He'd come close to facing it, would in fact be facing it now if Stella didn't possess certain skills, ones that had been passed down to her by her father along with the Smith & Wesson .357 Magnum that had been his service revolver during his decades as a Connecticut state trooper.

Understanding Cahill's grief, Tom gave his friend as long as he could, but their time to talk privately was ticking away. So after a moment, he said finally, "Why don't you tell me what exactly happened last night, Charlie."

Tom sensed the effort that was required for his friend to return to the present. He sensed, too, that Cahill wasn't back, at least not all the way.

"It's not just the firefight, Tom. There's something the Colonel didn't tell you. And he didn't tell you because he doesn't know. I saw something."

"What?"

Cahill seemed uncertain where to begin, so Tom prompted him. "Why don't you tell me how Ula was killed," he said. "Let's start with that. Let's start with the attack and work our way forward from there."

Cahill nodded and eventually spoke.

As he did, Tom removed his Colt from the Ziploc bag and proceeded to reload it.

"It was an exfil," Cahill said. "That's what I do now, that's all I do. Evasion and escape. Field medic when necessary. I was supposed to get Ballentine's brother safely out of the city, but he wouldn't leave without Ula. She'd fled to one of Raveis's safe houses with her daughter. As we were driving away, they hit us." Cahill paused. "They were waiting for us. And they hit us bad."

"Hit you how, exactly?"

"Fifty-cal through the engine block. Shooter firing from the sunroof of your standard black SUV parked about one hundred yards down the block. A second vehicle parked behind it had pulled out and charged to take a nose-to-nose position with us. That's when the shit really hit the fan."

Tom asked how many men were involved in the attack.

"Six men on foot, and the sniper and the drivers of the two vehicles, so nine total. The ground-assault team carried a mix of small arms. Some AKs, some Uzis, some short-barreled rifles. The initial attack, after the fifty-cal disabled our engine, wasn't exactly precision shooting—or that's what we thought until we concluded that their intent was to keep us inside the vehicle without causing any fatalities."

"They were pinning you in while they took position outside."

Cahill nodded. "Yeah. Our only chance was to go on the offensive. Ula took point. She exited and I followed. Our initiative paid off, because right outside the van's back door we made contact with the first of the shooters, catching him as he was transitioning from his AK to the tear gas gun slung on his other shoulder. Their plan was to gas us out. Ula dropped that first shooter before he even knew what was happening. Two shots to the chest, an immediate follow-up to the head. I took out the man next to him as he was bringing his weapon to bear on her. We'd only been out of the van for maybe two seconds, tops. Everything was happening that fast."

Cahill paused. Tom inserted the mag into the grip of his Colt, then pulled back the hammer to confirm that the firing pin was in place, a habit of his whenever his firearm was out of his sight for a period of time.

Racking the slide to chamber a round, he flipped the safety up into place with his thumb, then released the mag and topped it off with the loose round from the Ziploc bag.

He paused, though, before reinserting the mag into the grip and looked over at Cahill. "You okay?"

Cahill nodded, but Tom wasn't convinced, so he told Cahill to pull over.

"I'm good, Tom."

"Pull over, Charlie, please."

Cahill did, shifted into park, and killed the motor. He was looking straight ahead.

Tom inserted the loaded mag, leaned forward to holster the Colt, then leaned back in his seat again. He looked straight ahead as well.

Cahill was quiet, and Tom simply waited for him to continue.

Finally, after a long silence, he did.

Twenty-One

"We were in an all-out firefight. The four remaining men in the assault team panicked. Suddenly they were fighting for their lives. Their plan had gone out the window once that first shot was fired, like all plans do. They were shooting wild, opening up on full auto. Uncontrolled and prolonged bursts, not at targets but in the general direction of targets, the kind of shooting that works in places like Mogadishu, you know. Places that are target rich, and someone's bound to get hit. But there were just the two of us, and every one of those shooters was firing from the hip like an idiot.

"I immediately moved to take the only available cover, which was at the rear of the van, but Ula stayed right where she was. She didn't panic, didn't flinch, just calmly dropped to one knee and took out another man with two center-mass hits. Then she took out a third with a single head shot. It was like target practice to her. But I remember thinking that she needed to get the hell out of there. She was exposed, and I really needed her to take cover. Now. You hear all that bullshit about how women shouldn't be in combat because the men fighting with them will feel overprotective and that mind-set will reduce overall squad effectiveness. It wasn't that. Her skills were up there with any man I'd ever known. She was even better than most. And she had the kind of courage a man will never really know—the courage of a mother protecting her child. It was this calm ferocity. Do you know what I mean? Have you ever seen it?"

Tom hadn't, so he shook his head.

Cahill let out a breath before resuming. "But as I was looking at her, it wasn't her I was seeing. It wasn't her in harm's way. It was Erica. I was back there in that motel parking lot. It was that night all over again—the night I couldn't save her. That's where my mind was. That's what I was seeing. I moved to position myself so I could look around the van's rear quarter and target the remaining two men, but I couldn't move fast enough. I could see that Ula was pivoting in their direction, so it was just a matter of who targeted them first, her or me. I reached the corner and did a quick look around it and saw that these last two men were firing into the right side of the van. They couldn't see their teammates on the left side, so they didn't know they were dead. I didn't understand why they were doing what they were doing, shooting into the van's rear compartment like they were, and then I realized that Hammerton had stuck the muzzle of his SIG through one of the many bullet holes in the side panel and was firing at them. He was drawing their fire and they were returning it, not aiming high like they had been during their initial attack, but lower, straight into the rear compartment. You could see the panic—it was all over them, in the way they stood with their feet too wide apart and their shoulders held up high and their chins ducked down into their chests.

"And that's when something strange happened. Something I still don't understand. Before Ula or I could fire—before we could even get our weapons on those last two shooters—one of them was cut in half. He was standing there, firing, and then a second later his body was in two pieces on the pavement."

"The sniper took him out," Tom said.

Cahill nodded. "He'd taken out his own man, and with an armor-piercing round, by the way it split him in half. But why, right? I mean, that's the question. Was it to keep someone inside the van from getting killed? That had to be the reason. But who?"

Tom had no answer, so he offered none.

"The last man standing was just as confused as I was by what had happened to his partner. He froze for a second, looked around, and that's when he saw Ula to his right, kneeling and bringing her Kel-Tec up on him. He spun to face her, but he had pulled the trigger prematurely, firing before he even had his AK leveled. His first few rounds impacted the pavement right in front of her. Several of them fragmented; I caught some of the pieces in my face and neck. That caused me to turn away. It was reflex. I was out of the fight for maybe two seconds, tops. Even though the shooter had fired low, he was still on full auto, and the muzzle rise that caused solved his problem with aiming too low. The first round of his to hit her struck just as she had gotten him in her sight picture and squeezed the trigger. I turned back in time to see that. Even when she was under fire—even when rounds were impacting right in front of her—she took her time to aim. The first round struck her in the upper leg; the second hit her in the pelvis; the third caught her ribs on her left side. But her single shot—her only and last shot—went right through his mouth. He dropped instantly."

Cahill stopped there.

Tom waited.

"You know, I never felt rage in battle," Cahill said. "Back in Iraq, during my first tour, I once ran under fire to retrieve the severed hand of one of my men. I didn't feel rage at the asshole that had caused my man to lose his hand. I didn't feel rage at the assholes that were firing at me as I ran out into the street. Rage in the heat of battle gets you killed. It gets your men killed. Two tours of duty, one in Iraq and one in Afghanistan, then two more tours with Force Recon, and I never felt rage. But I did last night. Have you ever felt it, Tom? I'm talking about blinding rage. Rage that overtakes you, that disconnects you from any and all sense of reason."

Tom nodded. "Of course. Yeah."

"I didn't try to ignore it or stop it. I didn't want to. It felt so . . . justified. The sniper was still out there, and I wanted him. It was a disproportionate desire for vengeance—I mean, I didn't know Ula, I wasn't invested in her in any way emotionally, but none of that seemed to matter. It's obvious why, right? I mean, let's be honest. I was out of my mind. I was as far away from all my training as I could get. It was like I wasn't a marine anymore. It was like I had never been a marine."

Tom didn't say anything at first. He understood the significance of what Cahill had just confessed.

Finally, he asked what Cahill did next.

"You want to know what I did? I pulled one of the spare mags from my jacket pocket. I had managed to keep a count of how many rounds I had fired so far—that much I was able to do. I knew what I had left, but I also knew I'd need more. I *wanted* more. I wanted to fill every one of those remaining men—the sniper and the two drivers—with as many sixty-two-grain, steel-cored penetrators as I could. I wanted them mangled. So I held the spare mag in my left hand—you know the technique, pinning it to my palm with my ring and pinky fingers and supporting the forend of my carbine with my other fingers and thumb. I was ready for a fast reload, ready to just unload on them everything I had. I surrendered my covered position and ran out into the street, made my way around the left side of the SUV parked nose-to-nose with the van, and took aim through the passenger door window at the driver. He had a pistol drawn and fired twice at me, but I knew by the position of the muzzle and the way it jerked when he pulled the trigger that his aim was off. Because I was in motion my sights were wavering, so I slowed to a glide for a few steps and waited till the waver decreased enough and my sights were on target more than they were off. I let the air out of my lungs and squeezed off three shots, then another three. The instant I saw the driver slump, I turned and faced the SUV down the block.

"And there he was, his head just above the open sunroof, the flash suppressor at the end of his fifty-cal angling to stay on me as I moved. He'd have me in seconds, I knew it, and there was no way that I was going to get him, not at this distance and with me in motion, so I did the only thing I could, I bent down low, compressed myself into the smallest target possible, and veered right, taking aim at the windshield as I did. The driver's side of it was a big enough target that I knew I'd hit it, even at this distance. Then I just lay in on the trigger, again and again. The windshield was armored glass, but I wasn't looking for a kill shot at that point. The impact of each round left behind those little frosted stars, and that's what I was after. I wanted to disrupt the driver's view and cause him to panic. The instant the first few rounds hit the glass, the SUV lurched forward, and the sniper lost his fixed firing position. His head was still out, he was still making an attempt to zero me, but I maintained my fire and kept that running count in my head. When I knew the last round had chambered, I released the empty mag and slapped in the backup. This way I didn't have to bother with the slide release and could get back on my target with barely any interruption. I just hammered away at that windshield again and again as the SUV approached. I couldn't see the driver through the chips in the glass, which meant the driver couldn't see me, but he was barreling down on me, heading right for me, and when he was right there, maybe twenty feet away, I laid off just long enough to shift my front sight to the man in the sunroof. The instant I squeezed off the first round, he ducked down, but before he disappeared, I'd seen him. I'd seen his face. And he'd seen me. I continued to fire till the last minute, then jumped out of the way. The SUV passed me and I fired into it till my mag was empty. The driver's windshield was all messed up, but the passenger side was still clear enough. The sniper must have been directing the driver, because the SUV made the next turn and was gone.

"I pulled my last mag from my jacket pocket and reloaded, just in case, then hurried to Ula. She was bleeding bad, and in a lot of pain, but she looked at me, locked eyes with me, then raised her head up off the pavement and said, 'The Algerian.' She repeated it several times, and I realized that from her position she'd been able to see him, too. Which meant I had seen him, Tom. I had seen the face of the Algerian."

Tom understood the significance of what Cahill had just told him.

"The Colonel knows that she identified the Algerian last night," Tom said. "But you left out that you had seen him, too. The Colonel doesn't know about that."

"Correct."

"Why keep him in the dark about it?"

"Because if he knew I was the only one left who could ID the Algerian, he'd keep me out of the field, probably even lock me away someplace safe, and if I let that happen, if I went and hid somewhere, crawled into a hole and hoped for all this to work out somehow, then I'd never be any good to anyone again. I tried limiting my role—tried doing the least I could to help, literally—but I just found myself right back where I didn't want to be. You can't hide, not from who you are, not from what you're meant to be. I have no choice now, Tom. If I don't do this, then my fears will own me. Marines aren't owned by their fears. And if I'm not a marine, then I don't what I am. I don't want to know."

Cahill started the truck, shifted into gear, and steered back onto the road.

Tom asked what exactly he was going to do.

"We have a rogue agent in our operation. That's the only explanation for the Algerian waiting for us at a safe house with a hit team. A hit team that was instructed to spare someone inside that van. And that's the only explanation for what happened to Frank. He's not the kind to blow his own cover. He's not the kind to make a mistake. We find our rogue agent, we find the Algerian. We find the Algerian, and he leads us to the Benefactor. That's the mission here. That has been the Colonel's mission for a long time. All the intel Frank's kid brother brought us indicates that Frank was getting close to uncovering the Algerian. I'm going to do whatever it takes to get us the rest of the way. For him."

"You're sure you should go back undercover? I mean, after last night."

"I appreciate the concern, but I want to do this. I have to do this."

"Maybe I should go with you."

Cahill shook his head. "No. You keep an eye on the girl. My guess is she's the one they wanted alive."

"Why, though?"

"I don't know. There's the chance you'll find that out for us. She might open up to you over the next few days. I won't lie to you, Tom, that's what we're hoping for. You've been through what she's now going through. You'll know better than any of us what to say to her to put her at ease and get her talking."

Tom said nothing.

"I know, it sucks, right?" Cahill said. "That we're asking you to do this. Manipulate a girl who just watched her mother die. But we're at war, Tom. And it's a war we're losing."

Tom remained silent.

He'd been asked to do worse things than show kindness to an orphan.

At least that's what he was telling himself he was being asked to do.

"I'll help any way I can," he said finally. "You know that."

Cahill nodded toward the smartphone in Tom's hand. "We'll be clear of the blackout in a few minutes. You can power up then and call Stella, let her know what's coming her way."

The problem Tom had postponed was now facing him again. But while the Colonel and Cahill had addressed many of his questions, one had not been answered.

And it was an important one.

"The Colonel said Ballentine's brother got emotionally involved with his partner and her kid. And the Colonel seemed to almost, I don't know, coddle him. Have you considered you might be going into the field with someone who isn't up to the job?"

Cahill nodded. "I have, yes. But Raveis trained him. Personally, one on one, in secret. According to him, the kid passed everything with flying colors." Cahill paused. "Of course, training is one thing, and actual fieldwork is something else. No one can know how they'll react under fire until they actually are under fire. Some men remember their training, others freeze. But what the kid did for us was brave, Tom. We have to acknowledge that much. For the past six weeks, he's passed himself off as something he's not. He's done business with dangerous people. Undercover work takes guts. And the kid could have stayed in grad school, could have played it safe, but he didn't. He answered his brother's call. He volunteered for the same mission that probably got his big brother—his badass recon marine big brother—killed."

Tom thought about that, then nodded. "Fair enough."

"You're set where you live, Tom, right? Your place, I mean. It's secure. You've done your Seabee tricks."

"Yes."

"Do you have something more than your sidearm? A rifle or shotgun, anything?"

Tom nodded. "Yeah. We're good, thanks."

"It's best if I don't know where you actually live, so I'll be bailing in a bit. The Range Rover will take me back to the city. If either of us needs to reach the other, we'll stick with your protocol and go through Carrington. But for any number of reasons that might not be possible, so I'm going to show you a phone number. It's monitored twenty-four-seven. You call it, and they'll connect you to me right away. I go through burner phones quickly, and it's more efficient for me to provide a central person with new numbers as they come up."

Cahill reached into his jacket and removed a scrap of paper on which eleven digits were written in precise handwriting.

It took only a glance for Tom to memorize the number.

"You'll be asked for a code word before they'll connect you to me. The one I've assigned to you is 'Colt.' You good with that?"

"Yes."

"If I don't get back to you within thirty minutes, and if you need a safe place to go, you remember how to get to the compound, right?"

Cahill was from a wealthy family, and among the many properties they owned was a secluded home on Shelter Island, located between the north and south forks of eastern Long Island.

It was from this safe place that Tom and Stella had slipped away in the middle of the night, crossing to the mainland in a rowboat like two refugees, each torn by war.

That night was the last time Tom had seen the Colonel and Raveis. And while Cahill had brought him to the compound the day before, he had disappeared hours after that.

Tom's part was done, but Cahill's work was ongoing.

"I can get us there if I need to, yeah," Tom told him.

Cahill returned the scrap of paper to his pocket, then looked ahead through the windshield, searching the road as he drove. Tom knew he was looking for a specific landmark to indicate that they had cleared the blackout zone.

It took a moment, but Cahill spotted what he was looking for. "You can power up your phone now."

He steered the pickup to the side of the road and stopped.

The tailing vehicles lined up behind them.

Cahill extended his hand. Tom took it.

"Good luck," Cahill said.

"You, too, Charlie."

Cahill moved to exit, but Tom spoke, stopping him. "When you saw the Algerian, he saw you, too, right?"

"Another reason for me to be out front on this. What better way to flush out a hunter than to be what he's hunting?"

Tom said nothing.

Cahill smiled.

In it was a hint of that old recon marine confidence.

Whether it was an affectation or not, Tom could not tell.

He could only hope for the best for his friends.

"I'll see you, Tom," Cahill said.

He got out, and Tom waited until the Range Rover had made its U-turn and was driving away before he pressed the power button on his smartphone.

Twenty-Two

With the harsh headlights of the waiting SUV directly behind him lighting up the truck's interior, Tom waited for his phone to power up.

As he did, he was tempted to remember the last time he'd seen Frank Ballentine.

The chaos of battle—in this case a fighting retreat from a night-time ambush, in a desert as barren and as torturous as a moonscape.

Tom had done his best to forget the night he and Cahill were wounded—forget the horror of it, the excruciating pain and sudden rush of fear that had overtaken him in the moments that followed that grenade's explosion.

But he'd also forgotten something he maybe shouldn't have.

Fragments had torn through Cahill, losing much of their deadly velocity before coming to a stop inside Tom's torso.

Shallow wounds, for the most part, that had left him badly scarred.

The sound of the blast had temporarily deafened him, and the shock wave generated by it had forcibly voided his lungs of all air.

He'd been gasping, desperate to fill his lungs again, and looking up at the night sky cluttered with storm clouds and swirling sand when a solitary figure had appeared above him. Leaning close, the figure—Frank Ballentine—had eclipsed everything that was in Tom's view.

"I got you, Seabee," he said.

In his late thirties at the time, Frank had been the oldest marine in Cahill's unit, having completed four post-9/11 tours of duty before becoming a recon marine, after which he'd gone on countless missions, from South Africa to the Middle East to the Philippines to Latin America.

Force Reconnaissance Marines were deployed to places where other—and more high-profile—spec-ops units couldn't.

They were the true "quiet professionals."

Frank Ballentine had seen and done it all—and had lived to tell the tales, though he rarely spoke about himself or the things he'd done.

A legend is a man *others* tell stories about.

But that long-ago night in Afghanistan, Frank had dragged Cahill, the more badly wounded of the two of them, to safety first before coming back for Tom.

Those moments during which Tom had been left to wait—bleeding, burning, fighting an inner battle with his own primal fears—were among the longest of his life.

His only solace, other than that there would be no one to mourn him should he bleed out and die, had been that his life was in the hands of a man like Frank Ballentine.

If anyone could make it back for Tom, it would be him.

Ballentine had in fact returned to lug Tom to safety as well—or to the relative safety of Humvees waiting a half kilometer away.

And he had administered field first aid to Tom and Cahill as their Humvee carried them back to base.

The last Tom saw of the man had come as the stretcher bearers hurried him to a waiting chopper.

Ballentine had walked alongside Tom, saying something that Tom could not hear. A faint ringing sound had replaced his temporary deafness, and of course there had been the wash from the spinning rotors.

Finally, though, Ballentine had leaned close so Tom could see his face clearly, repeating one last time what he'd been trying to communicate.

Tom's eyes went to the man's lips.

"You saved our lives," Ballentine had said.

The next thing Tom knew, he was inside the chopper and it was lifting off.

Cahill had been on the stretcher beside him, the medics working frantically to keep the badly wounded marine alive.

It was a risk for Tom to remember this now—to remember what he had finally moved beyond—but he knew that he needed to, if only to put his current situation into perspective.

How could he not participate in the search for this man, especially since the role he was being asked to fill was one that would allow him to remain hundreds of miles back from what was essentially the front line?

A supporting role, nothing more.

There was no doubt in Tom's mind that Stella would feel the same way.

Or at the very least understand his feelings and recognize that, Tom being who he was, and why, meant that he had to do what he was being asked to do.

And anyway, they'd both known that this day would come—the day when the men Tom had killed for would find them, when they would need him again, and in one way or another draw him back into their world.

It was a day for which they had prepared in every way they could imagine.

Tom checked his watch, knew that by now Stella had finished up her workout and was likely chatting with Krista, as they often did for a few moments postworkout.

Of course, Stella was likely to also be holding her smartphone in her hand, waiting for Tom to contact her and inform her of the outcome of his meeting.

He wanted to relieve her of this anxiety as quickly as possible.

The phone had completed its powering-up cycle, and Tom shifted into gear and steered the pickup back onto the road.

The trailing SUV hung back slightly, sparing Tom the harsh glare from its xenon headlights in his rearview mirror.

Opening his text conversation with Stella, Tom pressed the small icon of a telephone receiver in the upper right corner of his display.

The screen lit up as his call was connected.

PART THREE

PART THREE

Twenty-Three

Still in their workout clothes, Stella and Krista were standing outside the restaurant when Tom pulled in. Parked by the front door, its lights on and engine running, was Krista's four-door Jeep Wrangler, rigged for off-road excursions. A kayak was usually strapped to the roof rack but had been replaced tonight by the mattress Tom and Stella needed for their guest.

Tom's pickup was followed by the SUV, which he led to the section of the gravel parking lot that wasn't visible to the main road—the tree-lined corner where the two dumpsters were located.

As Tom got out of his truck, Grunn exited the rear passenger-side door of the SUV. She was looking at the two women, who were now working together to take the mattress down from the Jeep's roof.

"Who's that with Stella?" she said.

Tom wondered how exactly Grunn knew what Stella looked like. As far as he knew, the only photograph of her in Raveis's possession was a private cell phone pic that Stella had once sent to Tom and that Raveis had intercepted.

But that was years ago, and there was for Tom a bigger concern at hand.

"That's Krista," Tom said. "She's our cook. And Stella's name isn't Stella. Krista only knows us by our aliases."

"Jim and Anne."

"Yes."

Grunn was staring at Krista. "And she's loaning you a mattress?"

"Yes."

Grunn looked at Tom. "And she just happened to have one lying around."

"She rents a room at the farm across the field. It's kind of a boarding house. Maybe they had a spare."

Grunn turned back and watched as Stella and Krista carried the mattress through the front door, Stella walking backward, Krista directing her.

The twin-size mattress was difficult to hold because of its floppiness, but the two women got it through the door.

Grunn continued to study Krista, sizing her up.

Once Krista was out of sight, Grunn shifted her attention to the front of the restaurant, which she scanned before surveying the parking lot and the perimeters of the property that were visible to her.

Tom knew she was searching for vulnerabilities; all properties had them, and theirs was no exception.

Grunn's partner exited the vehicle, as did the vehicle's driver.

She introduced the two men to Tom. Her partner was DiBano; the driver, Sheridan.

"All right, let's get moving," Grunn said.

There was urgency in her voice, and Tom understood why. With its lights on, both upstairs and down, the restaurant looked as if it might be open for business.

The last thing they wanted was someone looking for a place to eat to pull in as they were transferring their protectee inside.

The reaction to such an event by Grunn's men would be less than subtle.

Tom noted that Sheridan, unlike all the other bodyguards he had seen tonight, wasn't sporting the standard neat businessman haircut. Instead, he wore a freshly buzzed crew cut, which led Tom to surmise that either he had come to this job straight out of a branch of the military, or he was someone who was determined to always maintain his military edge.

Sheridan was young, maybe midtwenties at the most, and since Raveis generally only picked former service members, Tom was fairly confident that he was looking at someone who had signed up for service either as the only means out of his hometown or because it was the only place he could go once he'd left it.

For Tom, all those years ago, it had been the latter.

With their backs to the SUV, Sheridan and DiBano quickly scanned the surrounding area.

They wore their suit jackets open and held their hands in a manner that would allow them to reach quickly for their respective sidearms, should the need arise.

The only person remaining in the SUV was the girl. She made no attempt to get out, and Tom could only glimpse her through the open door.

But a glimpse was enough for him to recognize the face of someone who was both grieving and frightened.

It wasn't until Grunn stepped to the open door and waved to the girl that she moved.

Her movements were those of someone who was accustomed to being under close protection.

Head down slightly, she stood ready to follow the lead of those surrounding her.

Grunn said to Tom, "Lead the way, please."

He started toward the front door, had noted before he had turned that the two suited men were behind the girl, DiBano touching her shoulder and guiding her forward, Sheridan right behind DiBano and facing backward so he could cover their rear and observe the road as he walked.

The tight group of four individuals moved as one unit, their feet shuffling quickly and in sync. Once through the door, Tom stepped to the right and let them move inside.

As the girl passed by, he got his first real look at her. And he saw a face that was no longer that of a child but not yet that of an adult.

She was thin, maybe even a little gangly, but didn't strike Tom as frail. If anything, she was the opposite of that, which wasn't at all what Tom had expected to see, especially in a Syrian refugee.

What Tom did see was the look in her eyes, which was a mix of sorrow and fear and anger.

It was a look Tom had seen in his own reflection twenty years before, when he had found himself the only surviving member of his family.

A family taken by violence.

Unlike the girl, however, Tom wasn't alone in a strange country back then, being hustled around from one secret location to another by a pack of armed strangers.

All things considered, she was actually holding up pretty well.

Stella and Krista had come down the back stairs and were standing at the bottom step. Just as Tom had done, Krista stepped aside when Stella waved the detail forward.

They reached the stairs, and Stella led them up.

Krista, too, studied the girl as she passed, then looked at Tom.

It was one of the rare occasions when they were alone.

What was even rarer, however, was the fact that Krista was looking Tom in the eye.

Granted, the distance of the dining area was between them, but it was a small dining area, five booths long, and Krista usually averted her gaze nervously, no matter how far away or close Tom was to her.

But here she was doing the opposite, as if suddenly something had changed between them.

Tom couldn't put his finger on the nature of the shift in her.

One thing he did know for certain was that she seemed to regard him not as her boss or as an intimidating male, like she had always done before, but as an equal.

He couldn't explain it—there really weren't any words for it—but there was an air about her, a kind of recognition mixed with regret.

Maybe it was simply that, like Tom, she was a loner by nature, and there was now no escaping the obvious fact that the life he had made for himself was over, at least for now.

It had never dawned on him before that he and this odd girl—this *stray*, as Stella fondly referred to her—had something so fundamental to their personalities in common.

They continued to stare at each other, and then Krista said, "You look tired, Jim. You should get some sleep."

Tom had no doubt that he looked the way he felt.

But before he could say anything, Krista walked toward the door.

Passing him, she said, "See you in the morning."

He stepped to the door and watched through its window as she got into her rugged-looking Jeep and drove away.

Then he listened to the footsteps above for a moment, thought of those to whom the heaviest among them belonged.

Men he did not know but had no choice except to trust.

Fully vetted, the Colonel had said. *I trust them with my life, and so can you.*

Still, they were strangers who had entered the sanctuary he'd made for himself and Stella.

Their private quarters, where they didn't have to pretend to be people they weren't.

Where they could speak their real names to each other in more than whispers and do so without fear of being overheard.

Tom had taken solace in the fact that they had a place where they could rest in relative safety between their long shifts. He had come to rely on it, counting the hours as they worked till they could retreat to it and reveal to each other their true selves.

But he knew the day would come when they would have to abandon that.

He told himself now that at any hint of trouble—the first indication that something or someone wasn't right—he and Stella would bail, leave alone and do so without looking back.

More than that, having seen the girl's face, the mask of pain and sorrow she wore, he had no intention of using the horror they had in common in an attempt to get her to open up.

What he would do was aid in her protection in every way he could, but the girl had a security detail—a skilled one, from what Tom had observed—and Stella did not.

She had only Tom, and Tom had only her.

If it came down to it, Grunn and her men would likely sacrifice themselves for the girl. The training they had endured at Raveis's compound—identical to the training given to CIA special operatives at the secret facility known as "The Farm"—had no doubt instilled that in them.

They were also just as likely to sacrifice Stella and himself, if it meant saving the girl.

He would not—could not—risk Stella, not for anyone or anything.

What mattered to him—what could only matter—was Stella.

It was as simple as that, and Tom preferred to always keep things simple.

He waited a moment more before finally turning off the lights and casting the restaurant into darkness.

From outside, the business now appeared closed.

Tom would feel better when the upstairs was dark, too.

Locking the front door, he crossed through the dining room and headed up the back stairs.

It occurred to him then that their building had been unoccupied from the moment he'd left for his meeting to when Stella and Krista had driven up with the mattress.

Plenty of time for someone to have entered.

Tom had to consider all possibilities now.

Making his way to their bedroom, he made a quick sweep for listening devices, checking all the likely hiding places in which one or more could have been planted. But he found none.

To be certain, he double-checked, then checked again.

Finally, Tom hurried to the safe room and removed the Marlin Camp carbine from its secure location beneath the floorboards, carrying the weapon with him back to their bedroom and returning it to its place in the corner by his side of the bed.

His Colt was still in its holster inside his waistband, concealed by his sweatshirt, the spare magazines in the map bag hanging off his left shoulder.

The pistol would remain on him for the duration of his assignment, even as he worked clearing tables and washing dishes.

Twenty-Four

Later, Tom stood at their bedroom window.

He knew the view beyond it well, had studied it morning and night for close to two years now.

There was, however, one notable change tonight—the presence of a black Chevy Tahoe parked in the shaded corner by the dumpsters, not far from Tom's pickup.

Inside the SUV were Grunn and her two men, DiBano and Sheridan.

They had a long night ahead of them, sitting together in that SUV, waiting and watching and listening.

But there were, Tom knew, worse ways to spend a night.

Valena had been taken to the room down the hall, which was next to the bathroom and across from the safe room. Stella was with her, getting her settled in for her first night spent in hiding above a breakfast-and-lunch place in a small Vermont town.

Surrounded by people whom, like Tom, she had no choice but to trust.

Tom had not seen the girl since she was rushed past him downstairs, and he had no intention of seeing her again till morning, if even then. The process of opening the restaurant kept him busy, and her breakfast would be brought to her room, since there was no reason for her to leave it except for trips to the bathroom.

The very act of keeping her safe and out of sight while running the business, then, meant that Tom would have little to no contact with her.

This absence of any reason for interaction comforted him.

Maintaining that became his game plan: avoid as much as possible, for as long as possible.

He was grateful now for his long and busy days, and for Stella having taken point the way she had, seeing to their guest's initial needs. His only regret was that he hadn't pressed the Colonel for a more specific end date, something less general than his promise that it would take just a few days for them to locate a safe house that was known only to him and Raveis.

Tom was thinking about that—about the end of this mission and the resumption of their quiet life—when he heard a door down the hall open and then close, followed by the sound of footsteps. Stella entered the bedroom a moment later, closing the door as quietly as she could.

"She's asleep," she whispered. "Poor thing is spent."

She walked to the dresser and opened drawers, gathering together the clothes she would change into after her postworkout shower.

"It's the last thing you need," Stella said. "Something else to keep you up at night."

Tom told her that he'd be okay, then faced her and thanked her for taking care of the girl.

Stella shrugged. "Hey, what's another stray, right?"

"Yeah, speaking of, I want to ask you a question that's going to sound kind of weird."

Stella stopped and looked at him. "What?"

"Have you ever seen Krista's place?"

"What do you mean?"

"The room she rents. Have you ever gone up and seen it?"

"No. Why?"

"Just curious."

"What's on your mind, Tom?"

"She got that mattress awfully fast, that's all."

"Her landlord has a few unrented rooms in his house. I think he loaned it to her."

Tom nodded. "That makes sense, yeah. Ignore me—I'm just thinking out loud. Five minutes with Raveis and I start to get paranoid."

"You're just doing what you were trained to do, that's all. What that brain of yours does."

Stella watched him, waited for him to say more, but when he didn't, she began to undress.

"Where are—what's her name?"

"Grunn."

"Where are Grunn and her men?"

"In position. Out by my truck."

"Should I bring them something? Food, coffee?"

"No. They would have come prepared for a long night." He paused. "This is their job. They're paid well for it."

"You know me. I take care of people."

Tom fell quiet again.

Stella said, "You all right?"

"This was a mistake. Letting them bring her here."

Stella stopped undressing. She was down to her sports bra and boy shorts. "Why do you say that?"

"I don't know." He looked out the window again, then faced Stella. "We'll get a few hours' sleep, but after that, we're going to bug out."

"Are you sure?"

"Yes."

"Where to?"

"Anywhere but here."

"Grunn and her men, too?"

"No, just the three of us."

"But how are we going to get away without them knowing? You said they're parked right next to your truck."

"Text Krista when it's time, tell her to meet us in her Jeep down the road. You and I can slip out the back with the girl, and Krista can drop us off somewhere. From there we'll go somewhere safe; you can watch the girl and I can watch the perimeter."

"Won't they be pissed? Raveis and the Colonel."

"I don't care."

"If you had doubts about doing this, why did you say yes to begin with?"

Tom faced her. "Raveis offered us something."

"What?"

"Reinforcement of our cover."

"I didn't know our cover needed reinforcing. I thought Carrington said it was rock solid."

"It is, but we don't have government-issued passports. Raveis would get us those. But there was something else, too."

"What?"

"He assured me that no one would tip off the IRS about our situation. It was a threat."

Stella shook her head. "Yeah, well, fuck him, then. We can start over somewhere else, right? If it comes to that. Carrington can help us get set up again. He's the only one I really trust anyway."

"There's a chance we won't have to walk away for good. I'm still going to do what they want. I'm still going to keep the girl safe till they're ready for her. I just have to do it on my terms."

"So this is definite. We're going to bug out."

Tom nodded.

"I'd better take my shower," Stella said.

She resumed undressing.

Tom waited till she'd put her robe on and had picked up her change of clothes, then said, "I saw Cahill tonight."

"How is he?"

"Not good."

Stella took a breath, let it out, then crossed the room and stood face-to-face with him.

"I'm sorry your friend is suffering, Tom, but he can get help. His family has the means. He has the means. And he could go to the VA if he wanted to. Tom Sexton can't. Tom Sexton doesn't exist anymore." She paused, placed her palm on his wide chest, felt his heartbeat. "You know, maybe we should leave now. Maybe we should get far away from here, as far away as we can. That might put an end to your nightmares."

"No, we'll wait till morning," Tom said. "Krista usually gets here at four thirty. Text her right before that."

"Okay."

"Take your shower, then I'll take mine."

She smiled. "Or you could join me."

"I should keep watch."

Stella understood that he needed to do this, despite the presence of the security force parked outside. Tom's most driving need was guarding their perimeter. She knew that the seed for that had been planted before he'd even joined the Seabees and been trained to do that, to see the world in those terms.

She leaned close and kissed him once, then leaned back again to look at his face. "I love you."

"I love you, too."

Tom stayed by the window. A minute later he was listening to the muffled sound of water running through the pipes beneath his feet.

He thought about the work they had done together to bring this place up to code, and then the work they had done to transform the upper floor into something resembling living quarters.

He had lived in similarly rough conditions during his years in forward-operating bases in Afghanistan. And he had often lived out of his pickup during those five years of wandering the Northeast following his discharge.

As crude as this place was, it was their home, something they had put a lot of sweat into, along with nearly all of Stella's money.

Leaving what they had built wasn't something Tom relished, even if this was the best-case scenario and they'd be gone for just a few nights.

Even if it meant that he could find some degree of relief from his troubling dreams.

The sound of the water ceased, and a few minutes later Stella came back to the bedroom. Tom took his turn, though he barely spent more than a minute under the stream.

Returning to their room, he found that the lights were off and the single lemon-scented candle on Stella's dresser had been lit.

She was seated on the edge of the bed, naked except for her string of knotted pearls.

Tom had only a towel wound around his waist, and she looked him up and down.

He didn't immediately approach her, though he couldn't take his eyes off her.

Stella recognized that his obvious interest was mixed with hesitation. "We'll be quick," she said. "I just need to feel you on top of me. I've been thinking about that all day."

She paused, then added, "Life goes on, right?"

⁓

Afterward, Tom found sleep quickly—well, quickly for him.

But he dreamed that dream again, dreamed that he was a helpless witness to what he had not witnessed.

To the moment his life had forever changed.

In the weeks and months that had followed the murder of his mother and sister, a man Tom assumed was a detective would often come by in the evening to talk to Tom's father and bring him up to speed on the investigation.

In his bedroom, directly above his father's study, Tom had heard their voices through the heating grate.

He had heard the strain in the voice of his father—a man torn by grief and rage, a man whose desire for justice had been crossing over into the need for vengeance.

Tom had heard, too, the sympathy in the other man's voice.

It had been a well-intentioned gesture, the bringing of updates to a bereft husband and father, keeping him informed on the progress—or lack thereof, for the most part—of the investigation.

But how could this man not have known that he was feeding a fire?

How could he not have recognized what Tom was able to simply by eavesdropping?

Tom's father had been crossing into madness.

Over the course of those several months, Tom had overheard details that served to fuel his own imagination.

Four pairs of boot prints, so four men.

Entry through the front door, between midnight and two a.m.

A simple robbery gone wrong.

Or perhaps a home invasion.

On his last nighttime visit, the man had offered only one new detail.

Your wife put up a fight.

It was at that point that Tom had stopped listening to the voices downstairs.

By then, of course, it was too late, because the knowledge that his mother and sister had suffered before they were finally killed had been firmly planted in his mind and would never leave.

The dreams had begun then, had occupied Tom through his one year at Yale, after which his father had sought revenge and came close to accomplishing it, only to get himself killed.

War had put an end to Tom's bad dreams, had eventually replaced them with a new kind of bad dream.

Dreams of battle, lives saved, and lives shattered.

These had plagued Tom during the years that he had wandered, the years that he had unconsciously followed a meandering path that would one day lead him to Stella.

And from there back to his hometown.

He had believed all the bad dreams were gone for good, then, only to be proven wrong when they'd settled down here.

Tonight's dream begins the same—Tom is standing outside his childhood home, across the tree-lined residential street from it, watching as four faceless men stride quietly but steadily through the darkness.

Passing him, one right after the other, they head toward the front door.

It is a breezy autumn night, the long hiss of the leaves stirring on the swaying branches covering the sound of their footsteps.

Tom is helpless as they breach the door and pour through it.

He is helpless as they move into his home like a brutal, cold wind.

He wants to go after them, to pursue them and stop them, but he is unable.

All that he knows—all that he can do, all the skills he has acquired and maintained in his lifetime—don't matter, because he cannot follow.

He cannot follow because he wasn't really there.

No one was.

His mother and sister had been at the mercy of men who had none.

Men who hurt and killed for both greed and pleasure.

Standing across the street, frozen, Tom hears the first of the screams.

As Ula had done for her daughter, according to Cahill, so Tom's mother had done for hers.

She'd fought back.

———⌣———

Tom woke from the dream, his bare torso slick with cold sweat, his chest heaving.

Sleeping beside him was Stella.

He lay still, could hear only his breathing—a wheeze as air was drawn in through his nose, a gasp as he exhaled through his mouth.

It took a moment before he could think, and then another before he could hear anything more than his labored breaths.

And what he heard then was the sound of a dog barking in the distance.

Not the lazy baying of a hound, which he often heard coming from one of the nearby farms.

No, this was different.

This was what he'd been listening for and hoping never to hear since their first night in this place.

This was the unmistakable sound of a dog alarmed by the presence of something, or someone, an urgent bark coming from the south that repeated over and over without any change in pitch or rhythm.

Tom recognized this for what it was: a dog giving frantic warning.

Instantly, he was in motion.

Twenty-Five

Communication in battle was crucial, and Tom had taken that into consideration.

Much of what he would need to relay to Stella in a time of crisis he could do with prearranged hand signals, but for situations when they could not see each other—either because of darkness or separation—verbal commands, as short as possible, had been established.

All he needed to do once he'd woken her was to speak two words.

He touched her shoulder, and her eyes opened immediately.

"Safe room," he said. Their current situation, however, required that Tom add three more words—ones they hadn't worked out in advance. "Get the girl."

Stella looked at him for a brief moment, her eyes wide, but then she, too, was in motion, rising from their bed and grabbing her jeans and putting them on.

As she did that, Tom reached for the Marlin in its corner. Grabbing it, he laid it down on his side of the mattress, then dropped to his knees and reached under the bed for the ranger backpack he kept there.

He clutched the pack and pulled it out.

Unzipping it, he pulled out two plate carrier vests, each one housing a pair of quarter-inch steel plates, one in the front and the other in the back.

In a canvas MOLLE pouch attached to each vest was a handheld, two-way radio equipped with a throat mic and earpiece.

Tom tossed one of the carriers onto Stella's side of the bed. Her jeans on, she lifted the vest over her head and lowered it till it was fitted around her torso, then clipped together the side straps.

Instead of putting the other carrier on, Tom stripped it of its radio setup before tossing it, too, onto Stella's side of the bed.

He nodded toward the vest and said, "The girl."

Stella nodded to indicate she understood, then grabbed her Smith & Wesson revolver from her nightstand, along with a small shoulder bag containing a paddle holster and two boxes of ammo.

She looked at Tom one last time before hurrying out the bedroom door. The .357 was tucked into her waistband, and she was affixing the microphone to her throat as she moved.

Clipping his radio to his belt, Tom grabbed his 1911 and map bag containing a half dozen eight-round magazines, then slung the Marlin over his shoulder and moved to their only window, positioning himself to the left of it.

As he put on his throat mic, he leaned forward for his first look outside and saw the two dumpsters below, his pickup, and the SUV parked near them.

Scanning the line of pine trees just beyond, he saw nothing, though he was able to determine now that the barking was coming from the other side of their property, so he crossed the hall to the room opposite their bedroom.

As he did, Stella ushered the girl from her bedroom to the safe room directly across.

The space Tom entered was little more than a closet, crammed with cardboard boxes containing various paper goods. Wedging the earpiece into his ear, Tom ran a coms test, saying in a soft voice, "Check, check."

Stella's voice came through the earpiece right away. "Receiving."

Tom asked her to confirm that she was in position, and she replied that she was.

He said, "Stand by."

Taking the slung Marlin from his shoulder, he approached the window, drawing back and releasing the bolt, chambering a round.

The room was so narrow he had no choice but to stand directly in front of the glass.

This side of their property was lined with pine trees as well, though there was a broad opening in the center that allowed Tom to see a good portion of the farmer's field beyond.

His eyes went to that opening, focusing on the horizon and looking for silhouettes moving against the night sky. He saw nothing at first, but he trusted that if the dog's bark meant what his gut told him it meant, this was the spot where approaching attackers would appear.

Tom kept his breathing even and slow and let his mind go blank so that it could react faster to incoming visual stimuli. He couldn't *want* to see it, simply needed to be ready *when* he did.

A moment passed, then another—Tom counted a dozen barks before he finally spotted shapes against the sky.

"Contact rear," he said. "Coming from the south."

"Copy."

He began to count the men—one, two, three.

Then more appeared.

And still more.

He didn't want to relay how many were out there until he was certain, but by the time the count had reached nine, he saw no more appear in the break.

"We've got nine," he said.

From his earpiece came Stella's voice.

He heard the first hint of fear.

"Jesus," she said.

Tom grabbed hold of the cardboard box nearest to the window and dragged it beneath the bottom pane.

The box contained used hardcover books and old phone directories, all stacked tight like bricks, six long and dozens deep. The barrier, combined with the wall against which the box was pressed, would be sufficient to stop—or at least slow to a less-than-fatal velocity—a rifle round of intermediate power, particularly one designed to fragment.

Tom took a kneeling position behind the box, raised the window by a few inches with his left hand, then readied himself.

He watched as the men drew closer. Suddenly, they veered to their right, moving as a pack and abandoning the wide opening for the cover of the line of trees.

Maneuvering to the east, they headed to where the tree line was consistent and the cover it offered would allow them to get closer while remaining unseen.

Tom suspected that a handful of men would also peel off into a fire team and approach the back of the building, while the remaining men would continue around to the front.

Within a few seconds, that was exactly what occurred: a four-man team stopped, each man dropping down to a crouch and waiting for their cue to emerge and rush the rear, while five men continued on, quickly passing out of Tom's line of sight.

He immediately displaced, crossing the hallway and returning to the bedroom window, instructing Stella as he moved to get ready to hit them with the lights.

"Copy."

Standing to the left of the window, he leaned forward and surveyed the scene below. The SUV was still there, its tinted windows preventing Tom from seeing the three occupants.

He had no way of warning them—a flaw in their planning, he realized now, something that he or Grunn should have considered and taken care of with a simple exchange of cell phone numbers.

But it was too late for that.

His only hope was that someone inside the vehicle was looking out and would see the approaching men.

If that didn't happen, then the lights would alert them.

Of course, by then it might be too late.

Tom lost sight of the five men moving through the trees; it was just too dark on this side of their property. For several long seconds he had nothing, but then he detected movement—a low branch was jostled—and that was all he needed to reacquire them and determine their position and rate of approach.

Fifty feet from the SUV, which itself was another fifty from the restaurant.

The average person, moving at a sprint, could cross fifty feet in less than four seconds.

Not a lot of time to target and shoot.

Tom's Marlin was chambered in the .45-caliber pistol round, and though its effective range was roughly 150 yards, and these men were well within that, the .45-cal was a heavy and relatively slow-moving bullet.

To add to Tom's disadvantage was the fact that he would be shooting at a downward angle, a situation in which targets appeared closer than they actually were. He'd have to take that into account and make adjustments, if he was to have first-shot accuracy.

And he'd have only seconds in which to do that.

Tom focused instead on the advantages he had—the precautions he had taken with this very scenario in mind.

Kneeling, he raised the window a few inches.

It moved easily and quietly. During renovations, he had replaced the century-old pulley wheel with a brand-new one and updated the frayed rope with one made of nylon and coated with urethane.

He had also opened up the drywall and placed a half-inch-thick steel plate between the studs.

Readying his Marlin, he said to Stella, "Once you hear shots, displace."

"Copy."

Tom waited, controlling his breathing and heart rate, keeping his mind clear and ready.

He saw the first men emerge from the tree line—three of them moving shoulder-to-shoulder, dressed in full tactical gear.

Black clothing and boots, black vests and operator helmets. Walking like trained fighters, they moved at a steady pace.

He let them take four strides, needed that time to sight the center man, then said, "Hit them with the lights."

In the safe room was a panel that controlled every light inside the building as well as the eight 1,000-watt halogen spotlights mounted along the edge of the roof.

Stella flipped the switch marked FL, and instantly every corner of the property was transformed from nighttime into high noon.

The men reacted to the sudden change in environment by lowering their centers of gravity and picking up their pace, shifting from a soldier's stealthy glide to an all-out run.

Their weapons were raised and directed squarely at the SUV.

Their attack would begin by taking out its occupants.

Which meant that they knew what the SUV contained.

He couldn't think about what that meant, though, had to keep his focus, maintain his front sight on the center man.

Only seconds remained.

That target had taken just one step and was beginning his second when Tom squeezed the trigger.

Twenty-Six

The center man dropped fast, landing flat on his back, so Tom shifted to his next target—the shooter that had been to the downed man's right, closer to Tom by a few feet.

But the two men had obviously heard the shot, maybe even witnessed their teammate go down, and responded by fanning out, diverging from their straight path and taking wide and opposing, arcing ones toward their target.

They opened fire on the SUV with fully automatic weapons.

Tom was focused on bringing down the second shooter so he could move to the third, but there was a fine line between focus and fixation.

He was sighting in the second shooter when he realized he had succumbed to tunnel vision, knew he had to make a quick check of his surroundings.

When he did, he saw that the man he had shot was not dead.

He wasn't even wounded.

Rolling to his side, the man rose to a kneeling position and prepared to return Tom's fire.

The vests these men wore weren't a means of bearing extra magazines and other necessities.

Their full tactical gear included body armor, which pretty much guaranteed that the operator helmets they wore were Kevlar-lined.

Assuming a rating of II-A, those helmets would be more than enough to stop a .45 round, even one fired from a sixteen-inch carbine.

The instant Tom spotted the kneeling man, he dropped below the windowsill just as the man fired.

The multiple rounds shattered the panes of glass and tore through the upper ceiling of the bedroom, but then the shooter laid off the trigger long enough to lower his aim and open up again.

Tom heard the rounds impacting the metal plating inside the wall just inches from his head.

His position blown, he got into a crouch and hurried out of the bedroom, intending to head down the hallway to the safe room.

But just as he reached the door, the four-man team at the rear of the building opened up as well.

Several automatic weapons firing from several different positions, all of them trained on the part of the upper floor that Tom occupied, told him that the two teams were in communication.

It was as if Tom had stepped into a beehive.

He dropped to his stomach as the rounds flew above him and proceeded to crawl down the hallway.

Reaching the safe room, he pushed the door open.

The room was empty, just as it should be, with the escape hatch he had fashioned in the floor still open.

Rising back to a crouch, he hurried to the opening and looked down through it and saw Stella and Valena at the bottom of the emergency rope ladder.

They both looked up at him.

"Basement," he said.

Dropping the hatch, he moved to the wall.

The shielding of hardbacks and phone books under a layer of ceramic tile would withstand a steady barrage of intermediate-powered rounds.

Tom knew well the sound of the 5.56 NATO round being fired by a carbine, and that was what he'd been hearing so far. But given the level of gear with which these men were equipped, there was no reason for him to think that there wasn't a heavier weapon among them.

And what was it Cahill had said?

A .50-cal had disabled his vehicle.

The fire from the rear ceased suddenly, but the firing in the parking lot out front continued.

During renovations, Tom had cut out a small port in the wall, then blocked it off with a brick made of glued-together ceramic tiles.

A makeshift handle was affixed to that brick.

Grabbing the handle, Tom pulled the block from the gun port and positioned himself in front of it.

Six inches high and a foot long, the opening was just big enough, if he shifted his position, for Tom to have a full view of the front of the property, including the area off to the side where the dumpsters were located and his truck and the SUV were parked.

He saw that the three gunmen had reached the SUV—one standing behind it, another by the driver's side, the third by the passenger side.

They were burning through mags, shooting up the vehicle at near-point-blank range.

At this range and under continuous fire, it was only a matter of time before the windows of the fully armored vehicle fractured to the point of failure.

Tom had to act, and fast.

He slid the barrel of the Marlin through the port, did so just enough so the muzzle was clear, and took aim at the only man facing him.

The man standing by the driver's side.

He was wearing a helmet, and he had goggles on as well.

So Tom aimed for the only potentially fatal target not protected by body armor.

The imaginary triangle between his nose and his chin.

As Tom eased his breathing in preparation of firing, he heard the sound of pounding coming from below.

The clang of metal striking against metal.

The four-man team was attempting to breach the rear door with a handheld battering ram, but the door was heavy steel and seated in a frame constructed of the same material.

And the door opened out, not in.

They could bang on it all night and it wasn't going to give way.

The pounding, though, stopped after only four strikes—the men had obviously wised up and abandoned the battering ram, but it was possible that they were equipped with a hydraulic prying tool.

It was a slower process that required affixing the device and cranking it by hand until the door and frame were forced apart just enough to unseat the dead bolt.

If they had such a tool, he had maybe a minute, tops, before they were inside.

Emptying his lungs, he paused for a millisecond, then squeezed the trigger.

It took all he had not to blink as the weapon jolted, and if he had, he would have missed the sight of his shot landing true, entering right below the man's nose and, by the way the man dropped instantly, utterly destroying his medulla.

This drew the fire of the other men, but Tom was expecting that.

He withdrew his carbine and leaned clear of the window, pressing his back against the wall.

He trusted that the barrier he'd put there would protect him, so after taking a quick breath, he moved fast and positioned himself at the port again.

Resuming his shooting, he did not aim this time, instead laid down harassing fire to keep the three gunmen occupied.

And give Grunn and her men a chance to move.

The man to the right of the SUV had his back to the vehicle, and it was the rear passenger-side door that swung open first.

In the harsh light of the spotlights, Tom watched Grunn, still seated, shoulder her M4.

She was either aware of the fact that these men were clad in body armor, or she had simply made the assumption, because she didn't aim for the torso or the head but rather raked the back of the man's knees with a controlled burst, sweeping her weapon from left to right as it fired.

The man dropped, tried to roll onto his side so he could return her fire, but she had already emerged from the vehicle and wasted no time positioning herself over him and getting off another three-round burst.

All three struck just above his right cheekbone, killing him instantly.

The remaining attacker at the rear of the vehicle ceased firing at Tom's position, turning toward Grunn.

Before he could aim his weapon, she quickly ducked down, putting the armored SUV between them.

Tom was sighting the side of the man's neck when the driver's door opened enough for a hand to emerge.

In it was a pistol.

Handguns were difficult to shoot accurately, even at close range, and especially while under the pressure inherent in life-or-death situations.

The driver of the SUV began firing wildly.

Several rounds struck the third man in the torso, but the driver just kept firing and elevating his pistol until he happened to strike the man in the face.

Of course, once their final man was down, the two men holding back in the trees were free to open fire.

Their first shots sent Grunn to the front of the vehicle for cover.

The driver of the SUV scrambled out, swung his slung carbine to his shoulder and fired toward the trees as he retreated for the front of the SUV as well. Tom recognized Sheridan, which meant DiBano, the youngest of Grunn's men, was still inside.

It didn't take long for DiBano to join in the melee.

He stuck his M4 out the door that Grunn had left open and, with the weapon set on full auto, fired blindly toward the trees.

This had little effect on the two remaining gunmen, however; from their concealed positions, they continued to fire.

In battle, it was the side that could throw the most lead downrange that generally prevailed.

Here, Tom knew, was a slugfest to the end.

But he had achieved his objective of freeing Grunn and her men from the SUV.

It was now three against two down there—better odds than they'd had moments ago.

Coming now from the floor below, though, were the sounds of heavy footsteps moving through the kitchen.

The four men had breached the back door and were inside.

As were Stella and Valena.

Grunn and her men were on their own.

The battle outside was theirs to fight.

The battle inside—confronting the four armed men in pursuit of the two women Tom was intent on protecting—that was Tom's.

Twenty-Seven

Tom had lost count of how many rounds he had fired, so as he ran to the escape hatch, he released the eight-round magazine from the Marlin as precaution.

Taking a quick look, he saw that it was empty.

Since the bolt hadn't locked back in the open position, a round was chambered.

He exchanged the empty mag for one of the half dozen fully loaded eight-rounders in his map bag.

Nine rounds, ready to go.

He had to keep a better running count from now on, or else risk having to deal with switching out a magazine or transitioning to his sidearm in the middle of a close-quarters firefight.

There was no room for error here.

He said, "Location?"

Stella's voice came through the earpiece. "Basement."

"Coming for you now."

"Are you okay?"

"Yes. Hang tight."

Tom reached the hatch but opened it slowly. Below was a pantry off the kitchen.

If Stella had stuck to procedure, she would have closed the door as she exited to head for the basement.

Tom could tell by the near-total darkness below that she had done that.

Making use of the emergency rope ladder would be too slow and cumbersome, so Tom slung the Marlin over his shoulder and sat on the edge of the hole, then slid his legs through and began to lower himself with his arms.

Once he was chest-deep into the hole and confirmed that his carbine was clear, he pressed his elbows against the floor, lowering himself through even more. Then he raised his arms over his head and dropped the rest of the way through, landing on the balls of his feet to minimize the noise.

But he was a two-hundred-plus-pound man, and even though his full body weight had dropped less than three feet, the impact of his boots on the floorboards was audible.

Tom immediately lowered himself into a tight crouch, and the instant he did, automatic gunfire began to splinter the wooden door.

There wasn't time to unsling and shoulder the Marlin, so he drew his Colt 1911 and flattened out on the floor.

The holes being punched into the pantry door were at chest level, which meant his attackers had lethal intent, and the recognition that another person was determined to kill him caused a sea change in Tom.

It always did, and it had the same effect on every man he had served with and fought beside.

A mix of clarity and outrage overtook him, an equation that resulted in the determination that these moments would not be his last.

That his glimpse of Stella through the hole cut into the floor would not be his final look at her.

Or hers at him.

Tom aimed for a point in the door that was just below midway— whatever the height of the shooter beyond, this area would be the man's center.

Not his center mass, but the anatomical midpoint of his body, where the pelvis was located.

For the sake of mobility, this area would be lightly armored, if armored at all, and whatever level of protection was present, the impact of a .45-cal round striking any of the several targets located there—bones, abdominal and leg muscles, genitals—would force his target to fold and fall.

So Tom fired, putting a controlled pair through the door and following it up with a second pair.

The audible grunt coming from the other side of the door told him that he'd found his target.

Four shots down, four in the magazine, and one in the chamber remaining.

Tom displaced, rolling to his right, once, twice, then stopping and repositioning himself.

The area of the floor from which he had just fired was immediately riddled with bullets.

Tom heard only one weapon firing, however.

He sent two more controlled pairs through the door from his new location, then quickly transitioned to a seated position and crab-walked deeper into the pantry.

Eight shots fired, leaving a ninth in the chamber.

Tom ejected the empty mag, letting it drop to the floor, then slapped a loaded one into the grip. Rising to a kneeling position, he proceeded to empty the Colt, putting all nine rounds through the door, aiming once again just below midpoint.

He repeated the mag exchange, but he had emptied the weapon, requiring that he manually release the slide.

Engaging the safety, he holstered the cocked-and-locked Colt with his right hand as he reached around for the Marlin with his left. It took all of four seconds to complete the reload and transition.

Shouldering the Marlin, he rose to a shooter's crouch and moved toward the door until he was beside it.

The moment he hit the wall, the barrage he'd fired from the Colt was returned with another hail of automatic fire.

Again, only one weapon.

Staying trapped meant losing this fight, so there was only one thing he could do.

He shifted the Marlin to his left hand, then shoved the barrel through one of the many holes in the door and began to unload.

The fire coming from the other side temporarily ceased, and Tom made his move.

He withdrew the Marlin and pulled the battered door open with his right hand, then raised the Marlin and continued firing as he removed the Colt from its holster and searched for his first target.

What he saw was one shooter standing over a fallen shooter.

The fallen shooter had taken multiple shots to the pelvis and was clearly in agony.

The standing shooter had been attempting to return Tom's fire while dragging his wounded comrade out of the way.

It was close-quarters combat now, milliseconds counted, and Tom had no choice but to take advantage of the standing man's compassion.

He lunged forward with the Marlin raised like a fencer's foil, striking the man in the throat with the carbine's muzzle and simultaneously squeezing the trigger.

The angle was right, though this was more a matter of luck than skill, and his spine severed; the man dropped instantly.

Astride the downed shooter, Tom crouched just low enough to press his Colt into the gap in that man's armor, located just below the armpit. He angled the pistol so that the bullet would follow a straight path through one side of the man's upper rib cage and out the other, fragmenting as it went and tearing to pieces everything in between.

Only the infliction of maximum damage would do now.

He put a single shot into the man, then rose.

Both weapons up, he scanned the kitchen for more targets, but there was no sign of the other two men.

Tom's eye went to the one thing that mattered now.

The basement door.

It was open.

Looking back at the two downed men, he noted that night-vision goggles were affixed to their operator helmets.

But that wasn't what he was hoping to find.

He scanned the torso of the nearest man and saw attached to his tactical vest the exact thing Tom was seeking.

An M67 hand grenade.

Below it was another piece of equipment that instilled instant fear.

An incendiary grenade.

Tom ignored the fear and grabbed the M67. Clipping it to his belt, he broke into a run, heading toward the open basement door.

"Location, Stella," he said.

He received no reply.

He spoke just a little louder. "Stella, come in."

Still nothing.

Either the equipment had failed or she couldn't respond, and if the latter were the case, there were a handful of reasons why she couldn't speak, none of them good.

Tom was approaching the door when the first shots came up from below.

What he heard wasn't the crack of the 5.56 round fired from a carbine but rather the explosive boom of a .357 Magnum going off in a confined place.

Stella was fighting for her life.

Tom broke into a run. "If you can hear me, I'm en route."

He'd lost count of how many rounds he had fired from the Marlin, but there was nothing he could do about that.

He knew that he had fired only one from the Colt, though, so he holstered it, then ejected the mag from the Marlin and inserted a fresh one.

The weapon was shouldered and ready when he reached the open basement door.

Twenty-Eight

As the original foundation of the building, the basement was a long, rectangular box with a floor of packed dirt and walls of fieldstone and mortar.

A cold cellar, in the years prior to refrigeration.

Completely below ground, it was windowless—dark and cool and silent, and usually smelling of damp.

But the only smell that reached Tom's nose was fresh cordite, and the silence had been replaced by gunfire, the darkness by muzzle flashes.

In every way possible, the sanctuary Tom built had now been violated.

Stella's two shots from her .357 had elicited an immediate response from her attackers.

The gunshots Tom was hearing now were automatic carbine fire.

He felt a swelling rage, was seconds from being blinded by it and sent into frantic motion. Yet in his fury he was able to hang on to the understanding that he must do all he could to keep from crossing that fine line between purpose and recklessness.

Between rescue and suicide.

Tom thought of Carrington's mantra, the first thing his former commanding officer had taught him back when he'd joined Carrington's reconnaissance engineer team.

The only way out is through.

Tom cleared his head of everything but this and began.

The stairs were his first obstacle—a series of planks on an open frame of two-by-fours, they would offer him no cover as he descended.

More than that, a shooter could simply wait below them and fire up at Tom the moment he attempted to make his way down.

There was no time, though, to probe and determine whether someone was in fact there, waiting to ambush him.

And the steps were steep, more an angled ladder than stairs.

Tom did the only thing he could.

He flew into the darkness.

Landing on the hard dirt, he dropped into a crouch and spun to face the stairs behind him, but he lost his balance and fell against the rock wall, hitting the back of his head.

He ignored both the pain and the reflex to flinch, fixing his eyes on the stairs. The faint illumination coming through the open door above was enough to see that no one was beneath it.

He wasted no time getting to his feet.

Reaching into his map bag with his left hand, he removed his SureFire flashlight.

Six hundred lumens strong, the light was activated by pressing an easily reachable tab located on either side of the end cap.

A small amount of pressure from his ring finger was more than enough to engage the light.

Tom held the light in his left palm, then grabbed the Marlin's forend with a C-clamp grip—the support hand not under the barrel but off to the left side so that his thumb could hook firmly over the top.

Holding his weapon this way allowed for faster target acquisition in close quarters, as well as better recoil control, which would ensure accurate follow-up shots.

But more than that, it would enable Tom to keep the SureFire ready for exactly when he needed it.

The gunfire had ceased, and as best as Tom could tell, only one of the attackers had fired, which meant the other had likely attempted to maneuver through the maze they had found themselves facing.

A deadly maze Tom had constructed in the long months of renovation and alteration prior to the restaurant opening up.

Heading toward that maze, Tom found his way by memory, listening keenly as he moved one step at a time.

He had built the maze out of old wooden pallets he'd fashioned into crates, each one five feet tall and four feet wide.

Some of the makeshift crates contained nothing but a few gallon-size containers of water to give them a degree of stability, while others hid sandbags stacked in rows that were three deep—more than enough of a barrier to offer protection from all but the most powerful rounds.

And only Tom and Stella knew which crates to take cover behind and which, being easily shot through, were traps for anyone who attempted to use the maze against them.

Tom had practiced weaving from crate to crate in the dark, knew how many steps to take to reach the first crate, then how many diagonal steps were necessary to cross to the second, and from there to the third.

There were eight crates total, at the end of which was the last holdout position—a coal chute, the bottom of which was obstructed by a five-foot-tall cinder-block partition, each block hand-filled by Tom with a mix of ceramic tile bits and packed earth, after which the blocks had been cemented together.

A wall from behind which they could safely fire.

At the top of the coal chute was a steel hatch door, locked from the inside.

The hatch was just large enough for a person to escape through, but Tom had no doubt that Stella was still behind the partition wall.

The open hatch would have allowed some degree of ambient light from outside to spill into the far end of the pitch-black basement, and Tom saw none.

And the gunfire outside, sporadic now, was still muted significantly.

No, Stella was there, he knew that.

Ready to fight for her life and the life of the girl beside her.

Fight back, like Tom's mother had.

But Tom was here this time, had the upper hand, and was determined to make use of it.

Reaching the first crate, he crouched behind it, pausing to make sense of what he heard. Two men were talking—in English and with accents that were clearly American.

Tom couldn't let the fact that they were fellow countrymen affect him.

More than just countrymen, they were likely veterans like him.

But these two men had made their choice—the same choice Tom had once faced but ruled out when Carrington had offered him work as a private contractor.

There was, of course, a difference between a private-sector special operator and a mercenary, but it was a distinction that was too easily lost sight of by too many.

These men had either not seen that distinction or had but were indifferent to it.

They were here to kill because that was what they were paid to do.

Not for their country or as a last resort while protecting those who employed them.

They were here to murder without asking any questions.

Tom had decided long ago that he would never follow that path and become that kind of man.

The kind of man who had killed his family.

Their voices were low but not hushed. One man was telling the other to move, and the other was arguing that they needed to wait for reinforcement.

There was urgency in the first man's voice. It was clear that they were spooked by the maze they had suddenly found themselves in.

Spooked, too, by the shots that had been fired at them from behind a barrier wall.

By their conversation, Tom concluded that the brief firefight they had engaged in with Stella had covered the sound of his landing hard at the bottom of the steps.

These men were concerned with only what faced them, not what might be to their rear.

That distraction probably wouldn't last for long.

By tracking the voices, Tom determined that they were behind the fourth crate, which was one of the cover positions filled with a three-deep row of sandbags.

The next crate—the fifth—was a false position.

But Tom was behind the first crate, which was false cover as well, so he needed to get to the second crate before engaging them.

And while he was confident that Stella would recognize the difference between the sound of her attacker's 5.56 fire and his .45 fire—this was the reason for his not having taken one of the automatic weapons from the fallen men upstairs—he needed to be positioned behind actual cover in case she mistook him for them in the confusion of battle and opened fire with her .357.

Tom had only one option, and in the confines of the basement, it was a risky one.

One that would cost him.

But it was a sacrifice he had to make.

Removing the grenade from his belt, he held it and the SureFire light in his left hand—the light pinned to his palm by his pinky and ring fingers, the grenade grasped firmly by his thumb, index, and middle finger.

He grabbed the circular pull pin with his teeth, separating it from the detonator, then spit the pin out.

The grenade and light in his left hand and the Marlin in his right, he made his move, running from the first crate toward the second.

The sound of his motion was more than enough to expose his presence to the two men.

In the darkness he was blind, but he knew where they were and immediately released the grenade's safety lever.

The standard fuse delay of an M67 was between four and five seconds, and it would take maybe a second for the grenade to reach them once he tossed it, so he paused for the duration of one breath before lobbing the device in their direction.

For Stella's benefit, he said, "Grenade."

Though she and the girl were safe behind the reinforced cinder-block wall, protected from the countless fragments that were about to fill the air and spread out at a high velocity, the sound of the explosion, as well as the concussive force it generated, could be devastating to the unprepared.

Tom was certain Stella would hear his single word and grab Valena, pull the girl's head close to her chest and enclose her arms around her as she covered her own ears.

With a few steps remaining between him and the second crate, he shifted the SureFire in his hand until he achieved a functional grip.

Then he aimed the light at the men, flipping the power switch on.

Six hundred lumens of white light lit the dark basement like a camera flash.

He briefly saw the two men—saw them by the fourth crate, turning to face him.

He saw, too, that their night-vision goggles were in place.

The sudden bright light would overwhelm the night-vision system, temporarily blinding the two mercs.

Tom could tell by the reaction of these men that this was exactly what he had accomplished.

Quickly switching the light off, he reached the cover of the second crate and crouched behind it. He did his best to brace himself, but his Marlin was in his right hand and the SureFire in his left, and there wasn't even time for him to drop them, so all he was able to do was cover his left ear with the heel of his left hand.

His right ear would have to bear the effects of a grenade going off at point-blank range.

An experience that was all too familiar.

The metallic sphere had made no sound when it landed on the dirt floor, but the commotion of the men scrambling to save themselves was confirmation that his aim had been true.

Their frantic motion was audible for maybe two seconds, certainly not more, and then the grenade at their feet detonated.

Twenty-Nine

Tom was semiconscious, his lungs voided to the point of near collapse, and despite the last-second placement of his left hand, both ears were ringing sharply.

He had felt his legs go out from beneath him when the shockwave hit like a gust—that was the last thing he could remember, in fact, being hit by compressed air as dense as a wall that caused his internal organs to shift and force the air from his lungs.

Now he was flat on his back and staring up into a darkness that he could not at first understand, gasping for air but unable to draw it in.

His location unknown to him, he was looking for stars, his eyes searching for something—anything—resembling light.

He was desperate for it, maybe more so than he was for air to breathe.

There was no light, however, and the panic triggered by the seeming lack of air around him brought him back to reality.

He knew where he was, what he had done, and what he now needed to do.

All he had to do was get up, but he could barely lift his head off the dirt floor for longer than a few seconds.

It was as he was struggling against gravity that he felt someone touch him.

A hand on his arm.

His mind focused on the nature of that touch—gentle but firm.

He could see nothing, hear nothing, but the hand moved down his arm to his hand and pulled something from it.

Tom realized he had still been clutching the SureFire.

Within seconds of the flashlight being taken from him, there was at last something for his eyes to find.

Light was above him.

So, too, were Stella and Valena—Stella wearing her plate carrier vest, Valena all but lost in Tom's.

Keeping the bright light out of Tom's eyes, Stella illuminated his face.

She was studying him for wounds, feeling his head with her free hand and saying something, but Tom could only hear the ringing.

And even if he had been able to hear her speak, he simply had no air with which to voice a reply.

When Stella realized Tom was gasping, she quickly handed the flashlight to Valena, then placed both hands on Tom's solar plexus and pressed down, holding the pressure on his diaphragm for a moment before releasing.

As Tom's sternum rose, he gulped in air, filling his aching lungs.

It was then that he smelled the cordite.

More than smell it, he could taste it.

Stella said something to Valena, and together they worked to get Tom to his feet. It wasn't easy going; he weighed as much as the two of them combined, and his legs were still weak. But he did his best to help them, and once he was up, they each moved under an arm and wound it around their necks, propping Tom up like a pair of crutches.

Tom noted that the Marlin was still clutched in his right hand. Pointing it in the direction of the fourth crate, he muttered, "Light, there."

He couldn't hear his own voice, but he didn't let the loud ringing trick him into shouting.

He kept his voice even and low.

Valena shined the light on the two men lying on the dirt floor.

Blood was everywhere; they were either dead or unconscious and mere moments from dead.

That was all Tom needed to know.

He said, "Okay. Stairs."

Stella and Valena spun him, then maneuvered him around the first crate and toward the stairs.

Without being instructed to do so, Valena aimed the light at their destination.

Tom could tell Stella was looking at the side of his face frequently, watching him and trying to gauge his condition.

He kept his eyes on the stairs, though, his Marlin raised as high as he could manage.

They reached the bottom step, and Valena aimed the light at the door at the top.

Tom did the same with the Marlin.

No one was there.

He asked Stella what she heard, then looked at her.

She shook her head from side to side.

Tom watched her lips and saw her mouth the word, "Nothing."

Tom nodded. "Okay."

The steps were too narrow for the three of them to stand side by side, so Stella instructed that Valena get behind them, then helped Tom up one step at a time until they reached the open door at the top.

Tom scanned the room, then nodded toward the breached back door.

The ringing in his ears was still present, but he could hear other sounds now, too.

His own breathing, their footsteps, sporadic gunfire outside.

A few shots, a few more, then silence.

But the silence didn't last too long.

It was broken by the sound of voices.

Male voices barking commands.

Halfway through the kitchen, Stella stopped.

Tom looked at her.

He could hear the voices outside but not the words being spoken.

Stella had not only heard the words but also heard something that alarmed her.

Her face showed terror.

Tom said, "What?"

She spoke, but he didn't hear her, nor could he read her lips.

She put her mouth close to his ear.

"Someone is telling us to come out or they'll burn us out," she said.

Tom leaned back to see her face.

"He has an accent," Stella added.

"What kind?"

"French or something."

Tom remembered what the Colonel had called the man he had been seeking for decades.

The Algerian.

Stella leaned close again. "Who is he?"

But there wasn't time for Tom to explain.

Nor was there time for him to act, because something came crashing through the front window of the restaurant.

Tom grabbed Stella and the girl, pulled them down with him as he ducked.

Almost immediately after that, something came crashing in through the kitchen window, landed on the floor, bounced once, then rolled to a stop just a few feet away.

Tom was looking at a canister, identical to the one he'd seen clipped to the vest of the fallen man upstairs.

An incendiary device, it was now between them and the breached back door.

Tom rose, pulling the women with him, and said, "Go!"

His legs were back, for the most part, anyway, and he turned Stella and shoved her toward the basement stairs, Valena in front of her.

Stella got the girl through, then Tom got Stella through.

And just as he pulled the door closed behind, the device ignited, scattering a spray of white-hot phosphorous into the air.

Tom felt the wooden door heat up instantly.

It was almost too much to bear.

Stella and Valena were running down the steep stairs. Tom followed. He was barely halfway down when the door caught fire.

Tom said, "The coal chute."

They crossed the basement to the maze, wound their way through it, stepping over the two dead men by the fourth crate.

Valena was in the lead, using the flashlight to guide them to the barrier wall, which was pockmarked with dozens of scars from the grenade's fragments.

Making their way around the wall, Stella and Valena stopped at the bottom of the coal chute.

Tom hurried passed them, climbed the narrow, slanting chute to the steel hatch at the top and unlatched it.

Behind them, it was beginning to rain fire—the balls of phosphorus had burned through the wooden floorboards and were dropping like hailstones into the basement.

The planks and posts and beams, aside from a few recently replaced by Tom, were close to ten decades old. The entire place and everything it contained would be engulfed within minutes.

They had to move fast.

Above the ringing in his ears, Tom heard his own grunts from the effort of pressing open the heavy steel hatch.

He heard Stella instructing Valena to climb the chute first.

Tom was heartened by this.

If he could hear, he could fight.

If he could fight, he could save them all.

But what he wasn't hearing right now was a problem: the absence of gunfire coming from the front of their building, and the fact that the voice Stella had heard was likely the Algerian's, meant that Grunn and her two men had been defeated.

Whether that meant they had been killed or captured, however, remained a troubling unknown.

The coal-chute hatch was at the rear of the building, and beyond the border trees at the southern edge of their property was the farmer's field across which their attackers had first made their approach.

His only hope was to get everyone clear of the hatch and run for that field, then skirt the tree-lined edge of it to remain unseen.

But doing this would mean leaving any possible survivors behind.

Tom's mission, though, was to save the two women who were depending on him.

He thought only of that as he cleared the narrow opening, got to his feet, and quickly scanned his surroundings with his Marlin raised before turning back to the hatch and reaching in. Extending his left hand and grabbing Valena by hers, he pulled her up and out into the chilly night air.

He told her to get down, and she immediately lowered into a crouch, scanned the area like Tom had, then focused her attention on the corner of the building nearest to them.

The corner around which danger was likely to come first.

Tom grabbed Stella's hand and pulled her clear. Together, they crouched beside Valena, forming a huddle.

The grenade's explosion had blown out his communication gear, so he quickly ditched it.

Stella did the same with hers.

In a whisper, Tom said, "Make a run for that field. Stay by the trees, though. And be careful, because that's the direction they came from. Double back if you can, go around and make your way north to Krista's. If you can't double back, if you think someone's behind you, go to the twenty-four-hour gas station two miles past the farm. Call the police, then follow protocol."

"You're coming with us, right?"

"I'm going to cover you while you cross to the tree line."

"We'll wait for you there."

"No, keep going. I'll catch up."

Stella hesitated.

Tom was certain she knew what he was thinking.

How could she not?

Before she had the chance to express her objection, he said, "You know what to do, Stella. You know the procedure. I need you to follow it now, please."

Stella looked at him for a moment, then finally nodded and grabbed Valena by the hand, pulling the girl to her feet as she stood.

They ran across the open backyard, Stella setting the pace and the girl holding it.

Tom approached the nearby corner and peered around it.

The front of their property was illuminated by the spotlights Tom had mounted along the roof as well as the fire raging in the dining area.

It was as good as daylight there.

Tom saw nothing at first, but then a figure walked into his line of sight.

A man dressed not in tactical gear but dark pants and a leather peacoat.

Tom ducked back before the man could see him, watched as Stella and Valena reached the field.

Within a few seconds, they moved into the line of trees, disappearing.

Tom hesitated, torn between conflicting duties—catch up with Stella and lead her and the girl to safety, or make an effort to at least confirm whether or not anyone in Grunn's team was still alive.

And if someone were alive, he couldn't just leave that person in the hands of these men.

Tom looked again around the corner and saw that a second man had joined the man in the peacoat.

But that second man was not alone.

Someone was in front of him, being held like a human shield.

The light from the fast-rising fire inside the restaurant glinted off the blade he held to his captive's throat.

Grunn's throat.

Tom had yet to be spotted, but he had no doubt that it would be obvious to these two men that the rear of the building, which had yet to be consumed by the fire, provided the only avenue of escape for those inside.

The fact that one of them hadn't made it around to cover the rear meant that they didn't want to risk getting into a firefight with whoever had taken out so many members of their team.

It had to have crossed their minds that there was possibly more than one capable fighter inside.

Tom was thinking of a way to exploit that advantage when the man in the peacoat yelled, "Why don't we make a deal?"

His accent was as Stella had described.

This was the Algerian, then.

The dangerous man whom the Colonel and Cahill had spoken of.

But the Algerian was addressing the building, which meant he believed the occupants were still inside.

He wasn't sure why, exactly, they would believe that.

"One girl for another," the Algerian said. "That's fair, no?"

So they wanted Valena alive.

Tom said nothing.

"Or would you rather burn while this one has her throat slowly slit open?"

It didn't make sense to Tom that the Algerian assumed they were still inside when the rear of the building, and its already-breached door, was beyond his line of sight.

And yet the two remaining attackers stood there, showing no concern for the part of the property they could not see.

As confusing as this was, Tom knew better than to get hung up on that.

He glanced back toward the trees and saw no sign of Stella and the girl.

The longer he delayed the Algerian, the farther away the two women would get.

Stella could run all night if she had to, had been training for this since their arrival here. She had strong legs, powerful lungs, and a standing heart rate of fifty-eight beats per minute.

The girl at her side had youth.

And perhaps more importantly, the knowledge of what these men could do—having seen what men like these had done to her mother—caused her to experience gut-deep fear.

With fear like that came adrenaline.

Tom's protocol established that once Stella was safely away, she would contact Carrington, who would alert Cahill and Hammerton.

If necessary, Cahill would inform the Colonel, who'd move fast to dispatch local law enforcement.

Tom envisioned his friends—any or all of them—coming for her, then watching over her as she was transported to Cahill's safe house in Connecticut.

A place Tom knew well, having once been held captive there for a night.

If he had to stand his ground somewhere, or hide for a prolonged period of time, the old tavern wouldn't be a bad choice.

Tom needed to see that clearly in his mind, had to know that Stella would do her part so that the men he trusted could do theirs and get her to that stronghold.

Clarity as such was necessary if he was going to take the risk that was required of him now.

Thirty

Dropping to his right knee, Tom shouldered the Marlin, placing his left elbow on his left knee for added stability.

The man holding the knife to Grunn's throat was large, as big as a doorway, so his head was higher than Grunn's.

Though his face was visible, Tom's intended target—the area between the man's helmet and chin—was just five by five inches.

Added to that was the fact that the man was fifty feet away.

At that distance, a variance in Tom's aim of one-sixteenth of an inch would translate into a miss of six inches.

A fraction of an inch too high or to the right or to the left and he'd completely miss.

A fraction too low and he'd put a bullet into Grunn's head.

But the hard truth was, either way she was dead. Once they got what they wanted—Valena—any survivors would be terminated as unwanted witnesses.

What mattered—what could only matter—was buying Stella and the girl as much time as he could.

Tom let everything but the front sight become a blur.

He moved his index finger into the trigger guard, doing so carefully so as not to affect his aim.

He focused his mind, shutting everything out but the front sight, allowing the target beyond it to go out of focus.

Taking a breath and letting it out slowly, he placed the pad of his index finger on the trigger, poised to gently squeeze it.

But he had forgotten the first rule of combat.

He had traded in situational awareness for tunnel vision.

All he could see or think about was the target he was determined to hit.

So by the time he heard the sound behind him—the sound of motion, of something being swung through the night air by someone— it was too late.

Tom abandoned his shot and turned, but did so only in time to see the man standing over him.

He was wearing tactical gear like the others, but with one significant difference.

His face was hidden behind a mask.

All Tom could see was the depiction of a grotesque human skull.

The telescoping baton in his left hand struck the side of Tom's head.

Falling backward and landing on his back, Tom raised the Marlin toward his attacker, but the man was just too fast.

He moved in, parrying the carbine to one side, and knelt over Tom.

He lingered there for a brief second.

Only his eyes were visible, locked with Tom's.

But there was something about them.

Something . . . familiar.

Then the masked man raised his baton and struck Tom again.

The next thing Tom knew, he was being dragged across grass.

At some point the grass ended and he was on gravel.

Someone was holding him by one ankle.

Finally, the dragging stopped, and Tom rolled onto his back and looked up.

The masked man was standing above him, staring down at him.

Tom's vision was blurred, but he searched for Grunn and in the process spotted a vehicle parked nearby.

A panel van, its lights on and two front doors open.

No doubt this was the vehicle in which the masked man had arrived.

The open passenger door indicated that he likely had a partner.

Tom understood now why the Algerian and his man had made a show of calling toward the house as if they believed it was still occupied.

They were stalling, buying time for that newly arrived backup team to make its way around to the rear of the building.

Just as Tom had been buying time for Stella and Valena.

He wondered how far away the two women had gotten.

He'd bought them, what, two minutes?

So a half mile, maybe.

Each second that passed, though, got them farther away by a few more strides.

Every step they took increased their chances of getting out of alive.

Tom craved that, deeply.

He realized that the Marlin had been taken from him, but his Colt was still holstered inside his waistband at the four o'clock position on his right side.

Wedged between his back and the gravel, the weapon's checkered walnut grip dug into his skin.

To grab the Colt, he would have to do more than simply reach for it.

He would have to roll onto his left side or plant both feet on the ground and raise his hips, and either motion would not go unnoticed.

Another man dressed in tactical gear joined the masked man.

Tom assumed that he was the masked man's partner.

The second man had a pistol in his right hand. He pointed it down at Tom.

"Is that him?"

The masked man didn't speak, simply nodded.

Tom and he once again locked eyes.

The second man asked, "Should I kill him?"

Before the masked man could answer, the Algerian appeared beside him. "Not yet," he said. "We need the girl first."

The Algerian knelt beside Tom.

Tom looked up at him.

Now it wasn't just Cahill who had seen his face.

Tom made a point of memorizing every detail he could.

"Where is she?" the Algerian said.

The man holding Grunn moved to stand behind the Algerian, so Tom could see her.

His knife was still at her throat.

Tom and Grunn made eye contact.

Her face was bloodied, her hair matted by sweat. By the nature of her cuts, she had been punched multiple times.

The injuries were focused on the right side of her face, so whoever had beaten her was left-handed.

Tom looked again at the masked man. He knew those eyes, but from where?

The Algerian said, "Is the girl dead, or did she make it out?"

Tom played the only hand he had to play.

"She's dead."

Two more men appeared, but this pair was casually dressed, not clad in tactical gear.

One of them dropped something onto the gravel next to Tom's head. It was the communication gear he and Stella had shed at the back of the building.

"There are two sets of tracks in the grass," the man said to the Algerian. "Fresh. They lead to the field to the south."

"You'll never catch them," Tom said.

"That's why you will tell us where they are going," the Algerian said. "If these men have to chase them down on foot—chase them through fields and woods—they will be angry. And when they find them, which they will, they will act on their anger. Tell us where they are going, and unnecessary violence will be avoided. We will kill them quick, I promise."

Tom said nothing.

"Perhaps you would prefer it if these men were to demonstrate on your bodyguard here what exactly they will do to your woman and the girl, should you require them to exert themselves?"

Tom met Grunn's eyes again. She shook her head once, side to side.

The Algerian watched Tom for a moment. "You killed those men, no? The four sent in. And the shot fired from above, that was also you, correct?"

Tom remained silent.

When he got no reply, the Algerian nodded and said, "I see now why he fears you as much as he does. I see why he wants you dead. I, too, want you dead. I dislike loose ends as much as he. But before I get to kill you, I need you to give me the girl. How you die hinges on what you do right now. How everyone dies hinges on that. So I need from you now more than your silence."

"Fuck you," Tom said.

The Algerian stood and ordered his men to get Tom up. They pulled him to his feet.

The masked man held him while his partner placed the muzzle of his pistol behind Tom's ear.

The casually dressed pair stepped back, ready to assist, if needed.

"Check him," the Algerian ordered.

The masked man's partner patted Tom down, quickly finding his Colt and pulling it from its holster. He handed it off to the man who had informed the Algerian about the fresh tracks in the grass.

But the masked man snapped his finger, then extended his hand, making it clear that he wanted the weapon.

Tom took note that the hand the masked man had extended was his left.

And that the man was making a point not to speak.

The man with the tracking skills handed the Colt to him, and he slid it into his belt.

"Put them face-to-face," the Algerian said.

Tom was turned and positioned so he was facing Grunn. There was barely two feet between them. The Algerian reached into the pocket of his peacoat and removed a pistol.

A Walther PPK.

And though he'd gotten only a glimpse of its Bakelite grips, Tom saw engraved on them a gothic eagle, its wings spread and head turned to the left.

Even if he hadn't been a student of history, he still would have recognized the symbol of the Nazi Party.

"I am told that you are a man who has served his country," the Algerian said. "That you are descended from men who have served as well. Navy men, every one of you, all the way back to your country's founding. I never knew my father, so I do not know from whom he and I are descended. And I have no country to serve, so my cause is myself. My loyalty is to the man who pays me, so it is loyalty born of necessity, from the desire to survive, not pride. You would, I think, have been better served had you chosen a different path than that of loyalist. If you had, perhaps, been more like your father."

Tom didn't understand what the Algerian meant by that, but that was the last thing on his mind right now.

The Algerian pressed the Walther's muzzle against Grunn's temple.

"The choice is yours, Tomas Sexton. She is already a dead woman, there's nothing that can change that. You are a smart man, so you know this. But she can die quickly by my hand, or she can die slowly by the hand of my man here. She can die by drowning in her own flowing blood, while you watch helpless, or she can go as quickly and as easily as switching off a light." The Algerian paused. "So tell me right now, where is your woman taking the girl? I need something the girl has. Do you understand? Answer me truthfully and everyone dies easy. Don't answer me at all, or lie to me, and your woman won't die for days. None of them will. I won't ask again. Where will we find the girl?"

Tom saw fear in Grunn's eyes. And yet, like she had done a moment before, she shook her head from side to side.

A small but unmistakable gesture of defiance.

Then she braced herself.

Tom couldn't bear this, was ready to say anything to spare her from suffering.

He was ready to plead for her life.

But then he spotted something behind her. Movement in the trees surrounding the two dumpsters.

Someone had emerged from that concealment, only to move to another position and disappear from Tom's sight again.

A second later, that person was in motion yet again.

The Walther PPK was a double-action pistol, so the Algerian thumb-cocked the hammer and pressed the muzzle even harder against Grunn's head.

His finger was on the recessed trigger.

Tom said, "Let her go, and I'll tell you."

The Algerian opened his mouth to reply, though the expression on his face was one of doubt mixed with contempt.

But before the man could utter a word, the bright floodlights overhead suddenly went dark.

This was followed by a series of popping sounds from inside the restaurant. Compromised by the fire, the old-style fuses were exploding, the electrical systems failing. The only illumination now was from the fire as it consumed Tom and Stella's world.

Tom looked past Grunn again, and this time the fleeting movement he had detected was replaced by the sight of a figure carrying a rifle moving steadily from the dumpsters to the shot-up SUV.

Moving with a soldier's glide.

Dressed in jeans and boots, the figure wore a lightweight plate carrier over a Henley shirt. A cap, its bill tilted low, covered the head and obscured the face.

Unlike the vests Tom had acquired for Stella and himself, the one worn by this person was designed to offer bare-minimum cover in exchange for greater mobility.

The plate carrier of choice for someone who might need to cover a distance at a sprint.

Attached to the vest were three magazine pouches, and by the width of the magazines inside them, Tom knew that the ammo contained within them was not the smaller, weaker 5.56 NATO but the more powerful .308 Winchester.

The figure was close enough for Tom to see that the rifle was an AR-10 with an eighteen-inch barrel, suppressed.

Mounted to its flattop receiver was a scope, and close to the front edge of the floating rail forend was a folding tripod.

What really caught Tom's attention, though, was the shape of the figure.

The Henley was formfitting, and even partially covered by the plate carrier, it was obvious to Tom that the torso beneath was not a man's.

The figure was close enough to the SUV that the flames from the restaurant were bright enough for Tom to see her clearly.

And then she raised her head high enough for Tom to get a good look at the face the long-billed cap had obscured.

Tom estimated that the attack had started over ten minutes ago, which would have been just enough time for her to cross the distance between the farm where she rented a room and the restaurant where she worked.

It was a run that she had practiced nightly since the day she had showed up out of nowhere looking for a job.

Reaching the SUV and quickly taking a covered position, Krista expertly aimed her rifle, pausing to acquire her first target.

Tom looked at her and nodded once, indicating that he was ready.

And then she fired.

Thirty-One

Tom bent forward as the .308 round penetrated the base of the bigger man's skull.

The bullet exited, blowing out a chunk of the man's jaw.

The bending motion allowed Tom to avoid the escaping lead and flying pieces of bone and brain matter, but more importantly, it enabled him to slip out of the masked man's hold.

With both arms free, Tom reached up for the knife just as the dead man began to fall.

Yanking it away from Grunn's throat, he pried it from the man's hand, gripped the handle and swung for the man closest to him.

The masked man's partner, standing to Tom's right.

But the masked man stepped forward to intercept Tom's arm and stop the blow.

His partner wasted no time raising his pistol and quick-aiming at Tom's torso, point blank.

Before Tom could even react, Grunn moved in beside that man, clutching the top of his pistol's slide with her right hand and his forearm with her left.

It took only a small amount of pressure for her to cause the man's wrist to fold, and then his firearm was pointed safely away from Tom.

The man was about to counter by pivoting, which would prevent Grunn from turning his weapon to the point where its muzzle was directed at his midsection, but she stopped him midturn with a swift kick to the groin. Grunting loudly and dropping to the ground, he pulled Grunn down with him.

Tom didn't see what happened next, because the masked man moved under Tom's extended arm, driving his shoulder hard into Tom's ribs.

It was like a defensive end sacking the quarterback.

Forcing Tom back a few feet, the masked man suddenly stopped short, leaving a gap large enough for another man to come in and, blindsiding Tom, complete the tackle. As Tom hit the ground, someone else landed next to him.

It was one of that second pair of men—not the Tracker, the man who had spotted the tracks, but his partner.

And the condition of the dead man's skull told Tom that he had been taken out by Krista's second shot.

Two men down, three more to go.

Having wrestled during his years at military school, being on the ground wasn't a problem for Tom.

He quickly executed a reversal, putting the Tracker on his back with Tom on top of him.

But his opponent knew ground fighting as well and wrapped his legs around Tom's waist, then extended his hips high, keeping Tom at a distance.

As they struggled for control of the knife—Tom was holding it, the Tracker grasping Tom's hand and seeking a wristlock—a motion in the far left edge of Tom's peripheral vision caught his attention.

The masked man was on the move, escorting the Algerian in the way a bodyguard would, laying down suppressing fire with his own sidearm as the two men ran for the waiting van.

His rounds kept Krista's head down long enough for him and the Algerian to reach and enter the vehicle.

By Tom's count, the masked man had fired nine rounds before suddenly stopping, indicating that he had likely emptied his firearm.

Nine rounds meant an eight-round magazine with a round chambered.

That particular configuration was, with only a few exceptions, exclusive to the 1911 platform.

He had used Tom's Colt.

And he was making off with it.

Once the masked man's fire ended, he expected Krista to reposition and open up on the vehicle with her AR-10.

Even with the suppressor affixed, the sound of the high-speed round exiting the muzzle would make an audible sound, but as the van accelerated in reverse, charging across the gravel lot toward the road, Tom still didn't hear shots coming from Krista's location.

He feared she had been wounded or killed.

Taking a risk, he shifted his attention from the man he was fighting to the battered SUV where he had last seen Krista.

But he could see no sign of her.

Then he glanced to where he had last seen Grunn go to the ground with the masked man's partner.

She and her opponent were still grappling over control of his pistol.

At first she had been on top of the man, but he had rolled her and now they were both on their sides, facing each other.

It wouldn't be long before the man mounted her.

Tom had to get to her.

The Tracker's hold on him was a jiu-jitsu technique known as "the guard."

A solid defensive position, should one find himself on his back, but there were ways to pass it.

Tom initiated an escape, but the Tracker had been waiting for that because he immediately countered Tom's move, trapping Tom's left arm and beginning the process of applying a joint lock.

Tom countered that by keeping his trapped arm bent and grabbing hold of his left wrist with his right hand.

But as strong as Tom was, fighting against an attempted arm bar was fighting against leverage.

His opponent merely needed to wait for Tom's arm to weaken and his grip on his own wrist to falter, after which simple body mechanics would result in the man completing the lock and overextending Tom's elbow to the point of shattering the joint.

From Tom's bad position on the ground, he could still see Grunn, watched as her opponent took one hand off the firearm and quickly struck her in the face with his fist.

The blow stunned her briefly, and the man used that moment to scramble on top of her, mounting her like a school-yard bully.

Grunn recovered before he could snatch the weapon from her.

They continued their life-and-death struggle, but it was only a matter of seconds before he overpowered her.

Tom could feel the strain on his bicep, and his wrist was ready to slip from his hand.

His only hope was to hear the familiar clacking sound of a suppressed rifle firing.

He knew he was too entangled with his man for him to present a clear target, and though Grunn and the masked man's partner were also in close proximity, her opponent was better exposed.

Taking him out would free Grunn, who could then take out the Tracker.

This was all that needed to happen, but with every second that passed, Tom's hope that he would find his way out of this diminished.

He thought of Stella, of not getting to her like he had promised he always would, and felt a rush of anger, which increased to rage as he watched the pistol in Grunn's hand turn slowly, its muzzle closer and closer to being aimed at her chest.

Despite his rage, and the adrenaline surge it had triggered, Tom was helpless.

Barely maintaining his hold on his wrist, he braced himself for what would follow once his grip was lost.

In that moment, his world would end.

He'd be deprived of Stella, and she would be deprived of him.

He was sweating, his skin slick, and there was nothing he could do as his wrist slipped to his fingertips and the arm he was struggling to keep bent straightened slightly.

And then his hold on his wrist was gone and he felt his arm extend even more, felt the pressure on his elbow begin as his opponent applied torque.

Tom's arm was almost fully extended, and for an instant he thought he could hold out, maintain this stalemate, but it was a false hope.

His strength suddenly gone, his arm gave out, and he felt a sharp pain in his elbow as the Tracker prepared to apply the devastating lock.

Tom felt a scream building in his lungs when he heard a gunshot.

But it wasn't the clacking he'd been anticipating.

It was a loud cracking boom.

Specifically, the cracking boom of a .357 Magnum being fired just feet away.

Instantly, the man's hold on Tom was gone.

It was as if he had evaporated.

Tom slipped free and saw Stella standing over the Tracker, her Smith & Wesson in both hands. She remained poised for a follow-up shot, should it be necessary.

Tom looked at her in disbelief, but there wasn't time for that. He scrambled to his knees, rising so he could rush to Grunn and grab hold of that weapon before she lost her fight.

But he was too late.

Her opponent had torn the pistol from Grunn's hand, and sensing Tom's movement, turned and rose to one knee, quickly aiming at Tom.

The distance between them was maybe ten feet. Point and shoot would be all that was required.

Tom was between Stella and the last of the Algerian's men.

He heard her tell him to get down, but there wasn't even time for that. The man was squeezing the trigger, the weapon lined up perfectly with Tom, when Tom at last heard the clack for which he'd been waiting.

He watched the left side of the man's head explode.

Then his body dropped, the pistol landing unfired on the gravel.

By the time Tom looked toward the SUV, Krista was already hurrying to them, her AR-10 aimed at the downed man.

Tom faced Stella.

She was still holding her .357 in a two-handed grip, the muzzle now aimed safely at the ground.

For a moment all he could do was stare at her.

Once again, because of him, she'd been required to kill.

He could tell by her eyes that the gravity of what she'd just done was not lost on her.

Self-defense or in the defense of another, killing a man wasn't easy.

Or at least it wasn't supposed to be.

Stella asked if he was okay.

Tom more read her lips than heard her.

He nodded, then said, "Where's the girl?"

Stella looked over her shoulder at the corner around which Tom had briefly taken cover.

Valena emerged from behind it but did not move more than that.

Krista had reached them by then, extending her hand to Grunn, who took it. She pulled the injured woman to her feet.

"We need to exfil," Krista said. "Now." She spoke loud enough for Tom to hear.

Stella called to Valena, who ran toward her.

Krista told Stella to help Grunn, and Stella hurried to position herself beside the woman, holding her up.

"I'm okay," Grunn insisted, though she clearly wasn't. She could barely stand, and her eyes kept blinking.

Valena moved quickly to Grunn's other side and carefully took the woman's arm and wrapped it around her own neck.

Tom noted how fast the teenager had moved, jumping in to help without having to be asked or instructed.

She'd seen her share of violence even before her mother had been attacked and killed.

And that only reminded him that, like he had once been, she was now alone in the world.

"Stay with me," Krista said.

The awkwardness he'd always seen in her was gone, replaced with a sharpness that exuded confidence and efficiency.

She was a person who knew what she was doing, as well as what needed to be done.

A person comfortably in command.

Tom glanced at the battle belt around her waist.

Attached to it were a number of MOLLE pouches, one of which was marked with a red cross, the grips of trauma shears protruding from its top.

A bleedout kit.

The belt also held several magazine pouches, combos that contained both pistol and rifle mags.

And suspended from the belt's right side and secured to her quad by a strap was a holstered pistol.

Her loadout—choice of gear and placement of it on her person—was that of a patrol soldier.

Krista withdrew the pistol from its holster—a Heckler & Koch .45—and offered it grip-first to Tom.

"The weapon's hot," she said.

Despite the fact that she had told him it was loaded, he nonetheless proceeded with a brass check to confirm that a round was in fact chambered.

"I'll take point," Krista said to him, her voice raised so he could hear her.

Implicit in her order was that Tom was to cover their escape.

He deferred to her.

And he noticed then that all her piercings had been removed.

Krista led the three women away, and Tom followed.

They passed the shot-up armored SUV, beside which lay Grunn's two men, Sheridan and DiBano.

Both were dead.

Grunn looked at them as she was moved past.

Tom did the same before he came across the man he had shot and killed from the safe room shooter's perch.

When Stella reached his pickup, she paused, but Krista kept moving.

Turning back toward Tom, Stella had a confused look on her face. He knew she was wondering why they didn't take his truck to Krista's farm.

Tom said to her, "It's not safe."

"Why not?"

"It was out of my sight for too long. Someone could have attached a tracking device."

She nodded, then turned and continued on.

Tom stopped and faced the building behind them.

Engulfed by fire, it would be a smoldering hulk by the time the sun came up.

Right now, though, it gave off a heat that was almost unbearable as Tom watched everything he and Stella had worked for being consumed by flames.

His hearing still damaged, he suddenly detected a faint voice. Someone was calling his name.

"Tom! Tom!"

He turned to see that Valena was running back for him.

Stella and Grunn were still following Krista, though Stella was slowing and looking back over her shoulder at Tom.

Valena kept speaking, but Tom couldn't hear her.

It wasn't until she was right in front of him that Tom could make out what she was saying.

"Sirens are coming!"

Tom glanced toward the road and saw flashing blue and red lights approaching.

Maybe a half mile down the dark road, but moving fast.

Valena grabbed his arm and pulled him forward.

Together, they cleared the border trees and made the open field beyond. Tom slipped his arm free so she could run ahead as he held back and covered their retreat.

It had taken them a minute to cross that field, though, and the farm was still two miles away.

What was slowing them was their one wounded.

Tom caught up with Stella and took charge of Grunn, half carrying her, half guiding her along at a pace faster than she could manage on her own.

He spoke encouragements to her, and she was trying her best, but she was winded and broken and fading fast.

She stumbled several times, requiring Tom to slow till she could find her footing.

Finally, though, he hoisted her into a fireman's carry and set out on the long haul to safety.

Thirty-Two

Krista drove the Jeep, Stella beside her in the passenger seat.

Grunn was seated in the back compartment, Valena in the rear seat along with Tom, the AR-10 cradled between his legs.

Stella studied the mirror out the passenger-side window, while Krista checked the driver's rearview mirror.

They were looking for headlights on the dark road behind—anything to indicate they were being followed. It wasn't until they'd covered a few miles that it was safe to conclude that no one was after them.

Tom had Krista's bleedout kit and was using the small penlight he'd found inside to check Grunn's eyes.

The limited dilation of her pupils meant that she was concussed.

He instructed Valena that it was her job to keep Grunn awake.

Valena went right to work, leaning over the backseat and talking to Grunn, rubbing her shoulder, ready to jostle the woman if she began to slip into unconsciousness.

Tom moved between the two front seats. "I need some answers."

Krista looked at him in the rearview mirror and nodded.

"You're one of Raveis's."

"I was trained at his compounds. But he's not the one who gave me this assignment."

"Then who did?"

She hesitated. "Cahill."

"How did he know where to send you?"

"What do you mean?"

"When you first showed up, when we hired you, how did he know where Stella and I were?"

"I don't know. I'm just protection. I go where I'm assigned."

Stella was watching her silently.

It was clear that she was experiencing mixed feelings—gratitude, certainly, but confusion and even a little anger. Tom understood why.

The woman she'd known for nearly two years had been inserted into their lives by the very men they'd done everything possible to elude.

More than that, the employee she had befriended—taken under her wing because she just seemed so awkward and helpless—was far from the stray she had believed her to be.

"Does Raveis know our location?" Tom said.

"I'm not in communication with him."

"That's not an answer."

"I don't know what he knows. If he does, I didn't tell him."

"Have you been in communication with Cahill?"

"No. I was only to report to him when and if there was a problem. It was a deep-cover assignment."

Tom had other questions—countless others—but there was a more pressing matter at hand now. "Where are you taking us?"

"There's a safe house one hour north."

"Who knows about it?"

"Just me."

"Are you sure?"

Krista nodded. "Cahill told me specifically to keep its location from him."

"Why?" Stella said.

Krista looked at her. "I didn't ask. I just assumed it was for your protection." Then Krista said that she needed to collect everyone's cell phones.

Stella wanted to know why.

Tom answered that it was procedure.

"There's a Mylar bag in the glove compartment," Krista said.

Stella found the bag, and Tom collected Grunn's phone, handed it along with his own to Stella, who added hers to the collection and put them inside the bag.

Krista offered her own phone as well.

Stella said to Valena, "Do you have a phone, sweetie?"

Valena shook her head.

Stella folded the bag closed, effectively blocking any signals from being sent or received by the devices.

"Is there a GPS unit in this vehicle?" Tom said.

Krista answered, "Yes."

Tom nodded. "Good."

But he didn't ask for the device. Instead he touched Stella's shoulder.

She looked at him for a moment.

Then he sat back in his seat, and they rode on in silence through the last hour of darkness.

PART FOUR

Thirty-Three

The sun was rising when they arrived at their destination.

Tom felt the Jeep slow, turn, and come to a stop.

Only then did he realize that he had drifted off in the rear passenger seat, his head against the window.

Looking out, he saw an old church atop a small hill.

Built of Vermont granite, its two-story steeple stood like a sentry tower above a front entrance of double-arched doors.

Ornately carved doors, fashioned out of a heavy wood.

The rest of the building—a long rectangle with rows of narrow stained glass windows on either side—extended back a good one hundred feet.

Tom quickly studied the surrounding property.

There was a parking lot large enough to hold maybe two dozen vehicles, situated halfway between the back road and the sloping path leading up to the church.

On the right side of the structure was a brief yard; on the left, an old cemetery, its faded, tablet-style stones crooked, its ground uneven.

Beyond three sides of the property was a forest of evergreens and hemlocks.

Tom exited the vehicle first, followed by Krista.

He walked to the front passenger door and opened it, handing the AR-10 to Stella.

She gave him the .357, which he tucked into his jeans at the small of his back and concealed with his sweatshirt.

Krista had removed her battle belt before getting behind the wheel for the hour-long drive, but her HK .45 was now in a paddle holster she wore at the four o'clock position on her right side.

At the same position on her left side was a double-mag carrier.

Tom studied the church. "You own this?"

"No."

"Who does?"

She hesitated. "A man I know. A good man. He and his wife took me in and raised me. He came from nothing—worse than nothing—and now takes care of people when he can. Young people, mainly."

"What's his name?"

"Everyone calls him Mac."

"I need his full name."

"Declan MacManus."

"And where is he now?"

"He and his wife live up north, not far from the Canadian border."

"So you grew up in Vermont?"

Krista nodded. "One of the conditions Mac had for taking me in was that I had to find an after-school job. I started out washing dishes in a restaurant a lot like yours. After a year I made my way up to kitchen prep, then eventually line cook."

Tom thought about that for a moment—how perfectly suited she was for this particular assignment—then said, "So, this Mac guy just happens to own an abandoned church an hour from where Stella and I lived."

"No. I told him what I needed, and he found it for me. He's done well for himself, buys up distressed properties and sometimes gives them to people to make homes out of. My life would have been very different if he hadn't taken me in. He's the reason I joined the military."

"What branch?"

"Army. I was an MP."

Tom looked at the church, saying nothing.

He knew too well that what appeared to be a sanctuary could also be a trap.

What offered protection could also imprison.

Krista sensed his apprehension. "No one knows that I'm connected to him," she said. "Not Cahill, not Raveis, not anyone. This place is safe, I promise."

It was a moment before Tom spoke again. "How long since you were here last?"

"I came here on my day off last month."

"We need to make sure it's secure."

Krista led him up the path to the church. She unlocked the front door and entered, Tom behind her.

A keypad was mounted on the wall to the right of the door. Krista approached it and punched four numbers. The beeping of the security system ceased, and she led Tom through the foyer and into the main room.

The stillness and near darkness was like that of a cavern.

He saw rows of pews divided by a wide aisle, at the end of which was an elevated altar.

The layout was virtually identical to the Episcopalian church Tom had attended as a boy with his mother and sister.

To the right of the altar was the door to what had likely been the reverend's office. Another door was in the far left corner. In the church of Tom's youth, that had led down to the basement.

Above the foyer behind Tom was a balcony and organist's perch.

It was clear that this church had been shuttered for a long time, because the air was both stuffy and raw.

He asked Krista whether the heat worked.

"Yes," she said. "The thermostat is in the office. It's set low. I'll turn it up. In an hour the place will be warm."

As she walked into the aisle, Tom said, "I'm curious about something." She stopped and faced him.

"You're not the way you used to be," he said. "Toward me, I mean. You never used to be able to look me in the eye. You barely even spoke to me. I'm assuming this is the real you, but why the act? Why go out of your way to make things so awkward between us?"

Krista shrugged. "I really wasn't going out of my way to do that. I guess I'm just not very good at lying to people. I was afraid of slipping up. Cahill warned me that you guys were smart. And anyway, sometimes you'd look at me in that way you have of looking at people, and I'd wonder if you knew."

"I have a way of looking at people?"

"Yes. Stella calls it 'the Sexton Stare.'"

Tom said nothing.

"Yeah, that's the one," Krista joked. She paused. "She says your stare is what first attracted her to you. She says she could feel your eyes on her. I always felt like you were looking right through me. Like you knew." She paused again. "Did you, by the way?"

Now Tom shrugged. "I don't know. You showed up looking for a job exactly when we needed you. I guess maybe I was keeping an eye on you. I don't trust a lot of people."

Krista smiled. There was a genuine sadness to it, but there was also a hint of the awkwardness Tom had seen before.

"Yeah, it gets kind of lonely, doesn't it?" she said.

Tom recalled Stella's ongoing concern with the fact that Krista didn't seem interested in finding a boyfriend.

He now understood why.

More than that, he recognized the sacrifice she'd made while assigned to keeping him and Stella safe.

"Thanks," he said. "For everything. And for what you did this morning."

"It's my job."

"You do it well. I'll make sure Cahill knows that."

Krista nodded once.

"One more question," Tom said. "Did you know our real identities?"

"No."

Tom thought about that, then nodded and said, "I'm Tom."

"Nice to meet you, Tom."

"And is Krista your real name?"

"Yes. Cahill had said it needed to be that way, in case you ran a background check."

"He thinks of everything, doesn't he?"

"Pretty much, yeah."

"I'm assuming protocol requires that you'll need to contact him."

"I already did."

"When?"

"The moment I heard the first shots. I transmitted to him the location of my safe house. He should be here soon."

Cahill was likely airborne at this moment, heading by helicopter for what was now no more than a heap of charred timbers. From there he would be flown on to this location.

So Tom had maybe two hours, tops, to do what needed to be done. "You have some clean burner phones here, correct?"

"Yes."

"I'll need two. And Stella will need access to the Internet. That's her real name, by the way. Stella."

"It suits her," Krista said. "I have a laptop and a portable hot spot here. Everything's secured down in the basement."

"I'd like the phones as soon as you can get them. And then I'll need to borrow your Jeep, too."

Krista nodded. "No problem. I'll get the heat on first. After we get everyone inside, I'll make sure you're geared up." She paused. "Can I ask where you're going?"

Tom shook his head. "No. But I shouldn't be gone for long."

Later, Tom returned the .357 to Stella, who was seated in a pew with Krista's laptop beside her.

In her life prior to meeting Tom, Stella had been a successful realtor and investor.

The recession had put an end to all that.

But she still had access to the necessary industry websites, so it had taken her only a few minutes to complete the research Tom had requested.

She whispered to him, "It checks out. The property was purchased by a man named Declan MacManus. It was a cash sale."

"And the date?"

"The deal closed two months after we bought the restaurant."

Tom nodded. "Good."

They looked at each other for a moment, then Tom said a quiet goodbye and left.

Krista was on the level, so some of Tom's questions had been answered.

But more urgent questions remained. He needed those answered, too.

Using the portable GPS unit in the Jeep, he entered the coordinates that Carrington had shown him when they had shaken hands.

How long ago was that? Tom wondered.

It felt like days but was really only a matter of hours.

The device showed the location and the turn-by-turn directions to it. The map overlay indicated that it was a rural area thirty-eight miles to the southeast.

Due to the fact that the entire route was along secondary roads, the ETA was fifty-nine minutes.

Taking out one of the two phones Krista had provided—the second was in Stella's possession—Tom keyed in Carrington's number.

He recalled Carrington's instructions regarding how Tom was to contact him by text message.

According to Marcus Aurelius, what are the three disciplines contingent in overcoming any obstacle?

All Carrington wanted was one of the three words, so Tom keyed in one—the shortest of the three.

Will.

It didn't take long for a reply to come through.

Location.

Tom composed and sent his response: En route to coordinates. The reply to that came even faster.

Bring shovel.

Attached to the Jeep's hood just below the windshield were a pick and shovel.

Tom shifted into gear and drove.

He had the next hour to think and to organize the many questions he had, but really all he did was relive the end of the home he and Stella had made.

The last hours they'd spent in it—first falling asleep together, and then waking to the barking dog.

Then the hell that followed.

But everything he thought of—every moment he relived—only seemed to funnel him back to what the man he knew as the Algerian had said.

You would, I think, have been better served had you chosen a different path than that of loyalist.

If you had, perhaps, been more like your father.

What had he meant by that?

How did he even know of Tom's father?

But more came.

I see now why he fears you as much as he does.

I see why he wants you dead.

I, too, want you dead.

I dislike loose ends.

Who was this man?

And who was so afraid of Tom that he had sent a professional killer to murder him?

Not just him, but the girl, too.

Out of this cacophony of thoughts arose the question that concerned him the most. The question that both puzzled him and troubled him to his core.

How had this man—this Algerian—found him?

By the time he arrived at the location, Tom's mind was racing.

Despite its four-wheel drive and mud tires, the Jeep could take him only so far.

The last quarter mile he'd have to cross on foot.

Unhitching the pick and shovel, he walked through a sparsely wooded area, stepping over fallen trees and crossing rough ground.

The GPS guided him to the precise coordinates, and once there, he began to dig.

Thirty-Four

It took him only a few minutes to reach the buried cache.

The container was a four-inch-diameter, three-foot-long PVC pipe with caps on its ends.

Pulling it from the ground, Tom unscrewed one of the caps and upended the tube, pouring its contents onto the ground.

Everything the pipe contained was stored inside plastic Ziploc bags.

The heavier things came out first.

A pistol and loaded mags, one smartphone with a backup battery charge, a folding knife, several bottles of water and protein bars, and an IFAK—individual first aid kit.

Among the lighter things were a leather holster, a map, and a small compass.

The last to come out was the lightest of them all—a letter, also sealed in a Ziploc bag.

Tom opened the letter and recognized the handwriting as Carrington's.

The second thing he noted was the date at the top, which was roughly one week after he and Stella, with Carrington's assistance, had closed on the restaurant.

Tom,

If you're reading this, you're in trouble. Or maybe I'm the one in trouble, and you're hoping to help me. Whatever the case, here are some things you might need.

I know you're a 1911 man, but enclosed is a Glock 30S and four mags.

The sights are Trijicon HD night sights. They're a little higher than the stock sights, so keep that in mind. I know you're not a fan of polymer-framed subcompacts chambered in .45, but I've replaced the stock guide rod with one made of tungsten, and the added weight under the barrel should help reduce the muzzle flip.

Obviously, the Glock is smaller than your 1911, so you can conceal it more easily, but its mags hold ten rounds instead of eight, and that extra firepower might come in handy.

Let's hope, of course, you don't need the thing at all.

The pistol has a round in the chamber, and the mags are loaded. Couldn't find those lightweight, high-speed frangibles you like, so I've included these new polymer rounds that I find interesting. They're fluted, which helps build up kinetic energy as they spin through the air, and even though they're nonexpanding, the increased speed helps create a massive initial wound cavity upon impact.

Nothing but the best for us, right?

If you need my help, you know I will do everything I can. Recruiting you all those years ago was one of the best things I've ever done. Maybe the best.

I'm proud of the man you turned out to be. Always
remember that, no matter what.

    Your Skipper,
    J.C.

Tom folded and pocketed the letter, then proceeded to gather up
the gear.

It was too much to carry, so he checked the PVC pipe and found
a small backpack crammed deep inside.

He loaded the pack and slung it over one shoulder, then holstered
the Glock, sliding the holster into his waistband and clipping it to his
belt.

As he started to backtrack his way out, he powered up the
smartphone.

Halfway to the Jeep, however, he stopped to look around.

He needed to make sure of something, and this forest was as
secluded an area as he was going to find, so now was the time.

Stepping off the path, Tom drew the Glock from its holster and
sighted on a half-fallen trunk roughly twenty-five feet away.

This pistol's grip angle was significantly different from his Colt's,
so his initial aim was high and to the right.

It took a minor adjustment to place the orange dot of the front sight
just below his intended target.

Remembering what Carrington had written about the Trijicon
sights, Tom eased the muzzle up until the target was obscured by the
dot.

Then he fired a single shot, striking his target dead on.

The bullet's impact sent fragments of wood flying.

Even with the tungsten guide rod installed, the weapon's kick was
wild—certainly wilder than the kick from his heavier, all-steel Colt.

Fully extending both arms, Tom leaned forward more than
usual and this time went for a controlled pair—one shot followed

immediately by another, the goal being to place the second shot just above the first one.

The first shot was dead on, but the second landed high and to the right.

Tom knew this meant he was anticipating the felt recoil, so he made another set of adjustments to his two-handed grip.

Raising his right thumb in a wide sweeping motion, he wedged the webbing between his thumb and forefinger up against the spur.

This would help minimize the leverage created by the weapon's high-bore axis.

Covering his right hand with his left, Tom squeezed the heel of both palms against the grip, which allowed his right hand to relax.

This in turn ensured that he could manipulate his trigger finger without affecting the aim.

He sent another controlled pair downrange, these two hitting the target exactly as he wanted, the second shot landing just above the first one and creating a keyhole pattern in the wood.

Tom then shifted to a fallen tree that was twice as far away and fired another controlled pair, replicating the results.

He holstered the weapon.

Seven shots had been fired.

The Glock had held eleven—one in the chamber and ten in the mag.

He exchanged the nearly spent mag with a fully loaded one.

Out of the forty-one rounds he'd begun with, thirty-four remained.

Tom was approaching the Jeep when he heard a buzzing sound coming from his backpack.

He swung the pack around and pulled out the smartphone he'd retrieved from the cache.

It was vibrating, and while the number on the display was not one he recognized, it made sense that Carrington would use a burner phone to contact this one.

The message was another set of coordinates.

Tom entered them into the GPS unit.

By the time he reached the Jeep, the active turn-by-turn directions were in play.

His destination was just fifteen minutes away.

He was directed to a single-story motel in a small town.

The main street was all of five blocks long.

The motel had fourteen rooms, but only three cars were in the parking lot.

Just one of those cars—a Ford Escort—bore Connecticut markers.

Tom parked beside that vehicle.

Getting out, he stepped to the passenger door and glanced inside.

A rental form lay on the passenger seat.

The vehicle wasn't parked in front of a particular door but rather between two of them.

Of those two rooms, only one had a piece of black electrical tape stuck to the bottom right-hand corner of its door.

Tom approached and knocked gently, but the door was unlatched and the force of his knock was enough to swing it open slightly.

He moved the door back a little bit more with his toe and scanned the room, but he saw no one.

Entering, his palm on the grip of his holstered Glock, Tom made a quick search, ending with the bathroom, where he found a nearly empty bottle of Oban scotch by the sink.

He was back in the room and making another scan when he heard a cell phone ring.

The sound was muffled, but he tracked its location source—the bureau.

Stepping to it, he pulled open the top drawer.

Inside was a cell phone, resting on top of a stack of crisp twenty-dollar bills.

Tom answered the phone. "Where are you?"

Carrington ignored the question. "I left money for you, Tom. Take it and get Stella and go. I don't want to know where, just go somewhere safe and lay low. I'll start working on new identities for you two as soon as I can. I'll contact you by the phone in your hand when they're ready."

"What's going on?"

"We'll stick to a similar protocol as before. Turn this phone on between five and six every afternoon. But drive a few miles from wherever you are before powering up. And keep the battery removed the rest of the time, just to be safe."

"Skipper, what's going on?"

"Hammerton was attacked last night. At his apartment. I don't know the details. All I know is he's gone missing, just like Frank Ballentine."

"Jesus," Tom said.

"It's a shit storm."

"Men came for us, too."

"I know."

"How do you know?"

"Cahill contacted me. He told me about Hammerton. How bad? The attack, I mean."

"A dozen operators, full tactical."

"Stella?"

"She's safe. An operative Cahill had planted helped us get out."

"Yeah, Krista was one of my recruits."

It took Tom a moment to process what this meant.

"You told Cahill where Stella and I were living," he said finally.

"Yes. He wanted to assign a close-protection agent, so he came to me. I thought it was a good idea. And I knew the perfect person for the job."

"Who else knew where we were?"

"As far as I know, it was just me and Cahill. It's possible Krista was his private asset and that he paid her with his own money, didn't inform Raveis or the Colonel of his plan. But he also could have been acting on orders when he came to me—the Colonel's orders, Raveis's orders, orders from the both of them. They don't really tell me a lot these days."

"Then why did they go through you to contact me yesterday? If any of them knew where to find me, why didn't they just come to me directly?"

"I'm guessing so you wouldn't ever know that they knew exactly where you were. You made it perfectly clear to them on your way out two years ago that you wanted a private life. Letting you think they respected your wishes was a way to keep the peace so you'd be there when they needed you."

"Why didn't you tell me about this? About Krista being a close-protection agent. You could have reached out and told me back then. You could have told me when I saw you yesterday."

"I was under instructions not to tip you off."

"Whose instructions?"

"Cahill's. The cover we made for you and Stella was good, Tom, so I figured no one would find you and you'd never know about any of this. Anyway, I needed them to trust me again. The Colonel and Raveis. Following Cahill's instructions—all his instructions—was a way to start earning their trust back. The job was shit, and so was the pay. I was going fucking stir-crazy. I wanted to get back to what I do best."

"You said the job *was* shit."

"I can't go back there. It's not safe."

"Why not?"

"Because we're all marked men. Every one of us. Someone is making a move against the Colonel. Someone on the inside. That's the only way the Algerian could have found you. The Colonel's organization has been compromised, probably for even longer than they suspect. None of our secrets are safe. When you can't know who to trust, it's time to go dark."

"Any idea who came after Hammerton?"

"No. But if he was taken alive, I feel for the man, because whoever has him is going to do whatever it takes to get him to spill everything he knows. And Hammerton knows a lot." Carrington paused. "I'm starting to think that's what happened to Frank Ballentine. I'm thinking he was their first attempt at breaching the organization. They took him and wrung out of him everything he knew. If he's lucky, he's dead."

Tom said nothing.

In that moment of silence, he heard the sound of a tractor trailer approaching, then quickly passing.

An instant later he heard the same sound coming from the cell phone's earpiece.

Carrington was nearby.

Hurrying to the door, Tom looked in the direction the rig had gone.

He saw several blocks of two-story brick buildings—a mix of shops and restaurants with apartments above.

On top of a building three blocks away stood a sign: BONAZZA BUS LINE.

Tom began walking toward it.

"You there?" Carrington said.

"Yes." Tom needed to stall. "Did you drink that bottle of Oban yourself?"

"I left a little for you."

"You were supposed to stay sober. They won't ever take you back if you're drinking."

"It's not like you're going to tell on me, right? And anyway, it doesn't matter. It's all falling apart, Tom. So I'm disappearing, and I'm staying disappeared. I need you and Stella to do the same. I couldn't live with myself if anything happened to you."

"You're panicking, Skipper. That's not like you. There's something you're not telling me. What is it?"

Carrington paused before answering. "I hate to even think this, but there's the chance that Hammerton's disappearance might not be what it looks like."

"I don't understand." Tom crossed one block, two more to go.

"What happens to a mole when he's no longer useful? He's killed by those he served, right?"

"Hold on. You're telling me you think Hammerton is the rogue agent."

"Think about it. Four men were sent after Ballentine—four men Hammerton easily took out. That drew out Ula Nakash, who was killed by another team of men who, according to Cahill, seemed to be going out of their way to spare the life of someone in that van. At least, at first they were. And the minute one of those men got reckless and started shooting into the van, he was cut in half by the leader of the attack. Remember, Hammerton was one of the three people in that van. The next night the Algerian comes after the girl, has a whole team of men with him, hard hitters in full tactical gear. That's a wet team. That's annihilation, not abduction. So if she wasn't the one in the van they were trying to spare, and men had already come after Ballentine, then that leaves Hammerton, doesn't it? And how else did they find you so quickly, Tom? Someone had to have told them."

"Hammerton is not capable of betrayal. I know the man. I owe my life to him. He owes his to me."

"Men change, Tom. And he's getting on in years. He's got to be thinking about his future at this point."

"It's not possible."

"Don't let your sense of loyalty stop you from seeing what's in front of you."

Tom repeated, "It's not possible. And anyway, how would Hammerton know where I was?"

"He's a resourceful man, we both know that. But think about it. The attack on him happened around the same time you were attacked. That sounds like a purge to me. That sounds like someone looking to tie up loose ends."

Tom recalled what the Algerian had said to him about disliking loose ends.

He picked up his pace then, had no doubt that this exertion was audible when he spoke.

"Listen, I think we should stick together," he said. "We should go away together, the three of us. Safety in numbers, right?"

"No, it's better if we remain separate. One can move faster than three."

"What if I need to find you?"

"You can't. That's the way it has to be. For my sake as well as yours. Once I have new identities, I'll let you know where to pick them up."

"I need to be able to contact you, Skipper. With everything that's going on, I may need you."

Carrington hesitated, then said, "This phone will be on every day at five for an hour. Do you remember the four-digit code you texted me two years ago when I was hiding out in White Plains?"

Tom did.

The year that Benjamin Tallmadge, George Washington's spymaster during the Revolutionary War, had died.

"Yes."

"I'll reply when and if I can," Carrington said. "Good luck, Tom."

"Wait. The Algerian said something to me. Something about my father."

Tom heard only silence from the phone as he crossed onto the third block.

At its far end was the bus station. A bus was poised to pull out of the parking lot and onto the street.

"He seemed to know my father," Tom continued. "Or at least know of him. How is that possible? How would a man like that have known my father?"

There was more silence.

The bus began to pull out.

"Jesus," Carrington said. His tone was grave. "You're about to go down a road you shouldn't go down, Tom. The Colonel and Raveis, they've been manipulating you from the start. I couldn't tell you. I'm sorry. I wanted to. I almost did a thousand times over the years. Just listen to me and leave. I wouldn't trust anyone, not even Cahill at this point. Get Stella and leave and never look back."

The bus pulled out and swung right, passing Tom as he stood on the sidewalk.

His hope for answers was slipping away. "He said he understood why he fears me," Tom said. "Who is he talking about? Who fears me?"

He scanned the tinted windows but could see only the vague shapes of the dozen or so passengers within the bus.

When Tom got no reply, he said, "Are you there? Skipper?"

"You might not want to stay out in the open like that, Tom," Carrington said. "There's always the chance I was followed here." He paused. "Good luck, son. I'll be in touch."

The bus roared past Tom and rolled down the street, leaving a blast of air that smelled of diesel exhaust.

Tom could only stand silently and watch the bus go.

The call had been ended.

He looked around before turning to make his way back to the motel room.

He studied every car that approached and passed him, looked over his shoulder every few steps to make sure no one was behind him.

It took two minutes to reach the motel.

Inside the room, he grabbed the money, a stack of twenties that was three inches thick.

It had to be at least five grand.

Climbing into Krista's Jeep, Tom steered out of the parking lot and began to backtrack. He texted a single word to Stella as he drove.

STATUS.

If there was a problem, she was to reply one way, and if all was well, another.

Her answer came through in a matter of seconds.

Safe.

Still, as he steered out of town, he found himself pushing the speed limit as much as he dared.

Thirty-Five

Of the men Tom trusted, he had fought beside only three.

Carrington and Cahill and Hammerton.

He'd served under Carrington in Afghanistan.

He'd fought beside Cahill the night he led the rescue that saved Cahill's squad.

A rescue that had ended with Cahill attempting to shield Tom from the fragments of an exploding grenade.

And with Frank Ballentine carrying the two of them to safety.

Tom had fought beside Cahill again in New York City two years ago, after which he'd been taken to the Cahill compound on Shelter Island and reunited with Stella.

Tom's friendship with Hammerton was a more recent one—and the briefest.

But their bond had been forged within the same crucible of violence.

If not for Hammerton, Tom would have been killed in an abandoned machine shop in Connecticut.

And vice versa.

It was likely, Tom knew, that Stella would have never learned what had happened to him that night, and it tore him up to imagine her waiting for him, first for hours, then for days, then weeks and months and years.

Each man had sacrificed something for Tom.

And Tom had risked everything for each of them.

How could he not trust any of these men?

And how could he not defend one, even as they turned against each other?

Carrington's plea for Tom to get Stella and leave had its appeal. Of all the unknowns before him now, this was the one he could embrace.

The one he *should* embrace.

But he needed the truth, whatever shape that took, or he'd be running from an unknown, not just toward one, and that wasn't something he was willing to do.

That was no way for a man to live.

Even for a man who was as willing as Tom was to be nothing more than a ghost.

As he crossed the last few miles, Tom focused on those three contingent disciplines necessary to overcoming any obstacle.

Perception, action, and will.

All he had now were those parts of himself.

He was the only person—the only man—that he could trust.

Tom parked the Jeep and looked up at the solitary church atop the small hill.

There was plenty of space for a helicopter to land in the surrounding open ground, but Tom saw no sign of one.

Exiting the Jeep, Tom began to climb the hill.

Reaching the church, he moved along its right side, listening as he went for voices coming from within but hearing nothing.

The majority of the windows were stained glass, but one just past the halfway point had a missing panel that had been replaced with a pane of clear glass.

Tom looked through that window and saw Krista standing by the main door, guarding it, her AR-10 ready.

Shifting his position, he spotted Stella in the front row of pews.

She was with Valena and Grunn.

Tom walked to the front door and knocked. Krista unlocked it and let him in.

He asked whether there was any word from Cahill.

"He's almost here," she answered.

"Good. I'll need your HK."

Without hesitation, Krista drew her sidearm from its holster and handed it to Tom.

He walked down the wide aisle to Stella, took her hand and squeezed it.

"Everything okay?" she said.

Tom nodded and looked at Grunn. "How are you?"

Grunn shrugged. "Alive."

"Do you think you need to see a doctor?"

She shook her head.

Then Tom addressed Valena. "How are you holding up?"

"I'm fine," she said.

Tom could tell she was anything but that.

He also understood her reason for bravado.

He'd felt the same defiant self-reliance when he'd been left alone in the world. "Do you have any family in the United States?"

Valena shook her head.

"Anyone here your mother was close with? A friend? Woman or a man?"

She hesitated, then glanced at Stella. "No."

Tom took a breath, let it out, and said, "A friend of mine is coming here. He and I are going to talk. Whatever happens, you might be with us for a few days. Maybe even longer. Are you okay with that?"

Valena nodded.

Tom offered a smile. "You don't talk much, do you?"

She shook her head.

"Me neither," Tom said.

Krista was still by the foyer, guarding the front entrance. He gestured toward the door to the left of the altar. "Is there a way out of the basement?"

"No. Why?"

Tom heard the distance drumming of helicopter rotors, approaching from the south.

He said to Stella, "Take Valena into the office, okay?"

Stella released Tom's hand and took the girl's. Standing, she led the girl toward the door to the right of the altar.

Tom waited till they were in the room and the door was closed before he held out the HK45 for Grunn to take.

"Anyone other than Cahill walks through that door, open fire," he said.

He turned to Krista. "Same goes for you."

Grunn took the pistol.

Tom said, "When Cahill gets here, tell him I'm waiting downstairs."

The drumming grew louder, was starting to sound now like distant thunder.

"You sure you're okay, Grunn?"

"Yeah."

"Good. I'll see you after."

Tom walked to the basement door.

Moving through it, he headed down the stone stairs.

By the time he reached the bottom step, he could no longer hear the rotors.

Thirty-Six

Tom waited in the dimly lit basement.

The space was empty, save for Krista's gear, which was stowed in several lockable storage containers stacked on a single pallet not far from the stairs.

There was nothing Tom could use to build a maze or take cover behind, should it come to that.

The air was dank and chill, but he unzipped his hooded sweatshirt anyway so he could more easily reach Carrington's Glock.

Then he stood with his hands hanging at his sides and listened.

The sound of the rotors, muffled but unmistakable, reached him as the helicopter landed somewhere outside. That noise ceased as the powerful engine was shut down.

There was nothing for a moment—Tom counted a minute, then another—but then he heard the church door open and close.

He waited for some kind of commotion from above—voices raised, running feet, shots fired—but all he heard were calm voices, two of them, male and female.

Cahill and Krista.

Tom could not make out their words but didn't need to; Krista had more than proven herself to him.

Eventually, the door at the top of the stairs opened. Cahill moved through it, closing the door behind him and proceeding down the steps.

Reaching the bottom, he looked at Tom before scanning the basement to confirm that they were alone.

Then he faced Tom again.

He made no motion, simply stood still and stared at Tom. "You look like a man with a lot of questions."

"It would be best if you kept your hands where I can see them."

Cahill nodded. "I'm not your enemy, Tom."

"Where's Hammerton?"

"You spoke with Carrington."

"Yes. Where's Hammerton?"

"That's one of the many unknowns we're dealing with."

"What happened, exactly?"

"Some men came to his place. He was keeping an eye on Ballentine for me. Despite his injuries, Hammerton killed the men and fled."

"What about Ballentine?"

"Unknown as well."

"Hammerton lives in New York. You can't move a block in any direction there without being caught on surveillance cameras. Piecing them together will tell you if he left the city or if he's still somewhere in it."

"We're working on that. Gathering all that footage takes time."

Tom nodded. Finally he said, "Who else did you tell about Stella and me?"

"No one."

"Then how did those men find us so fast?"

"That's another unknown we need to figure out. It would help if we knew exactly who they were."

"The leader was an Algerian. And someone else was with him. He wore a ski mask, but there was something about his eyes."

"You recognized them."

"Not exactly. It was more of a context thing. Like a vague feeling of déjà vu. I can't explain it any better than that."

"At what point did you have that feeling?"

"When he was above me, with the night sky behind him."

Cahill thought about that, then said, "Did you get a good look at the Algerian's face?"

"Yes."

"I'm going to reach into my jacket for something, okay?"

Tom nodded.

Cahill removed a folded piece of paper, held it out, but didn't make a move toward Tom.

Tom stepped to him. Taking the paper, he unfolded it and saw that it was a photocopy of a charcoal sketch of a man's face.

"Is that the man you saw?"

Tom said it was and handed the paper back to Cahill, who folded it and returned it to his pocket.

"Did he say anything to you, Tom?"

"He said a lot."

"We'll need to debrief you while it's still fresh in your mind—"

"Whose idea was it to send Krista?" Tom interrupted.

"We'll fill you in, I promise. There isn't a lot of time, we should get moving."

"Fill me in now."

Cahill took a breath, let it out. "It was the Colonel's idea. But he didn't know the details of the operation. He wanted to be kept in the dark."

"You paid her with your own money."

"Yes. Her salary was transferred by wire every month out of a trust I'd set up through an attorney, so it was untraceable. She knew where you were, obviously, but she had no idea who you were. So the only people who knew the location of Tom Sexton and Stella Quirk were, in effect, me and Carrington."

"Are you sure about that?"

"As far as I can be, yes."

"Which means?"

"I can only be sure about my actions. Carrington, on the other hand, is an alcoholic. He's the wild card here, Tom. One of the reasons why I got him the job at Taft was so that Sandy Montrose would be able to check his urine regularly."

Tom had forgotten that Sandy didn't just live on a farm less than a mile from the school—she was its resident physician.

"And?" Tom said.

"He was always clean."

"But you're still suggesting that he got drunk and shot his mouth off to Hammerton."

"What does Hammerton have to do with this?"

"Carrington raised the possibility that Hammerton is the rogue agent you've been looking for."

"Do you believe that?"

"I don't know what to believe. That's the only reason I'm still here."

"What else did Carrington tell you?"

"That the Colonel has been manipulating me from the start."

Cahill's pause indicated that he had not been expecting that.

"Is it true, Charlie?" Tom said. "Has the Colonel been manipulating me?"

"You should talk to him about that."

"He's not here, you are."

"I'm not at liberty to discuss that."

"Don't give me that."

"Tom."

"I need to know, Charlie. Please."

It took a moment for Cahill to answer.

He was obviously searching for the right words. "Certain events in your life weren't as innocent as you were led to believe."

"Which means?"

Cahill hesitated again.

"What does that mean, Charlie?"

"It means that when Carrington found you all those years ago and recruited you to his recon engineer team, it wasn't your then-commanding officer who had recommended you to him, like you'd been told. He wasn't the reason why Carrington came looking for you at the range that day."

"Then who was?"

"The Colonel, Tom. The Colonel was the reason Carrington was there. He sent Carrington to recruit you."

"Why?"

"So someone could keep an eye on you. More than that, though, he wanted someone to begin the process of grooming you."

"For what?"

Cahill gestured to the space in which they stood.

The dark basement of a hidden safe house.

"For this," he said. "For the day in the future when he'd need you. Didn't you ever wonder why Carrington retired right before your eight-year enlistment was up? He bowed out before he'd put in his twenty years. He forfeited his pension, Tom, with only a few years to go. He did that because the Colonel offered him the money he needed to start his own security firm, which of course was just a cover so Carrington would have the means to recruit you and others like you into the intelligence community. Everything Carrington did for you—transfer you to his recon team right out of boot camp, offer you work as a private contractor after your discharge, help set up you and Stella in your new life here—everything he did for you, he did on the Colonel's orders. Every moment he was at your side, during and after Afghanistan, he was doing so as the Colonel's man." Cahill paused. "He was guiding you, Tom, without you even knowing it. He was making sure that when the day came and the Colonel needed you, you'd be right where he could find you. And you'd be ready."

Tom uttered the only words he could. "Why me?"

Cahill didn't answer.

"Why me, Charlie?"

Once again, Cahill made a point of choosing his words carefully.

But there really was no delicate way to put it.

"Because of your father."

"My father was an engineer," Tom said. "He helped governments around the world plan and rebuild infrastructure. He was a consultant."

"He was that, yes. But that was just his cover. In reality, he worked for the Colonel. Raveis was his handler. For a time there, in fact, Raveis and your father were apparently close friends."

This time Tom couldn't find even a single word.

Cahill gave him a moment before continuing. "Your father was in the navy before you were born, correct? That's why you enlisted after you dropped out of Yale, right? Your father entered the navy as an engineer, but by the time he left it, he was part of naval intelligence. The Colonel recruited him right away. This was back when the Colonel was still CIA, before he saw the way the world was going and left for the private sector, where he wouldn't be constrained by laws and treaties and senate oversight committees. He knew things were going to get bad, and he wanted to be free to do what the CIA or NSA or DHS couldn't do."

Tom barely heard this, had on his mind only one question.

What he didn't have was the will to ask it.

Or more accurately, he lacked the courage to hear the answer.

But he had no other choice; he'd come here for answers.

"My mother and sister weren't killed in a home invasion, were they?" he said finally. "They were killed because of him."

Cahill nodded. "The police settled on a home invasion as the explanation because that's what the evidence bore out. The killers staged it to look that way. Of course they didn't know what your father really was, and maybe it wouldn't have changed their conclusion if they had known. Small-town cops tend to think small-time. But the Colonel and Raveis had no doubts that it was an attempt on your father's life. The four men weren't criminals who randomly targeted your house. They were a hit team sent to assassinate your father in his home. A last-minute business trip had kept him from being there."

Tom had always wondered how differently things might have gone that terrible night had either he or his father been home.

Sometimes, in the years immediately after the murders, he'd catch himself fantasizing about a scenario in which he and his father had both been there. Tom a competitive wrestler, his father a combat veteran.

Could they have fought the men off?

Tom had never before felt what he was feeling now, though.

He was overwhelmed with resentment, angry that his father's secret life was what had brought that terror into their home.

It was an impossible thing to comprehend—that this two-decades-old event was something other than what Tom had always believed it to be.

Just as impossible to process was the fact that his entire adult life had been directed, to a significant degree, by forces of which Tom had been largely ignorant.

But he knew that he had to clear away the emotions triggered by this seismic shift in those long-held perceptions.

Of the many things that Carrington had taught him, the words of Marcus Aurelius were what mattered now.

Perception, action, and will.

In that spirit, Tom needed to know one final detail. "Who sent them?" he said. "Who sent those men to kill my father?"

"The Colonel doesn't know who carried out the hit. Or if he does, he hasn't shared that with me. Considering the lifespan of men in that line of work, though, chances are they're all dead by now. But the Colonel knows who ordered it."

"Who?"

"Tom, I think you should hear this from him—"

"*Who? Who ordered it?*"

Cahill remained calm, spoke in an even voice. "It was ordered by a man the Colonel has been hunting ever since."

"The Benefactor," Tom said.

Cahill nodded. "So you understand now, right? Why the Colonel has invested in you the way he has. Who better to send after a murderer than the son of one of his victims, right? That's the mission he's been grooming you for. And that's why the Benefactor sent men to kill you last night. At some point he became aware that George Sexton's son was one of the Colonel's most-guarded assets. He had to kill you before you could be activated—before you even knew what it was the Colonel wanted you for. What we need to determine now is not just how he knew where to find you, but how he knew about you in the first place. We need to know who tipped him off to you and when, because as it stands now, it could have come from one of only two people. I'm standing here, unarmed, and the other has gone into hiding."

"We've been here before," Tom said. "You thought the same thing about Carrington two years ago. You were wrong, and men got killed. Carrington ended up risking his life to save mine."

"So maybe it wasn't him, Tom. Maybe there's something we can't see yet. He fits the profile of a double agent, though. Disgruntled, broke, alcoholic. I think we can all agree on that much. But if not him, then who? Hammerton, somehow? Would that scenario really be any better? And I'm not just talking the damage either one of them could do because of what they know. I'm talking about the cost to you because of what they mean to you. And let's not forget, Hammerton didn't know where you were. Or did he, Tom?"

"He didn't."

"I'm curious, how did you and Carrington communicate? What were your protocols this time?"

Tom explained the procedure.

"So anyone who knew that number, and knew when the phone was powered up, could have determined your location."

"I never gave Hammerton that number."

"Maybe he accessed Carrington's phone. For that matter, anyone could have done that. So much for narrowing the suspects."

Tom said, "I want to talk to the Colonel."

"And he wants to talk to you. He's waiting for us at a secure location. My orders are to take you there."

"Stella and the others are coming with us."

"They'll be safe here."

"You had to file a flight plan before you left. Anyone who knows where to look could be able to find out where you went."

"I falsified my destination, Tom. And I flew below radar from your place to here."

"I'm not taking any chances. The men who tried to kill me also tried to kill Stella. And there's the girl to take into consideration. The Algerian came there to kill her, too. Anyway, there's only one place they'll all be safe, Charlie, and you know it. I'm guessing that's where the Colonel is waiting for me right now."

Cahill studied Tom for a moment. "Okay. They come with us."

"Everyone. Grunn and Krista, too."

Cahill nodded. "Everyone, Tom." He was still studying him. "You look a little beat, man. Are you sure you're up for this? Because you might have to make a tough decision before this is over."

Tom ignored the question, though he couldn't ignore the statement. "We should get going," he said. "I need them safe as soon as possible."

He walked past Cahill and headed toward the stone stairs.

Thirty-Seven

The helicopter was a Eurocopter EC155.

As Tom approached it, he looked for a pilot or crew standing by but quickly realized there was none and that Cahill had flown here solo.

Climbing into the pilot seat, Cahill began the preflight check.

Krista took the copilot seat and assisted him.

It was obvious that she, too, knew her way around a cockpit.

Tom and Stella helped Grunn into the passenger compartment.

As Stella buckled Grunn in, Tom turned and saw that Valena was still standing outside. She seemed hesitant to get onboard.

Cahill started the engine, the rotors beginning their slow spin. Still, Valena didn't move.

Over the high-pitched engine whine, Tom shouted, "C'mon," but Valena simply shook her head.

Moving in beside Tom, Stella extended her hand, and eventually the girl took it and was pulled onboard.

Tom buckled her in, then took a seat and secured himself as the helicopter lifted off.

The flight path was to the southeast, and Tom knew it was possible they'd pass over his hometown.

He waited, watching the landmarks pass below.

Twenty minutes after takeoff, he was looking down at a familiar place.

The house he'd grown up in was on the other side of town, so he was spared having to see that.

But the cemetery in which his mother and sister and father were buried was visible.

It was a small but old cemetery, historic, and it held the remains of a number of Tom's ancestors. Men who had fought for their country, women who had borne their children, children who had then married and borne children of their own who had fought for their country, and so on.

Tom was the last of that line, a thought that he'd never considered much before now.

But this was not yet the end of his life, he knew that much.

Not done, not by a long shot.

It wasn't a desire for revenge that instilled in him the strength to keep going.

It was the woman beside him.

And the other women around him.

He would fight for them, just as they would—and had—fought for him.

No one spoke for a long time, and lulled by the motion and sound of the helicopter, Tom fell into a deep sleep.

He woke with a vague sense that he had dreamed but with no memory of what, at least at first.

He decided maybe to call that an improvement.

But it didn't take long before Tom remembered.

He'd dreamed not of the home of his youth under attack—the dream that had tormented him since settling down so close to his home—but rather of the event that had for a time replaced it.

That night in Afghanistan when he had led the rescue that saved Cahill and his recon marines.

He saw and heard what he always saw and heard—the chaos of a fighting retreat through a desert. Tom and Cahill had been covering the rear when the grenade landed. After that, Tom's dream was just a series of snippets. He saw the night sky above him, Cahill torn up beside him, and then he saw the face of the man who had run back to get them.

Frank Ballentine was leaning over Tom, locking eyes with him, speaking words that Tom couldn't hear.

Tom had never been so happy to see a face in his life.

Ballentine had taken Cahill first, leaving Tom to face that dark desert sky alone.

Leaving him to wait for either salvation or death.

Only one of those had seemed certain.

When Ballentine had reappeared, he'd made a point of locking eyes with Tom.

He'd done so in a way Tom would never forget and could never describe.

Then he'd hoisted Tom into a fireman's carry and run with him toward the nearest Humvee.

At one point they had come under fire, because Ballentine had turned, drawn his sidearm, and emptied his weapon into the darkness behind them.

Looking over at Stella now, Tom saw that Valena's head was resting on her shoulder. And Stella's head was resting on top of Valena's. They, too, had fallen asleep.

Grunn was looking out the window, lost in thought.

Tom knew that she was likely thinking about the men she'd lost, as well as her own brush with death.

The muzzle pressed to her head, the weapon in the hand of a professional killer.

A monster with no hint of remorse.

The line of people who wanted the Algerian dead—wanted to kill him or at least wished him dead—was long.

Cahill, Valena, Grunn—they had all lost someone, either by the Algerian's hand directly or by the actions of someone under the man's command.

This lack of emotional investment would allow Tom to feel removed from this group.

He could think rationally when these souls might not, and this, he was determined, would be his role.

He would advise, then do just as Carrington had told him to.

He'd get Stella and leave.

It took Tom these moments to realize that he'd slept for close to an hour.

If they weren't yet over Connecticut, it was only miles away.

———

Thirty minutes later, they were approaching the farmhouse known as the old tavern.

Tom had been there before, when a wounded Hammerton was in dire need of medical assistance.

This was back when Tom had been sent to find Cahill, when the Colonel and Raveis had made their first overt appearance in Tom's life.

A simple search and rescue, he'd been told, that had turned out to be anything but.

Tom had been little more than a pawn, then.

He was much more than that now, though.

The EC155 landed, and they were greeted by Sandy Montrose and her husband, Kevin. The couple led the passengers into the farmhouse and brought them to two rooms upstairs.

Grunn and Krista in one, Stella and Valena in another.

Tom knew that fresh clothes and towels would be waiting, as well as medical attention for those who needed it.

Cahill and Tom, however, headed for the renovated barn at the end of the dirt driveway.

Tom had been there before, too.

The barn housed vehicles and equipment, as well as Kevin Montrose's large animal veterinarian hospital.

Beneath the barn, though, was a fortified bunker that also served as Cahill's command center. Underground, unreachable by any and all electronic signals, it was a safe place to talk.

The Mercedes and Range Rover SUVs parked just inside the barn door told Tom whom he'd be talking to.

Farther into the same bay as the vehicles was an old Hughes 500 helicopter.

A fast and maneuverable chopper, it was the basis of the US Army's MH-6 Little Bird attack helicopter.

Unlike the Little Bird, which had no rear seats inside the cabin, requiring its passengers to sit on benches mounted outside the open rear door, the Hughes was a four-seater with a closed cabin.

Fully refurbished, it was painted glossy black.

Tom wondered briefly what it would be like to have hundreds of millions of dollars, like the Cahill family did.

Unlimited resources with which to accumulate any and all gear one could possibly need or want.

He thought of the Cahill family compound on Shelter Island— private, secure, tranquil.

As appealing as something like that was, what he really wanted was to reclaim the life that had just been burned to the ground.

Or build another just like it.

Moving to the back of the barn, Cahill opened a heavy steel door.

Tom stepped through and descended the steep steel stairs to a second steel door.

Cahill was right behind him.

The bunker was as he remembered it, comprising three shipping containers welded together and buried twenty feet underground. The first container was the communication center, the second a sleeping area, the third a medical bay and galley.

Waiting in the med bay was the Colonel.

And with him was Sam Raveis.

Thirty-Eight

The two men stepped from the med bay to the galley.

Raveis and the Colonel stood in the small eating area while Tom remained in the narrow doorway with Cahill behind him and slightly to his right.

The Colonel smiled. "It's good to see you, Tom."

Tom neither smiled nor responded, simply stared at the man.

The Colonel's eyes shifted to Cahill, who said, "He knows, sir. I told him."

Focusing on Tom again, the Colonel said, "It's a lot to process, son, I know. But a promise was made long ago, and I had every intention of keeping it."

"Whose promise?"

Raveis answered, "Mine."

Tom looked at him.

The Colonel said, "Your father had Raveis swear that he'd take care of you. It was the last thing he said to Raveis. After that, your father went off to hunt the Benefactor and got himself killed."

"You let him go?" Tom said to Raveis. "Alone?"

"I couldn't stop him," Raveis answered. "Believe me, I tried. Believe me, I wanted to. I had tracked him to a hotel in New York. He was in the city to meet someone who would lead him to the men who'd been hired by the Benefactor. It took him two years to track them down. These were the actual men who had come to your house and murdered your mother and sister. His pretense was that he wanted to hire them. I thought I'd talked him out of going—he was supposed to stay put, said he would, but he slipped away on me later that night. He went through with the meeting, was brought to those men, but his rage wasn't enough. He only killed three of them. The fourth one killed him and got away."

Tom knew only a few details of his father's death, some it from the visiting New York City detectives who had filled him in, the rest from newspaper articles.

What he did know was that his father had been found dead in a small hotel room in New York City.

Three other men had been with him, all dead, and all signs indicated that there had been a life-and-death struggle between them.

Gouged eyes, flesh torn by teeth—as brutal and bitter as hand-to-hand combat can get.

Tom had neither sought nor desired to know anything more than that.

Even back then, at the age of nineteen, he had known that he, too, could find himself as consumed by the need for revenge as his estranged father had been.

It had been a conscious choice to turn away and do what he could to forget.

"The Benefactor is old school," the Colonel said. "As the surviving son of a man he'd had killed, you were already marked for death by him. That's the way he does things. No loose ends. That's why we didn't come forward and pay for Yale. We could have done that anonymously, funded your entire education. But you'd have been exposed if you stayed there, an easy target, especially in a city as violent as New Haven. So we were relieved when you joined the navy right after your father's death. We knew you'd be safe for at least eight years. And when you got out and wandered around, we knew you'd be safe then, too. It was a calculated risk when we activated you to find Cahill two years ago, but we had no other choice. And when you left Cahill's compound in the middle of the night and disappeared yet again, well, as long as you were safe and we could reach you through Carrington, then Raveis's promise to your father would be kept."

"And you could use me when the time came."

The Colonel nodded. "That, too, yes. Your father was one of the smartest men I'd ever met. He was born for this work. By all accounts, you're even smarter than he was. And everything I've seen tells me that you inherited his innate skills."

"Your father's murder was our first major loss to the Benefactor," Raveis said. "It signaled his arrival on the world stage. It was the beginning of his rise to what he is now."

"Which is?"

"Chaos," the Colonel answered. "Greed. Brutality. Everything men like us stand against."

"Everything your father was helping us fight," Raveis added.

"I left the CIA, Tom, because your father's murder taught me that in order to fight an enemy who is unconstrained, we needed to be free, too. We needed a team that could and would do whatever it took, even if that meant at times meeting the enemy on his level. We needed a private special activities division, as good or better than the CIA's SAD, but one that had no connection with our government and therefore wasn't bound by any laws or treaties yet could serve national security in ways our government couldn't. A force like that—well funded and completely under the radar—could at the very least act as a check against men like the Benefactor. In the two decades we've been operating, we've had successes and setbacks. We've taken out career assassins and would-be terrorists and black market arms dealers—everyone the Benefactor employs or does business with—but we've never gotten close to the Benefactor himself. In fact, the only times we've ever been close to him are the times he's come close to us. And he was always gone before we even knew he was there. The attack on you, however, that's the closest he's ever gotten. He's getting bolder. He knows things he shouldn't, he's found a way in. We need to know how. We need to know who betrayed us and continues to betray us. We're at war, Tom. It's a secret war, a shadow war between two ghost organizations, but it is war nonetheless. We can't lose, not this one, not to him."

"How can I help?" Tom said.

The Colonel nodded to Raveis, who put on a pair of gloves and removed a phone from his pocket.

He powered the phone up.

"I thought you couldn't get a signal down here."

Raveis didn't answer, just pressed a few keys with his thumb, then turned the phone so Tom could read the number on the display.

It was the number of Tom's burner, the one that for nearly two years he had turned on one hour every afternoon.

"This phone was found in Hammerton's apartment," Raveis said. "That number is the only number stored in it. Do you recognize it?"

Tom nodded.

"It's yours?"

"Yes. I don't understand. How did Carrington's burner phone end up in Hammerton's apartment?"

"It's not Carrington's phone."

"Then what is it?"

"It's a mirror copy of it. And it was made recently. Which means someone got access to Carrington's phone and copied everything stored in it onto this one. Whoever had the mirror copy would not only know every number the original phone contacted, but would be able to monitor any calls and texts to or from that phone. And he could determine its location via GPS."

"More to the point," the Colonel said, "someone with the right resources could locate any of the numbers contacted by the original phone. Hammerton has connections in both US and UK intelligence communities."

Tom shook his head. "I have a hard time believing Carrington would just leave his burner phone lying around, unencrypted. And I don't buy that Hammerton would just leave evidence like that out in the open at his place, either."

"He would have left in a hurry," Raveis said.

"It doesn't matter. I know both men."

"So do we, Tom."

The Colonel asked, "What are you thinking?"

"I'm thinking this isn't adding up. At least not to what you think it adds up to."

"There's a chance that we can use this to bring Hammerton out in the open. If the attack on him and Ballantine is what it looks like—the Benefactor ordered a hit on him to tie up loose ends—then maybe he'll be in the mood to cooperate."

"Either way," Raveis said, "we need to find him. Cooperation or not, we need to know what he knows."

"Then let me go talk to him," Tom said. "We'd have to find him first, so press your contacts in the NYPD for the surveillance footage. Once we know where he is, I'll go meet him. I'd be dead if it weren't for him. And he'd be dead if it weren't for me. If he did betray me, then I doubt it was easy for him. If I'm right, that means I have the best chance of anyone you can send of getting close enough to him to talk."

"And if you're wrong about him?" Raveis said.

Tom didn't answer.

From behind him, Cahill said, "I'm going with you."

"It would be better if I went alone."

The Colonel thought about that, then shook his head. "No. Cahill goes with you. That's the way it has to be."

Tom looked at the two men standing before him, then looked over his shoulder and glanced at Cahill behind him.

Facing the Colonel again, he said, "If something happens to me, I need your word that you will take care of Stella. Give her a new life, maybe set her and Krista up in a restaurant somewhere far away from all this, if that's what they want."

"Of course."

"Call it an investment, otherwise she might not take it. You'll make your money back, I guarantee it."

The Colonel smiled. "We're not worried about that."

"Just trust me on this, okay. She likes to work for what she has. She's not big on charity."

"I understand."

Tom breathed in, exhaled. "So let me know when the surveillance footage has been analyzed and you know where Hammerton went."

The Colonel nodded. "You should try to get some sack in the meantime."

The Colonel and Tom shook hands.

Then Raveis extended his.

Tom hesitated at first, then took the hand of his father's friend and shook it, too.

———

Alone, Tom was approaching the farmhouse when Sandy Montrose exited and met him in the dirt driveway.

"It's been a long time," she said.

Tom smiled as best he could. "Not long enough," he joked.

Sandy laughed, then asked whether she could get Tom anything.

"You can, actually, yes," he said. "Is my old room free?"

Thirty-Nine

The room was small, barely enough space for a bed, and had no window.

Access to it was by a set of narrow stairs located behind a hidden door in the pantry off the kitchen.

During the Civil War, runaway slaves on their way to Canada had spent long nights here.

Tom's one night at the farmhouse two years ago, himself in hiding, had been spent in that room.

Separated from Stella, all he had wanted then was to get back to her.

Now he was waiting to leave her and face the challenge of making his way back to her once again.

Overcoming—or plowing through—whoever tried to get in his way and stop him from doing that.

It was a sick feeling in his stomach, even though he knew she'd be safe here.

Safe from danger but not from the anguish of knowing that a loved one was in danger.

Tom recalled leaving his hometown after enlisting in the navy.

He remembered walking away from his home for the last time, then the bus ride out of town.

Everyone he had ever cared about was dead, so there was no one to miss him or, should he be killed, mourn him.

There had been freedom in that, but there had also been an overwhelming feeling of emptiness.

It was what allowed Tom to do the things he'd needed then to do, and do them without a second thought.

His life wasn't about that anymore—a hollow courage.

It was about fullness.

But right now, that fullness was also an ache. Like a homesickness, but worse—almost painful.

He couldn't dismiss or ignore it, knew he would have to carry it with him as he made his risky journey out and back.

If it was a burden, his love for Stella, then it was one he would bear.

———

Tom and Stella had been alone in that room for more than six hours.

It had to be night by now.

They had talked, then slept, talked some more, and slept again.

At one point, Stella was looking for a tissue and opened the top drawer of the table beside the bed.

She didn't find a tissue there, but she saw a Smith & Wesson M&P Bodyguard chambered in .380, resting next to a fully loaded mag.

Now she and Tom were seated together on the bed with the lights off, listening to the sounds of voices coming up from the kitchen below, waiting for the inevitable sound of footsteps on the hidden stairs.

"There's something I've been wondering," Stella said.

"What?"

"Is it possible that Carrington was the masked man?"

"No," Tom said. "Carrington is right-handed."

"Cahill's right-handed, too. And Hammerton was in New York at the time, so it couldn't have been him."

"Correct."

"But you've seen his eyes before."

"Something like that, yeah."

"Why would he wear a mask, though? I mean, whoever he was, if he was there to kill you—to kill all of us—why bother concealing his identity? Why would it matter if you saw his face?"

"People wear masks for three reasons. The first one is so they can't be identified. The second is to shock or instill fear. His had this grotesque human skull for a face. It was like the face of death. The third reason someone wears a mask is so they won't be seen. It gives them a sense of anonymity. Maybe he couldn't do what he came to do with me looking at him."

"You mean with you recognizing him."

"Yeah."

Stella watched him for a moment.

"I'm sure you'll find the answers," she said. "You always do."

Tom waited a moment, then said, "How are you holding up?"

"The last time we went through something like this, it was a shock. I didn't see it coming. But I know who you are, and I mean that in a good way. I know what being with you means. I wouldn't be here if I didn't. And I don't think either of us fooled ourselves into thinking this day would never come. It was always just a matter of time, or at least that's what I thought. I'm just glad we were prepared when it did." She smiled. "And I'm glad we hired that weird girl with tattoos. She's something, huh?"

Tom nodded. "She is."

"You wonder how a person can do that, you know. Be someone they're not, maintain their cover day in and day out. No wonder she seemed so . . . lonely. And all this time I thought I had taken her under my wing, when really she had taken me under hers. Everything we did, all that training, she was just prepping me."

"That's why I stayed away from this line of work. No one is ever who they seem. At least your surprise was a good one."

"And she learned how to do all this from Raveis?"

"Him and his people, yeah. He has compounds around the country, that's where they do their training. Why do you ask?"

Stella shrugged. "Just curious. You meet people like that, see what they can do, and you wonder if you have what it takes to be like them."

"I don't think you ever have to wonder that about yourself, Stell." Tom paused. "Thanks for before, by the way. For ignoring me when I told you to keep running."

She smiled. "Yeah, well, you should know, Tom, I don't always do everything you tell me."

The voices downstairs ceased.

The outside door opened and closed, there were footsteps in the kitchen, and a moment later, the door at the foot of the stairs opened as well.

Stella and Tom listened as someone climbed the stairs.

She smiled and kissed Tom.

A long kiss that neither wanted to end.

But it had to, and leaning back, Stella said, "Come back to me, Tom. In one piece. That's an order."

Cahill led Tom through the kitchen.

Grunn and Valena were seated at the long wooden table with Kevin and Sandy Montrose. Several dishes of food were spread out before them.

Tom looked at Grunn and Valena as he passed.

"I'll see you guys in a little bit," he said.

Exiting the farmhouse, he walked beside Cahill toward the three-story barn. Instead of entering it this time, they headed around to a small landing pad behind it.

On the pad was the Hughes 500, and in its cockpit running through the preflight checklist was Krista.

Tom said to Cahill, "I thought we were going alone."

"We need another pilot."

"Why?"

"Where Hammerton is, there's enough room to land the Hughes, but we can't leave it there. She'll set us down, then take off and assume a holding pattern above. Also, if he's hurt, I can't fly and apply first aid at the same time."

Tom nodded as they reached the helicopter.

Krista started the engine.

"Where is he, by the way?" Tom said.

"He's hiding out in the Bronx."

"Where exactly?"

"The last place anyone would look for him," Cahill said. "Ally or enemy."

PART FIVE

Forty

The Hughes touched down in a fenced-off courtyard surrounded on three sides by the shuttered Baychester Motel.

Tom saw that the pavement was riddled with cracks through which tall grass had grown.

He and Cahill exited and stepped away from the helicopter, and within seconds it was airborne again, rising high above them.

It wasn't long before the sound of the rotors was just a muffled thumping in the distance.

Cahill was wearing a small ranger backpack containing a full field-med kit.

As always, he was armed with his subcompact Kimber.

Tom had the Glock 30S that Carrington had given him, along with the spare mags.

Cahill led the way to the center of the three buildings. Reaching the concrete steps to the second floor, he spotted a blood trail.

He and Tom followed it up to a room in the middle of that wing.

Moving to one side of the door, Cahill removed his Kimber and stood ready. Tom took the other side but didn't go for his Glock.

"Hammerton, it's Tom," he called. "I'm coming in, okay?"

Tom waited, repeated himself when he got no reply, waited again.

Finally, he opened the door, letting it swing back a few inches by its own weight, and peered around the door frame.

He saw a room void of all furnishings, but to the left of the door was a makeshift wall comprised of stacks of concrete mix.

Stepping inside, Tom scanned the room, then stepped forward so he could see what was behind the stack.

Slumped against the wall was Hammerton, the floor around him blood-smeared; his eyes were closed.

Beside him was his Belstaff shoulder bag, on top of which lay an open bleedout kit, its contents scattered.

Tom hurried toward Hammerton. "Get in here, Charlie."

He knelt down at Hammerton's left side. Cahill entered, rushed around the stacked bags of concrete, and knelt at Hammerton's right.

Swinging off his backpack, Cahill laid it aside and immediately began to assess the man's wound. To do so, he had to peel back the Israeli battle dressing that Hammerton had applied to a gunshot in his abdomen.

The dressing was soaked with blood.

Hammerton opened his eyes then, or tried to; he could raise his lids only halfway at best.

"It's about time," he muttered.

"Don't talk," Tom said. "We've got you. You're going to be okay."

As Cahill looked at the wound, the expression on his face turned from concerned to grave.

Hammerton's eyes closed again. Breathing was difficult; he could only manage rapid but shallow inhalations.

Tom glanced at the location of the wound.

It was an inch below Hammerton's right rib, meaning it was likely that the round had struck his diaphragm. If it had pierced his lung, the wound would be making a sucking sound every time he breathed in.

"We're going to get you out of here," Tom said.

"All of our safe houses were blown," Hammerton whispered. He was rambling. "I didn't have anywhere else to go."

Cahill asked, "Why didn't you call for evac?"

"They took my phone. Didn't have a backup."

"Who took your phone?"

Hammerton didn't answer.

"Hang tough," Tom said. "We're going to stabilize you, then get you out of here."

Hammerton shook his head, then forced his eyes open and looked for Tom.

His doing so, Tom knew, was an act of pure will.

Tom shifted so Hammerton could see him without having to strain. "I'm right here. I'm right here."

Hammerton said, "You need to know something."

"Save your breath."

"I need you to listen to me." His voice was hoarse. "I didn't hang on this long for the fun of it. I've been watching the door for . . . I don't know how long. I've been waiting for someone to get here . . ."

Again, Hammerton's eyes fluttered and closed.

Tom remembered lying in the Afghan desert and waiting for Ballentine to come back for him.

In reality, it had been only minutes for the recon marine to return, but they were the longest minutes of Tom's life.

Hammerton had been here bleeding and in pain for eighteen hours.

Tom felt a wave of compassion for his friend, could well understand the fear and aloneness he must have felt, wondering whether he had been abandoned, minutes turning to hours, hour after hour.

Cahill said, "He needs to stop talking, Tom."

Before Tom could say anything, Hammerton spoke.

"The kid bolted," he said. "Ballentine. He bolted."

Cahill shook his head in disgust. "I never understood why Raveis put him in the field," he said to Tom. "He just wasn't ready. They rushed him. Unless they were using him as bait. Or maybe they were counting on him being motivated, like they were with you."

Hammerton let his frustration show.

To have waited so long only to be unable to make himself understood had to be maddening.

He put everything he had into his voice. "*No.* It wasn't that. He didn't bolt when the attack started. He bolted before it started. Like he knew what was about to go down. Like he knew it was coming."

Tom and Cahill looked at each other.

Tom leaned close. "What are you saying?"

"One minute he was standing there in front of me, asking if he could borrow my phone. The next thing I know, he's running off with it. By the time I figured out what he was up to, it was too late."

Neither Tom nor Cahill spoke.

Hammerton turned to Cahill. "It always bothered me that they didn't shoot into the van. That bothered you, too, right? I figured they wanted the girl alive for some reason. But now I know the person they didn't want to kill was him. The kid. Ballentine."

"But a hit team came after him," Tom said. "Just a few hours before. You stopped them, remember?"

"I'm good at my job, but I'm not that good. Those men didn't know what they were doing. Pros wouldn't have filed into a doorway one right after another the way they did. Their last man in certainly wouldn't have put his back to the street."

"Ballentine was wounded," Cahill said. "You're saying he let himself get shot."

Hammerton shrugged. "I don't think he's as inept as he made himself out to be. I don't think his mistakes were mistakes at all."

"Why do you say that?"

"You can tell how deadly a man is by the way he stands. It's just a feeling I had, I'd see him sometimes and there was something there. And anyway, Raveis trained him. Raveis could make a commando out of my dead granny." Hammerton shrugged again. "It's possible he didn't let himself get shot. Those men could have panicked and forgotten their orders. Or they could have gotten carried away. You get what you pay for with thugs, and those men were the bottom of the barrel in every way."

"The attack was staged," Tom said.

Hammerton nodded.

"Why?" Cahill said.

"To set everything in motion. Draw the real targets out into the open."

"Valena and her mother."

"Maybe," Hammerton said. "Or maybe one of us. Or all of us. Because this sure feels like hunting season to me. Like someone wants every person in the Colonel's organization dead."

"You're saying Ballentine works for the Benefactor," Cahill said. "But the Benefactor had his older brother killed. That's why Ballentine came to us. He wanted to help find Frank."

"How much help was he, really? Ballentine shows up with a sad story and all the documents we're desperate to see, and we buy it. Meanwhile, he's doing everything he can to derail the search he volunteered for. And learning the identity of our best operators and the location of every safe house in the Colonel's network in the process."

"He's the breach," Tom said.

Cahill shook his head. "But that doesn't make sense. Why would he do that? Why would he work for the man who had his brother killed?"

Hammerton said, "It could be his brother isn't dead. What if he didn't disappear? What if he switched sides? The Colonel only just told us about the breach, but I'm guessing it started long before the kid came on board."

"Why would Frank do that? Why would he betray us?"

Hammerton shrugged. "Why does anyone do anything? For the money."

Cahill needed a moment to process that. "But how could the Benefactor even approach him? He was one of our best. He was undercover. I can't imagine him slipping up."

Hammerton shrugged again. "Maybe someone sold him out. Someone who knew the Benefactor was looking for someone to turn."

Cahill thought about that, then said to Tom, "The kid signs up, feeds intel back to our enemy, and when the time is right, the Benefactor makes his move. And he starts by going after the only person who can identify his number one assassin."

"The attack on Ula pushes everyone out into the open," Tom said. "Like dominos falling."

"And exposes you to the Benefactor. Suddenly he sees his chance to eliminate the son of a man he'd had killed. A son the Colonel has been protecting and grooming for over two decades. You become a priority-one hit, so he sends a team of men to kill you and the girl, men led by his best assassin."

Tom froze for a second, his eyes looking off to the right.

Then he quickly snapped out of it and looked at Cahill.

"What?" Cahill said.

"Shit," Tom muttered.

"What?"

"I knew I'd seen his eyes before."

"Whose eyes?"

"The masked man."

Tom remembered his attacker hovering above him in the dark last night.

He remembered, too, Frank Ballentine appearing that night in Afghanistan as Tom lay wounded.

Frank had left to carry Cahill to safety, had been gone for what felt like an eternity.

But then he'd finally returned, his shadowed face all but obscuring the night sky.

His eyes, all that Tom could see of him, had locked in a way Tom would never forget.

Those were the same eyes he'd seen last night—a context that was both similar and different.

He remembered one final and damning detail.

Frank Ballentine hoisting him into a fireman's carry and starting toward the waiting Humvee. Turning when they came under attack and raising his sidearm, firing into the dark desert behind them.

And there it was now for Tom to see, as clear as if he were back there.

Frank Ballentine's marine-issue Colt 1911 had been in his left hand.

"Frank *is* alive, Charlie. He was there last night. At my place. He got the Algerian out of there when Krista opened up."

"Jesus," Cahill said.

Tom leaned close to Hammerton again. "Do you know where the Ballentine kid would go?"

"No."

Tom turned to Cahill. "It's possible they could track him with the surveillance footage, right? Like they did Hammerton."

"No time for that," Hammerton said.

Tom looked at him. "What do you mean?"

Hammerton was fading. It took everything he had now just to draw breath.

"I need to stabilize him or he can't fly," Cahill said.

He reached into his backpack and pulled out a fresh dressing, tearing open the vacuum-sealed wrapping with his teeth.

Working fast, he applied the dressing over the bleeding wound. "Christ, he has lost a lot of blood."

Tom waited for as long as he could, then leaned closer still to Hammerton. "What do you mean there's no time for them to track him?"

"When we were at the old tavern the day after our attack, I saw something. Raveis's men were about to put the girl into the Colonel's caravan. I was watching from a window. Ballentine came over to say goodbye to her. I saw him whisper something into her ear. She nodded, and he leaned back, and it looked to me like she was slipping something into her pocket. Something he handed her."

"What?"

"I couldn't see. I didn't think too much about it at the time. He was close to her and her mother, you know. Closer than we're supposed to get. But if it was a cell phone, maybe what he whispered was something like, 'Don't lose this or let anyone take it from you.' Or he could have been assuring her that he was only a phone call away. I mean, the poor girl had just watched her mother die. She was suddenly surrounded by a bunch of strangers in suits holding automatic weapons. He was the only person she knew, and she probably thought she could trust him. He probably did everything he could to cultivate that. Which would mean developing an attachment to her wasn't Ballentine screwing up, it was Ballentine doing the job he'd been sent to do."

Hammerton paused to catch his breath. "And if it was a cell phone he gave her," he said, "then Ballentine could be using it to track her. Everywhere she went from yesterday on—wherever she is now, wherever the Colonel has put her for safekeeping—Ballentine would know. And what Ballentine knows, the Benefactor and all his goons know."

Tom thought about what the Algerian had said.

The girl has something I need.

Tracking a cell phone could cut both ways, revealing the locations via cell towers of the person being tracked and, via the metadata stored in the phone's memory, the location of the one doing the tracking.

Their enemy would know that as well.

Killing the girl wouldn't be enough.

To fully conceal their tracks—to remain as ghosts—they'd need to secure the phone she'd been given as well.

No loose ends.

When Krista had asked for cell phones as they'd departed for her safe house, Valena had simply shaken her head.

Obviously, Cahill had reached the same conclusion, because he said to Tom, "Go. Now."

Tom was torn, didn't want to leave his wounded friend.

The man to whom he yet again owed so much.

"I'll help you get him downstairs," Tom said. "We'll fly him back to the old tavern with us, Sandy can patch him up."

"He wouldn't survive us carrying him to the copter, Tom, never mind the flight back. I'll get an ambulance here, ride with him to the emergency room. He needs more than I can do anyway." Cahill pulled a small radio from his pocket and spoke into it. "Tom needs immediate exfil."

From the radio came Krista's voice. "Copy. Coming in."

Cahill returned the radio to his pocket and withdrew his cell phone, punching in *911* with his bloodied thumb.

"You need to be gone before the cops get here," Cahill said. "Go. Call Stella now. Tell her to get everyone in the bunker and not come out for anyone but you. At top speed, you can be there in thirty minutes."

Tom was still looking at Hammerton.

"Thank you," he said.

Hammerton nodded, closed his eyes, then opened them again. "Do me a favor, huh? Kill that little fucker for me."

Tom rose and sprang for the door as Cahill completed the 911 call.

His smartphone in hand, Tom stepped out into the chilled spring night.

He ran the length of the landing, then down the concrete stairs, and was in the courtyard and keying in Stella's number as the Hughes descended.

It touched down on the cracked pavement, the overgrown grass fluttering under the rotor wash.

Tom had the phone to his ear as he climbed in next to Krista.

Forty-One

Stella was seated alone at the kitchen table, her eyes on the clock above the stove and a cup of hot tea in her hands. The table was oak, old, and long enough to seat six people comfortably.

On it, right in front of her, was the cell phone that Tom would text when he was on his way back. Not far from that was her .357. When she wasn't looking at the clock, she was looking at the phone.

The farmhouse was quiet, Grunn and Valena in the living room, Sandy and Kevin in a small office just off the front entrance.

The place had been still like this for hours, and Stella was reminded of the silence in which she and Tom had slept in their rooms above the restaurant.

A tranquil and hidden world that was now gone.

She couldn't remember the last time she'd been alone for this long; Tom was almost always with her, or at least always nearby.

And when she wasn't with Tom, she was with Krista, either working or training after work.

The next logical thought was that Tom might not return—not in the next few hours, not tomorrow, not ever.

But she could not let her mind go to that horrible place.

What was about to happen—what he would have to endure and overcome in order to make it back to her—was out of her hands.

It was an understanding she didn't much care for.

Her tea was cold but only halfway gone when she heard the sound of commotion coming from the front of the house.

A door was opened, followed immediately by footsteps moving quickly.

Seconds later, Sandy was hurrying into the kitchen, Kevin close behind her.

There was no mistaking their urgency.

Professional and calm and well practiced, but urgent nonetheless.

Stella asked what was going on.

Sandy answered, "We have wounded incoming."

Stella's heart stopped. "Who?"

Kevin exited through the kitchen door and started toward the barn.

Sandy said, "He didn't say."

"Who didn't say?"

"Hammerton. He's bringing someone in. They're just minutes away."

Stella was confused. "Why would he wait till just now to alert you?"

Sandy opened the pantry, reached in, and grabbed a backpack off the shelf. She was a flurry of activity, her mind focused on the tasks at hand. "I don't know. The text came from his phone. The emergency code was correct."

The backpack over one shoulder, Sandy exited, following the same straight line toward the barn her husband had.

Rising from the table, Stella moved to the kitchen door and drew the curtain aside. Through the window she could see that Kevin was already at the barn.

Sandy was crossing the dirt driveway, moving now at an all-out run. Then she, too, entered the barn.

Grunn appeared in the living room doorway. "What's up?"

"Someone's coming in."

"Who?"

"I don't know."

"Wounded?"

"Yes."

A moment later, a vehicle turned into the driveway and began to slowly roll past the house toward the barn.

As the vehicle stopped at the oversize door, Sandy and Kevin rushed out to greet it.

Sandy went around the nose to the driver's side, Kevin around the rear to the door behind it.

Valena entered the kitchen and stood beside Grunn. "What is going on?"

Grunn told her that someone was here.

The driver's door opened, and a person Stella did not recognize got out.

Opening the kitchen door, she moved through it and stepped onto the small porch.

Sandy seemed to know the driver.

He was young, dark-haired, handsome.

He had a middleweight boxer's build and moved fast.

Stella knew Hammerton, and this wasn't him.

She heard the driver say to Sandy, "He's in the back."

Kevin moved to open the back door, and Stella stepped off the porch.

Drawn forward, she was desperate to see who exactly was in the backseat.

Desperate to know whether or not it was Tom.

Kevin opened the rear door but blocked Stella's view.

She took a step, then another, was ready to break into an all-out run toward the car but stopped short when she heard a clacking sound.

The sound of a suppressed gunshot.

Kevin dropped to the ground, and before Sandy could react, the driver grabbed her and placed one hand over her mouth.

In the other hand was a subcompact pistol, which he pressed to her temple.

Face-to-face with her, he told her to shut up as the occupant of the backseat emerged.

The man with the suppressed firearm—another man Stella did not recognize.

But there was a second man inside the vehicle, and he had gotten out of the passenger side the instant the driver had grabbed Sandy. As this man came around the rear of the vehicle, Stella saw him and felt her gut tighten.

His face was hidden behind a mask.

A mask depicting a grotesque and grinning human skull.

The mask of death.

Turning, Stella ran back to the kitchen door. Valena was standing there, looking past Stella at the driver.

Stella could tell by the look on the girl's face that she had reached the door after the shooting.

"That's Dante," Valena said.

She seemed pleasantly surprised to see him.

But her look of surprise was replaced by recognition that something was not right when Stella grabbed her by the shoulders and pushed her into the kitchen, then closed the door and locked it.

Valena could see through the parted curtain the men with weapons drawn coming toward them.

She could see, too, Ballentine with his pistol held to Sandy's head.

Rushing for the kitchen table, Stella grabbed the .357 and said to Grunn, "Help me get the table to the door."

Grunn met her at the heavy table. Together they began to push it across the floor.

Valena watched, confused, but then she joined in.

Her added strength made the difference.

They got the table to the door, then flipped it onto its side, setting it up as a temporary barricade.

The phone flew off the tabletop, landed on the wood floor, and slid under a hutch.

And only then did it ring, indicating an incoming call.

But there wasn't time to get it.

Stella grabbed Valena and guided her to the pantry, pulling her through it and to the hidden door at its far end.

Opening the door, she pushed Valena through. "Go up the stairs. Lock the door behind you. Don't come out for anything, okay?"

Valena nodded and climbed the steep stairs.

Closing the concealed door, Stella first made sure that it fit flush with the wall before returning to the kitchen.

Men were already at the door, though she had no idea how many.

Grunn was waiting at the entrance to the living room, Krista's HK45 in her hands.

She whispered, "C'mon," but just as Stella began to cross the kitchen, someone kicked the door.

Two kicks were all it took to splinter the wood around the dead bolt.

The door opened a few inches, and in the space between it and the door frame was the masked man.

That limited view was more than enough for her to see that he was a large man with a powerful build.

And he was readying for a third kick.

Raising her .357, Stella took quick aim and applied smooth pressure with her index finger to the trigger.

The hammer moved back, then sprang forward, striking the cartridge primer and firing the round.

But the masked man had seen her and used the time it had taken her to work the double-action trigger to move from her line of sight just as the revolver went off.

Stella recovered from the recoil and was re-aiming when a breaching shell fired from a shotgun shattered the top door hinge.

An instant later, a second shot did the same to the bottom hinge.

Flying wood splinters struck Stella in the face. Ducking and turning away, she didn't see the door being pulled outward, leaving an opening that was obscured only by the upturned table.

As heavy as the thing was, it wouldn't be much of an obstacle for that man.

The masked man kicked the table back and was poised to enter, but that changed when he saw something off to the right of the kitchen.

Grunn was on the move, firing the HK one-handed as she rushed toward Stella.

The pistol was large for her hand and heavy, plus the recoil of the .45-caliber round was too much for one-handed shooting.

But it was suppressing fire she was laying down, so accuracy didn't matter.

Reaching Stella and pulling her to her feet, Grunn backtracked toward the living room as she continued to fire toward the kitchen door.

The full-size HK held a thirteen-round mag, so with a round chambered, she had fourteen rounds at her disposal.

Grunn had unleashed eleven by the time she had gotten Stella to the living room, leaving only three.

And she spent those last three as she moved through the door.

But she had no backup mag, so she dropped the pistol and guided Stella farther into the dimly lit room.

Mounted on a wall was a cabinet containing a half dozen hunting rifles. Grunn hurried to it, opening the glass door and removing a double-barreled shotgun.

Stella's cheek had been cut by the flying fragments of door and hinge, but she rubbed the blood away with her left hand and aimed the .357 at the door with her right.

Opening the break-action weapon, Grunn proceeded to search the drawers beneath the glass cabinet for ammo.

It was the third drawer she opened that held what she was seeking.

Lunging for the box, she grabbed two cartridges and was feeding the first one into the shotgun when they heard the sound of footsteps in the kitchen.

Forty-Two

Heavy footsteps, closing fast.

Grunn had gotten only one shell loaded, but there wasn't time for the other, so she swung the breach closed and shouldered the shotgun.

The first hint of a shadow appeared and she fired, the double-aught buckshot taking chunks out of the door frame.

Grunn pushed the top lever aside with her thumb, opening the breach and ejecting the spent shell.

She was loading the second one, her eyes on the door. Stella was looking there, too, her .357 now held by both hands.

Neither of them saw the man making his way down the hallway that led past the small office and to the front entrance.

The entrance neither had paid attention to.

The man took a step into the room, raised his pistol—a Walther PPK—and aimed at Stella.

Right behind him was the driver, the man Valena had identified as Ballentine.

He was holding Sandy roughly by one arm and pressing his sub-compact to her temple.

"Drop the shotgun," the first man said.

Stella had heard that accented voice before, outside their home as it had burned around them, set afire by men who had come to kill them.

Grunn laid the shotgun, still unloaded, on the floor.

"Now you," the Algerian said to Stella. His voice was calm to the point of monotone. "Put the revolver down. Please."

As Stella did, the masked man entered the living room from the kitchen.

In his hand was a pistol fitted with a suppressor.

Stella recognized it as a 1911, similar to Tom's but newer, its finish a glossy black.

The masked man walked up to her, and she saw tucked into his waistband yet another 1911.

The wear pattern on its walnut grip was identical to Tom's.

The Algerian said to Stella, "Where is the girl?"

Stella didn't answer.

Taking a step back so he was beside Sandy, the Algerian placed his PPK to her head as well.

The masked man moved even closer still to Stella and raised his 1911, aiming it between her eyes.

Looking at the women, the Algerian said to Ballentine, "Is she here?"

Ballentine lowered his pistol and reached into his jacket, removing a smartphone. Looking at the display, he said, "She is."

"Where?"

"The signal is coming from the back of the house." He nodded toward the door to the kitchen. "Through there."

"Go," the Algerian ordered.

Ballentine went into the kitchen.

The Algerian pushed Sandy to where Stella and Grunn were standing.

Sandy was in shock, Grunn defiant.

Stella couldn't take her eyes off the masked man.

But the three women stood together, facing the men.

A moment passed before the Algerian called out and asked what the holdup was.

Ballentine returned to the doorway. "The signal says she's there, but I can't find her, can't get to where it says she is."

"Maybe she is upstairs or down below."

"GPS only determines location on the map, not height. Anyway, there aren't any stairs off the kitchen. The only door opens to a pantry."

The Algerian crossed to the three women.

He looked at Grunn. "You again." Then he faced Sandy. "This is your house, no?"

When Sandy didn't answer, he aimed his PPK at Grunn but kept his eyes on Sandy. "Where is the girl?"

Sandy was frozen, more by shock than fear.

The Algerian thumbed the hammer back and placed his index finger inside the trigger guard.

Stella thought of her hours with Tom in that hidden room, the voices below at times clearly audible.

She thought, too, of the compact Smith & Wesson in the top drawer of the table by the bed.

"I'll get the girl," she said.

The Algerian nodded to Ballentine. "Go with her. Secure the device. Bring me the girl."

Ballentine pocketed the smartphone, held his Beretta subcompact ready as he followed Stella into the kitchen.

She entered the pantry, but he waited outside, watching as she walked toward the back, wary that it was some kind of trap.

Stella reached the back wall and pushed against one side of it, causing the wall to swing back on a hinge like a door. She stepped aside so Ballentine could clearly see the darkened stairs beyond.

He gestured into the pantry, said, "After you."

She climbed the stairs as he followed, making no attempt to walk softly on the old planks.

Each step creaked, each creak echoed in that narrow stairwell.

At the top, a small landing, three feet long, was all that stood between them and the closed door.

The stairwell they'd climbed had been narrow, but the hallway was even more so. Ballentine brushed against Stella as he moved around her to the door.

She was certain that he did so more than was necessary to get by her.

For a second they locked eyes, and he almost smiled.

Facing the door, Ballentine said, "Valena, it's me. Come out, everything's okay."

But he got only silence.

Ballentine knocked on the door gently, then tried the knob, but it wouldn't turn.

"C'mon, Valena, open up. It's me. We're going to get you out of here, to someplace safer. The two of us. I promised you and your mother, remember? I promised I'd take care of you. So let me take care of you."

Nothing at first, then the sound of the door being unlocked.

Yet the door remained closed.

Ballentine hesitated.

Stella thought of the bedside table, envisioned it just inside the door and to the right.

If she could get to it first . . .

"I'll go in," she said.

Ballentine moved around Stella again, brushing against her, then positioned himself behind her, using her as a shield.

Stella turned the knob and opened the door.

The windowless room was pitch-black.

Stella stepped through and shifted slightly to the right, feeling for the bedside table.

She found it, but what she felt didn't make any sense at first.

The top drawer was open. And it was empty.

The dim light spilling into the room from the hallway barely diminished the darkness, but Stella knew it was enough to make clear silhouettes out of herself and Ballentine.

He remained behind her, though, the muzzle of his pistol pressed into her lower spine.

"Turn on the light," Ballentine said.

Stella felt for the lamp on the table, found the small chain, and pulled.

She knew the room, knew that there was only one bare corner for the girl to back into, so she saw her a split second before Ballentine did.

Not cowering but down on one knee, the .380 held expertly in a two-handed combat grip.

But Stella's advantage didn't last long. Ballentine saw Valena and had enough time to grab Stella and pull her in front him.

Then he aimed his pistol at the cornered girl.

He could only grab Stella with one hand, though, was holding the pistol with the other, and that meant Stella had two hands free.

She needed only one.

Pivoting her hips slightly, she had a clear path to his groin and took it, striking him there with a swift backfist.

Then she lunged for his right arm, threw her torso against it and pushed his pistol off target.

Driving farther to his right until she was no longer in front of him, Stella left Ballentine a wide-open target for the daughter of Ula Nakash.

Valena did what her mother would have done.

What her mother had no doubt taught her over the years they had pursued the man who'd killed her father.

Valena opened fire.

Forty-Three

The shots echoed sharply through the farmhouse.

Two, one right after the other, then two more.

This was followed by the unmistakable sound of a body dropping to the floor.

The Algerian glanced at the masked man, who kept his eyes on the two women before him.

A few seconds passed but no more shots came.

The Algerian said to the masked man, "Go and see."

Following his orders without hesitation, the masked man left the living room and entered the kitchen.

His suppressed 1911 raised, he scanned the room before moving to the door he had broken down.

Standing to the side of it, he peered through.

He detected no movement, saw only the dead man in a heap on the driveway.

Turning back to the kitchen, he identified no other means of egress or entry. The only door at all was an open one that led to a narrow pantry, the two long walls of which were lined with sturdy shelves.

He made his way to the pantry, stopping just outside it when he heard a sound from somewhere within.

A creaking sound—specifically, a wooden step bending under the weight of a foot.

Entering, he paused to listen, heard the sound again, though this time it ceased abruptly, as if someone had stopped midstep.

The only explanation was that the wall straight ahead was a false one and someone was behind it.

The only question that remained was whether it was the woman and the girl or his kid brother.

He took a step closer, then another, only to hear another creak.

But this one didn't come from behind the wall. It came from beneath his own boot. He realized his mistake, but it was too late.

The wall dead ahead began to burst as multiple rounds were fired through it.

Rounds fired from Ballentine's Beretta by Stella.

Several of the initial shots missed, and the masked man turned and ran, bent at the waist. He was nearly clear of the pantry when his luck ran out.

A hollow-point round caught him in the shoulder, another went into his back.

It was the third one that did the most damage, piercing his right lung and lodging in his ribs.

He staggered for a few more steps, enough to clear the pantry, but then dropped face-first onto the kitchen floor.

Stella pulled back the door, keeping the girl behind her as she moved through the pantry.

Blood was flowing from the motionless man's chest as she and Valena stepped over his body.

Stella was aware that the Algerian was still in the next room—just steps away.

She quickly led the girl to the kitchen door and gestured for her to go through it.

Valena didn't move.

Stella mouthed, "Run," but the girl shook her head and remained.

From the living room, the Algerian said, "Frank, what's going on?"

The man was moving.

Stella placed her hand on the girl's shoulder and led her through the door and onto the porch, then made a shooing motion with her hand.

The girl looked at her, but she wouldn't run.

There wasn't time, so Stella reentered the kitchen and positioned herself, taking aim at the door to the living room.

She waited, did her best to control her breathing, but adrenaline was in her blood now.

Surging through her, it caused her heart to pound as if she had just run miles.

But she was used to that.

She was used to pushing herself.

The steps she heard were slow and deliberate but getting closer.

She had no idea how many rounds Ballentine's pistol held or how many she had already fired, but since the slide hadn't locked open on an empty mag, she knew at least one remained.

She scanned the floor, looking for her .357, just in case.

After spotting it on the other side of the room, she put her eyes back on the doorway.

And as she did, someone appeared in it.

Forty-Four

It wasn't the Algerian who crossed the threshold first.

It was Sandy.

Her shock had worn off and tears were streaming down her face now.

Fear and grief gripped her.

She was followed by Grunn, and behind her was the Algerian, his weapon against the base of Grunn's neck.

Stella held her ground, the subcompact Beretta raised and aimed.

The Algerian was squarely behind Grunn, so all that Stella could see of him was one eye as he peered around Grunn's head.

She held the front sight on that eye.

The Algerian told her to drop her weapon.

Stella shook her head.

"I will kill her, and I will kill the other," the Algerian said. "And then I will kill you."

From the corner of her eye, Stella detected motion. Valena had been standing outside the kitchen door, but now she was gone.

The direction she had run—toward the front of the house—told Stella what the girl intended to do.

Just as the Algerian and Ballentine had, she was making her way around to the front entrance.

A short walk down the hallway to the living room, and she'd have a clear view of the Algerian's back across that open room.

But the girl needed time.

"Go fuck yourself," Stella said.

The Algerian was at first confused by this—by her defiance—but then he smiled. "That is what he said to me. Your man. Tom. You two are meant for each other."

"He's on his way," Stella said.

"Good. I hope he arrives soon. In the meantime, I will enjoy causing you agony. And humiliation. I can cause all kinds of both. The sounds of your cries will bring him right to me."

Stella ignored that—or at least wanted it to appear to him that she did.

In reality, fear was like a fist in her gut. "You need the girl," she said. "The phone she has, that Ballentine tracked her with, you need that. Why?"

The Algerian's answer was to lower his PPK and aim it at the middle of Grunn's back.

Stella remembered the feel of the muzzle of Ballentine's Beretta pressed against her spine, the instant and unbearable thought of a bullet severing it, paralyzing her.

"You shoot, she goes down, I shoot you," Stella explained. "Go out the way you came in, and no one's going to chase after you. Get in your car and drive. If you don't, you die."

"Arrogant American woman."

"Like I said, go fuck yourself."

"I'm going to count to three," the Algerian said.

"This is your last chance."

"One."

"Turn around and leave."

"Two."

"Suit yourself."

Before the Algerian could speak, a voice came from behind.

A woman's voice.

A *girl's* voice.

It was Valena, and she was just a few feet away. "Three," she said.

Startled, the Algerian turned, bringing around his PPK, but it was too late.

Valena's first shot was a center-mass hit at point-blank range.

He was a strong man, though, and the .380 round fired by the Bodyguard lacked the power to knock him down.

Grunn quickly grabbed Sandy and pulled her clear of the line of fire, shielding the woman with her body, just as she had been trained to do.

The Algerian was bringing his weapon to bear on Valena, but Stella had more than just one eye to target now.

She put a nine-mil into the Algerian's right rib.

But that shot emptied the Beretta, and he was still standing.

Stella ditched the empty pistol and scrambled across the floor for the .357.

She heard two more shots from Valena's .380, which emptied that weapon as well.

The Algerian was still standing, determined to return the young Syrian's fire—determined to kill every one of these women.

Spoiled American women who dared to oppose him, talk back to him, think they could bring him down.

He had his target in his sights and was placing his finger inside the trigger guard when someone tackled him.

It was Grunn, throwing herself into him and slamming all her weight into his freshly wounded rib, driving him backward. He stayed up for a few steps, but then he came down hard.

Quickly mounting him, Grunn landed several vicious elbow blows to his head, bouncing his skull off the wide planks and stunning him.

Then she went for the weapon in his hand, prying the Walther free with little resistance.

Her right hand closed around the Bakelite grips and her finger covered the trigger as she brought the PPK to his head, pressing the muzzle against his temple.

The hammer was already drawn back, so only a slight amount of pressure would be required.

Leaning close, she looked the Algerian in his eyes and said through gritting teeth, *"Moi encore."*

Me again.

Then she pulled the trigger, killing him instantly.

Stella had grabbed her .357 when she heard the shot.

Getting to her feet, she rushed to the doorway, reaching it as Grunn was rising to her feet, the dead Algerian beneath her.

Both she and Valena were staring down at the man, their chests heaving, their faces blank.

Stella turned to Sandy. "Are you okay?"

Her only reply was to say her husband's name. "Kevin."

She moved past Stella and into the kitchen, but she had taken only a single step before stopping short and gasping.

Stella turned and followed her line of sight to the puddle of blood by the pantry door.

The masked man was gone.

She grabbed Sandy and pulled her back into the living room.

Grunn had ditched the Walther and was already at the gun cabinet, the shotgun she'd been forced to drop once again in her hands.

She loaded two shells, closed the breach, and handed the weapon to Valena, who took it and stepped aside.

Stella joined Grunn at the cabinet, as did Sandy.

They each grabbed a rifle and began loading them as quickly as they could.

After that, they took positions around the room, covering every door and window.

And there they waited, ready.

Though the man was wounded, he was still armed, could be outside right now planning to ambush anyone who exited.

Or he could be looking for another way in.

Whatever the case, he was an active shooter, and setting a perimeter and guarding it was the right thing to do.

It was, Stella knew, what Tom would do.

Minutes passed—long minutes—before they heard any sound.

What they heard wasn't an indication of the masked man returning for them.

It was the steady thumping of an approaching chopper.

Coming from the south and moving fast.

Forty-Five

Tom could finally see the farmhouse below.

Krista banked to circle, maintaining an altitude that would keep them out of the range of small arms.

But Tom spotted a vehicle parked in front of the barn.

Three of the vehicle's four doors were open.

Next to it was a body, facedown.

The body was to the left of the vehicle, between it and the farmhouse.

Then Tom saw something else.

Another prone figure, but this one was in motion, crawling from the farmhouse toward the vehicle.

Then the figure got up, staggered for a few steps, only to fall again.

After that, the crawling stopped.

Tom ordered Krista to land.

She banked around again and brought the copter down in the open field to the right of the barn.

The vehicle was a good three hundred feet away.

Tom exited, his Glock drawn, and began to close the distance.

Krista paused only to kill the engine, then was right behind him. Running, she drew back the charging handle of her AR-10, chambering the .308 round.

As they neared the vehicle, she said, "Going left."

She veered in that direction and took cover behind the rear right bumper. Tom veered right and quickly cleared the vehicle's interior before taking position by the front right fender.

Krista scanned the farmhouse and announced, "All clear."

She and Tom rose to their feet, moved in sync around the vehicle to the man lying facedown next to the rear passenger door, and knelt beside him.

His head had turned sideways, and Tom looked down at the lifeless face of Kevin Montrose.

He muttered, "Shit."

But that was all he had time for. He rose again, Krista with him, and together they ran toward the man Tom had seen crawling across the grass.

They were steps away from him when Tom knew exactly who he was looking at.

Reaching the masked man, he knelt, rolling him onto one shoulder, while Krista covered him with her AR.

Tom looked into the eyes he had seen the night before.

The eyes he had seen a decade ago.

He pulled off the mask and looked at the face of Frank Ballentine.

Gasping for air, he was looking up at Tom.

Tom glanced toward the farmhouse, saw Stella standing in the kitchen doorway. Relief surged in his chest.

With her in the doorway were Grunn and Valena and Sandy, every one of them holding a rifle.

Tom said to Krista, "Go. Secure the house, find the phone, and shut it down. Then get everybody ready."

"We are we going?"

"Shelter Island."

She started toward the house as Stella stepped out on the porch, Sandy close behind her.

Ballentine was still conscious, so Tom held up his hand palm out, indicating Stella and Sandy should stay put.

Looking down at the fallen man, he remembered that night in Afghanistan, Ballentine's face appearing above him, eclipsing the stormy night sky.

I got you, Seabee, Frank had said.

Tom wondered whether his own face was obscuring the clear night sky above them.

He wondered, too, if Frank had lain bleeding in the dark, waiting and hoping as he felt the life draining out of him.

Felt the world and everything in it slipping away.

Ballentine struggled to speak. Finally, he said, "It wasn't personal."

Frank looked at the Glock in Tom's hand.

Nodding toward it, he said, "Finish the job, Seabee."

Tom shook his head. "The Colonel will want to talk to you."

"I have nothing to say to him."

"Raveis won't care."

"I saved your life. You owe me."

Tom rose to his feet.

"I'll make it easier for you," Frank said.

He rolled onto his back and reached for the 1911 in his waistband.

Tom's 1911.

Despite his wounds, Frank Ballentine moved fast, with deadly intent.

He was drawing the Colt and releasing the slide safety with his thumb when Tom pointed the Glock at his head and pulled the trigger.

Ballentine dropped the pistol onto the grass.

Tom stared at the dead man's face, then tossed the Glock next to the 1911 and turned away.

Sandy broke into a run, hurrying toward Kevin.

Tom fixed his eyes on Stella as they started toward each other.

Meeting halfway, they embraced.

When he opened his eyes again, he saw Krista, Grunn, and Valena exiting the farmhouse.

Krista held up a cell phone and nodded as she led the other two toward the EC155.

All that remained was Sandy.

Kneeling, she was leaning over her husband's body.

The only sound that could be heard now was her weeping.

PART SIX

PART SIX

Forty-Six

Tom slept in a white room.

Whitewashed walls and plank floors, white wicker furniture, white bedding, white clapboard ceiling.

He and Stella had been in this room before.

This time, Tom slept for days, pulled deep into the plush mattress by his own weight, which seemed almost unconquerable.

He'd never before known such complete exhaustion, the cause of which, more than physical activity or sleeplessness or violence, was the elation he'd felt upon seeing Stella again.

Returning for her—for all of them—and bringing them, with Krista's help, to this safe place.

It was as the Cahill compound on Shelter Island had come into view below them that Tom finally felt the full force of his profound exhaustion.

And once he and Stella had been brought to their old room, it was as though a trapdoor had opened beneath his feet, dropping him suddenly into an unconsciousness that felt like succumbing to death.

He saw faces as he slept—his mother and sister, his father.

But he did not revisit his childhood home and see again those things he had not witnessed.

Those four men breaching the front door.

Nor did he see his father, driven mad by grief, fighting to the death in some New York City hotel room with those same men.

He saw only what he had actually seen—his mother and sister happy, his father proud.

He saw himself, too, as a young man, one-fourth of a family of four, with his entire life ahead of him.

For the three days he'd slept, this was what Tom had dreamed.

Even when he had recovered from his exhaustion he still forced himself to seek more sleep, if only so he could spend as much time as possible with these memories.

Finally, when he'd had enough and it was time to again face the world, he looked at himself in the bathroom mirror and saw a man who was ready for whatever was to come.

⁓

They ate meals family style, at a long table.

Tom and Stella; Krista, Valena, and Grunn; Cahill and his parents, who were the kind and gracious people Tom remembered them to be.

People who took genuine pleasure in caring for their guests.

The majority of their efforts were at first directed toward Sandy, who spent a great deal of time in her room.

Cahill visited her frequently, sometimes got her to come out and go for walks with him, and every time Tom saw them together, he considered the terrible bond they now shared.

Both had lost what Tom could not imagine losing.

If anyone could guide Sandy through her grief, it was Charlie Cahill, a man she had known since they were teenagers—he a student at Taft, she the daughter of the boxing coach and school physician whose friendship had turned the onetime troubled rich boy around, setting him on the path that would both prepare him for and ultimately lead him to his life's purpose.

Over the course of a few days, Tom watched the forming of a new family.

Stella and Valena spent much of their mornings together, often taking walks down to the water, while Tom and Cahill and Cahill's father sat on a porch and talked history over coffee.

Afternoons were private time, during which Tom and Stella took to their room and a calming silence fell upon the entire house.

Where the others were, Tom didn't know or care.

He had Stella in his arms, and that was all that mattered.

At five o'clock every day, he secretly turned on the phone Carrington had given him, sent the prearranged coded text of 1835, then kept the phone in his pocket till six, when he powered it down as secretly as he had powered it up and put it away in the drawer of his bedside table.

He'd yet to receive any reply from the man.

There was no way of knowing whether this meant something had happened to Carrington, but all Tom could do was power up the phone at the appropriate time, send the coded message, and wait and hope.

If something had happened, Tom was certain news of that would eventually reach him.

But if Carrington thought it was best to maintain silence for now—to ignore Tom's daily attempts at opening communication—then there had to be a good reason for that.

One day, Tom would receive a reply, and until then, he would continue to follow protocol.

Dinners were spent together, as were the evenings.

Tom would watch everyone as they drank a little too much, let down their guards.

There wasn't a person in that room who hadn't faced death or been forced to become it.

They would forever be bonded because of this, and yet it was their laughter that lingered in his mind when bedtime came.

He and Stella retired to their room at ten every night, slept beside each other in that white room, and woke together to mornings that smelled of sea air and cooking breakfast.

It was during one of those mornings that Tom awoke to find Stella already in the shower.

Leaving their room to use the bathroom down the hallway, he saw Krista quietly exiting Grunn's bedroom and closing the door carefully.

She turned and saw Tom.

They looked at each other for a moment before she nodded once, then crossed the hall and entered her bedroom.

Later, when Tom mentioned to Stella what he had seen, she simply smiled and said, "Good for them."

A week had passed, the weather getting warmer, when visitors came to the island.

Tom watched from the bedroom window as a Mercedes SUV turned into the compound and headed up the long gravel drive.

It stopped at the gatehouse, where the driver showed his ID to one of a pair of armed guards before continuing on to the main house.

Tom had known it was only a matter of time before the world intruded.

His first question when meeting with the Colonel and Raveis in a small greenhouse a few hundred feet from the house was about the status of Hammerton's recovery.

"He's coming along," the Colonel said. "It'll be a long road, but he's walked longer ones."

Tom understood that this reference was to the selection process that Hammerton had endured on his way to becoming an SAS trooper.

Months of surviving in the Scottish Highlands with only what he could carry to sustain him.

Tom was lucky to have such an ally. "Whatever he wants or needs."

The Colonel nodded. "Of course."

"And he should be brought here when he's ready. He deserves to be part of what we all have now."

Raveis said, "It'll be a while before he goes anywhere, Tom."

Tom looked at Raveis, the man who'd years ago known his father, who'd done his best to stop the man from getting himself killed.

And who'd promised to take care of his surviving child.

Then Tom looked at the Colonel, the man whose invisible hand had sent Tom down his own long road.

But it was a road at the end of which was the diner in Northwest Connecticut where he'd first seen Stella and found himself entertaining the idea of maybe having the kind of life that other people had.

Tom knew, though, not to pull at such threads. There was a new-found belief germinating within him that everything happened for a reason. It was, for a man like him, a novel way to view the world.

"What's going on?" Tom said.

The Colonel spoke first. "I wanted you to know that the data we're finally getting from the cell phones is proving invaluable."

"Why finally?"

"It took a few days to find the right hackers to get us into the devices. And it's not just the phone they planted on Valena that we're mining, it's the phones belonging to the Ballentine brothers and the Algerian, whose name, thanks to you, we now know."

"What was it?"

Raveis answered. "Anton Gateno."

Tom nodded but said nothing.

A part of him wished he hadn't asked.

Men like the Algerian were better forgotten.

The Colonel continued. "We've been able to chart their whereabouts via cell-tower pings going back months. One location in particular we were led to was an airport hangar just over the border, in Massachusetts."

Raveis said, "We found the body of a woman there. She'd been shot execution-style and buried naked behind the hangar. Time of death is estimated to be the same day you and Stella were attacked. Obviously, no cell phone or ID was found, but as it turns out, she had hidden a flash drive inside herself. An encrypted flash drive."

"Inside herself how?"

Raveis shrugged. "It's an old trick, easier for a woman than a man."

The Colonel said, "Our hacker friends are working on getting into the drive as we speak. It may be nothing, it may be something."

"Does any of what you have lead you to the Benefactor?"

"Not yet, no. But a pattern is emerging. We know what areas his men frequent. And maybe one of the many numbers stored in those devices is his. Either way, his operation is less invisible now, and that makes him less invisible. This is the first break we've had. The first real break, anyway."

"What do you mean by the first 'real' break?"

"Everything Frank Ballentine acquired, everything his kid brother brought with him when he came to us, was all misinformation. We have no idea at what point, exactly, that Frank turned, or why, for that matter, but we now know how he was turned and by whom."

Tom waited.

"Carrington," Raveis said. "Carrington planted the mirror of his phone in Hammerton's apartment, we assume to set Hammerton up to take the fall for his crimes. And it was Carrington who sent the team to kill Hammerton, because dead men can't prove their innocence. Everything Carrington has done, he's done in an effort to cover his tracks. That includes contacting you for us. And that includes everything he did to help you after that."

Tom recalled the survival cache, the money in the motel room, everything Carrington had said to Tom as his bus pulled out of town. "How can you be sure?"

"GPS doesn't lie, Tom. We've brought printouts of all the data from the mirror phone, if you want to see it for yourself."

Tom needed a moment before he was ready to ask the one question on his mind. "Did he lead the Algerian to Stella and me? To our place?"

The Colonel shook his head. "The data clears him of that much, at least. They found you by the phone Dante Ballentine had given to Valena."

"A strange thing for me to be the one to defend James Carrington," Raveis said, "but it looks like he was bending over backward to keep his betrayal from affecting you. His beef was with the Colonel and me. I believe he thought he was helping the Benefactor eliminate a witness in Ula Nakash, and that was it. There was no reason for him to believe it would catch up with you the way it did."

The Colonel took a step toward Tom. "We need to know if you have any way of contacting Carrington, Tom. We need to find him, and you're our best bet at getting him to come out of hiding."

A similar request had been made of him two years ago when Cahill had gone missing.

Tom said, "Find him for what reason, exactly?"

Neither the Colonel nor Raveis answered.

Of course, they didn't need to.

The Colonel and Raveis operated outside the law. It was their mandate, the unique service they provided their country in its time of need.

Carrington's crimes weren't the kind that could be resolved in a court of law. And there was only ever one punishment for treason.

"The last time I saw him was in Vermont," Tom said. "He was on a bus, heading out of town."

"Any idea where he was going?" the Colonel said.

"No."

"And you have no way of contacting him?"

Tom shook his head.

"No code you can text to a cell phone?" Raveis said. "No hidden communication via a newspaper or websites or anything like that? We know he loved his clever codes."

Tom shook his head again.

Raveis studied him, then said, "Would you mind if we looked through your things?"

Tom smiled. "What things? Everything I own burned."

"Then maybe we could take a look around your room here."

"That won't be necessary," the Colonel said. "Tom's word is all I need. And anyway, he's a clever guy. If he had something he didn't want us to find, we wouldn't find it."

Raveis continued to look at Tom. "I understand why you'd want to protect the man. I get that this would be your initial instinct. He was family to you—the only family you knew for a long time. You're who you are in large part because of him. But he was family to us, too. And there's no man more dangerous than a man who'd betray his own family, for whatever the reason. With or without your help, I will find him. And he will pay the price for what he did."

"Since when is assassination justice?" Tom said.

"He's guilty, Tom."

"Yes, it seems that way. But things aren't always what they seem, are they?"

"We can't afford to be so . . . evolved," Raveis said. "Because of what he did, a lot of people are dead. And a lot more could have gotten killed. That's what I see. That's what the intel tells me. That's all I need to know."

He understood Raveis's need for absolutes.

But he also understood the danger in that thinking.

It was what got his father killed, and Tom wasn't his father.

He'd never let himself be so consumed by vengeance that he'd abandon those who needed him.

"I need your word that you won't interfere," Raveis said. "I can't do what needs to be done if I have to worry about you getting caught in the cross fire."

"Do what you have to do," Tom said.

"And we'll have no problem, you and I?"

"This is your business. It doesn't have anything to do with me. Whatever you do, whatever you have to do, we won't have a problem." Tom looked at the Colonel. "Sorry you came all the way out here for nothing, sir."

"It wasn't a wasted trip," the Colonel said. "It's always good to see you, son. And we have some things for you."

"What things?"

"You and I had a deal," Raveis said. "And a promise is a promise."

Forty-Seven

Tom waited for sunset, then slipped out of the house and walked to the water's edge, where he tossed the pieces of Carrington's disassembled cell phone into the harbor.

Severing contact in this manner wasn't enough, though.

Carrington could already know that Tom was here.

And with Tom were the others.

There was no staying now.

More than that, there was no keeping this family together.

The only thing that would keep them all safe was to scatter.

Returning to the house, Tom quietly told Stella that, and together they asked Cahill to walk with them and broke the news to him.

Tom told his friend everything, including the fact that he had lied to the Colonel and Raveis about not being able to contact Carrington.

"I'm hoping that if things go bad for me someday, I'll look over and see you sitting right there in the jury box," Cahill said. He paused. "Maybe I would have done the same thing, Tom. Anyway, no reason for me to tell them otherwise. The phone's destroyed. What's done is done."

"Thanks."

"We'll close up the compound for a while," Cahill said. "It's the safe thing to do. My parents can go live in our place in the city. Or maybe I'll send them on a tour of Europe or Asia until all this plays out."

"Please apologize to them for me."

"They'll understand. They know the risks they're taking. The risks we're all taking. They're proud to play the part they play." Cahill smiled. "And a long trip is no hardship."

"What about the others? What about Valena?"

"We've pulled some strings, my father and I. As distinguished alumni. She's enrolled in Taft starting next fall, if she wants that. Full scholarship. We'll pay for college, too, when the time comes."

"How could any of that be safe? Not just for her but for the other students and the staff?"

"We've provided her with a new identity. It's hers if she wants it. And anyway, fall is a long way off."

"And in the meantime?"

"Krista apparently has an adoptive father I knew nothing about. A guy named MacManus. She and Grunn are going to stay with him for a while. They offered to take Valena with them. Krista thinks it would be a good place for her. Someplace she can call home. She needs that, don't you agree?"

Tom nodded. "And you?"

"There's work still to do. The ground beneath the Benefactor's feet is shrinking. My guess is that will only make him more dangerous. And Sandy needs me." Cahill looked at Stella, then back at Tom. "How soon will you two want to leave?"

"Before dawn."

"Okay. Same route as last time?"

"Yes."

"I'll take you to the train station on the mainland."

"You don't have to do that. We can make our own way."

"I know you can. But I want to. The first train is at five thirty. I'll come for you guys at four."

Tom nodded. "Maybe we shouldn't say anything to anyone right away. Let them all have one last night together before the real world comes crashing back in."

"I'll tell them in the morning. All of us can leave together." Cahill smiled. "It'll be like the Exodus. And I'll be Moses."

"Sounds good."

"You guys should come inside. Everyone's just sitting down to dinner."

Tom glanced at his watch.

Stella saw him do that.

"We'll be right in," he said.

Cahill left. Tom and Stella watched him approach the well-lit house.

Once Cahill was inside, Stella said to Tom, "We're not waiting for dawn to leave, are we?"

The last train to New York City departed East Hampton at 11:30 p.m.

Tom had slipped out after dinner and secured the rowboat they'd use to get from the island to the mainland.

When he rejoined everyone, no one seemed the wiser.

He and Stella had already packed their few possessions.

Among the items the Colonel and Raveis had provided them were new driver's licenses, social security cards, and passports.

Also included were pistol permits for a variety of states—those in New England that required permits, as well as New York and New Jersey.

There were also nonresident permits from Florida and Utah, both of which had reciprocity in dozens of other states.

This combination of permits would allow them to legally carry in forty-one of the fifty states.

It mattered to Tom that he broke no laws, and the Colonel and Raveis knew this.

Breaking such laws would make Tom no better than those he'd been required to fight.

As well as those he wanted to avoid having to fight.

And yet never for a second did he think he could again wander unarmed, even if he wanted to. Those days were over, never to return.

The pieces of documentation fit into the pockets of their jackets, as did the $5,000 in cash that Carrington had given Tom, so all that remained were the firearms and ammo they'd been gifted.

A Kimber K6s for Stella.

A six-shot .357 Magnum with a two-inch barrel, it was lightweight and hammerless, making it a revolver that was powerful yet concealable.

Tom's weapon was a Heckler & Koch compact .45, along with a mix of eight-round and ten-round magazines, all fully loaded with high-velocity hollow points.

Even for an all-steel-government-model-1911 man like Tom, the polymer-framed HK45c was an acceptable replacement.

Accurate and durable, it was also more concealable than Tom's preferred Colt.

These items went into a plastic shopping bag, which Tom hid in a cupboard by the back door just before dinner.

Their plan was to excuse themselves at ten, as they always did, under the pretense of going to bed, only to instead grab their belongings and slip away.

But at nine thirty Cahill was informed that a call had come in for him on the secured landline. When he left to take it, Tom saw their chance.

He told the others that he and Stella were calling it a day, said as they stood to leave, a quick good night to those he'd come to call his own.

Krista and Grunn, Valena and Sandy Montrose.

His four sisters-in-arms.

He realized that he couldn't leave without shaking the hands of each one of them.

It was the same for Stella.

As he went from one to the other, Tom did his best to pretend that this was just another night and not their last.

Not an easy thing, which was odd for him, but he managed to pull it off.

Finally, he and Stella left the room, and instead of heading upstairs, they grabbed their bag of items and left through the back door, making their way through the darkness to the rowboat waiting at the small dock behind the house.

Stella was onboard and Tom had released the mooring line. He was about to step aboard himself and push off when someone appeared behind him.

It was Stella's look of recognition and surprise that alerted Tom.

Turning, he stood square with Cahill, seeing on his face an expression he'd never seen on the man before.

Tom knew something was wrong—something more than his and Stella's attempt at slipping away without saying goodbye.

Tom asked him what was going on.

Cahill took a step toward the dock, then stopped short. "That was the Colonel on the phone," he said.

"What's happened?"

Cahill glanced at Stella, then said to Tom, "Listen, we should go back inside. We'll talk there."

"What's going on, Charlie?"

As he had done in the basement of Krista's church, Cahill searched for the right words.

But the look on his face was even graver than it had been then.

Tom's gut tightened, and a wave of impatience ran through him. "What, Charlie?"

"The woman they found buried behind that hangar, the woman that had been executed, it turns out she was the Algerian's courier. The encrypted flash drive she had—this morning, the Colonel's hackers got into it. It contained a single document. One long document. And in it were the names of everyone the Algerian had killed, along with the identity—sometimes just physical descriptions—of whoever had hired him. Most of his early hits were in Europe, but the first hit in the United States—the first hit he did for the Benefactor—it was . . ."

Cahill stopped short.

He looked again at Stella, as if for help.

Of course, she had none to offer.

"It was what?" Tom said.

"Gateno . . . he killed them."

"Killed who?"

"He was one of the four men who came to your house that night, Tom. He was the one who killed your mother and sister. He used that same Walther. The ballistics match."

It took Tom a moment to even begin to process this.

He had looked upon the last face his sister and mother had seen, and he had done so without even knowing it.

He had stood inches from the man whose shadow had been cast over his entire adult life—a shadow that was even longer than the Colonel's—but he had done nothing.

Up till now Tom believed that he had no desire for revenge, that he was in that way unlike his father, and yet had he known what the Algerian had done, what risks might he have taken just so he could reach out and kill him with his bare hands?

This revelation gave rise to another question, but it was one Tom almost couldn't ask.

It was one he didn't really need to. "And my father?" he said finally.

Cahill nodded. "Gateno was one of the four men your father tracked down in the city two years later. He was the only one to walk out of that hotel room alive."

Tom stared at his friend.

What could either man say?

After a moment, Cahill spoke. "I didn't know, Tom. No one did, not the Colonel, not Raveis. I don't think they would have kept that from you. If anything, it would have helped them get you to do what they'd been grooming you to do." Cahill paused, then said, "No one would have known if not for Valena keeping the phone Ballentine had given her. Without that, we would have never found the courier, and without her . . ."

Cahill didn't finish his thought.

Stella was out of the rowboat and on the dock, approaching Tom. She reached his side, but he was still staring at Cahill.

Then Tom let the line drop from his hand, and the steady nighttime current began to pull the small boat away.

⌒‿⌒

Nothing was as it was, nor would it ever be again.

Stella knew this just by looking at Tom.

As did the others.

Word had spread through the house by morning, but preparations for a quick departure kept everyone busy.

No one had time to do more than quickly seek out Tom's eyes, and when they did, he made certain to acknowledge each of them with a grateful nod.

If not for them, after all, the Algerian would not be dead.

And their own lives, like Tom's, would never be the same because of the Algerian.

Either by the man's hand or command, someone they cared for was dead.

Theirs was an order to which no one wished to belong, but they did now and always would.

While Stella was grateful she did not belong in that club—Tom was alive—she knew that she was a member of another.

She had played a part in killing the Benefactor's best man.

And she had played a part in the death of the other men he'd sent.

Of course, the Benefactor would not know the specific details of those two events, but how could a man like him not want any and all who had dared to stand against him to be destroyed?

And how could he fail to recognize that Tom had not made his stand alone?

Stella's life, too, would never be the same.

As long as Tom was beside her, though, she didn't care how deep they had to hide or how far they had to run.

She was strong enough for all of that.

And she would only get stronger.

But their real strength was in numbers, and Stella needed Tom to finally see that.

The safest thing wasn't to scatter but to remain together, face whatever was to come as a force.

So as they waited to depart with the others, Stella brought Tom to the dark study and made her case.

"I'm done running, Tom," she said. "And I'm done hiding. So let's not fight it anymore. Raveis wants you, always has, so he'll take me, too, if it means getting you. We'll learn what he has to teach, because no matter what we do or where we hide, the Benefactor will find us. So let's be ready for him when he does. Or better yet, let's save him the trouble and find him first. Let's end all this or die trying, because what else is left for us? He pushed, and now we have to push back. We'll bring them the Benefactor's head, and then we'll go somewhere and live our lives in peace. It's the way this has to go, and you know it.

It's been leading to this from the very start. I'd rather die beside you than live without you. Maybe if we do this, we won't have to do either."

Tom looked at her but said nothing.

"So let's call Raveis now, because there isn't a lot of time to waste. He's out there, Tom, and you know it. The Benefactor is out there, and he wants us—all of us—dead."

It was six a.m. when the vehicles arrived—a convoy of black SUVs sent by the Colonel and driven and protected by men Raveis had recruited and trained.

To Stella's eye, each and every one of those heavily armed men possessed the zeal of a true follower.

Hardened disciples of Sam Raveis, these men would not betray them.

And may God have mercy on them if they tried.

The Cahill estate on Shelter Island was closed up by the time the vehicles departed again thirty minutes later.

The SUV that Stella and Tom occupied was the last to leave the grounds.

She watched through the rear window as the guards that would remain behind as caretakers closed the gates.

The home that had once been full of life and light and healing was now silent and empty.

Abandoned, like so many of the places in which Stella had lived over these past years.

But what was behind them didn't matter.

She told herself this, believed it now more than ever.

What did matter was who was beside her, and who was around the two of them.

She was among warriors, was herself one, now.

Nothing was as it would be, nor would it ever be again.

About the Author

Daniel Judson is the Shamus Award–winning (and four-time finalist) author of *The Temporary Agent*, his first novel in The Agent Series, as well as *Avenged, The Poisoned Rose, The Bone Orchard, The Gin Palace, The Darkest Place, The Betrayer, The Water's Edge, The Violet Hour*, and *Voyeur*. Judson's immersive research method lends his work a distinctive authenticity and has fostered an ever-expanding, eclectic skill set that includes Vipassana meditation, Filipino knife fighting, and urban-evasion techniques. A Son of the American Revolution, former grave digger, and self-described onetime drifter, Judson currently lives in Connecticut with his fiancée and their rescued cats.